THREE HEART ECHO

KEARY TAYLOR

ALSO BY KEARY TAYLOR

THE HOUSE OF ROYALS SAGA

THE FALL OF ANGELS TRILOGY

THE EDEN TRILOGY

THE McCAIN SAGA

WHAT I DIDN'T SAY

———

"These violent delights have violent ends
And in their triumph die, like fire and powder,
Which as they kiss consume: the sweetest honey
Is loathsome in his own deliciousness
And in the taste confounds the appetite:
Therefore love moderately; long love doth so;
Too swift arrives as tardy as too slow."

-William Shakespeare

———

CHAPTER ONE

IONA

You'll love me for forever? His voice echoes through my brain as my fingers tighten around the steering wheel. *Are you sure?*

I'm sure, I vowed with a smile.

Promise? He said as he traced his fingers along my cheekbone before tucking a lock of hair behind my ear.

Promise.

I rest my elbow on the door of the car beside the window and run two fingers over my lips. One conversation after another rushes into my mind, making it difficult to focus on the road passing beneath my tires.

The day is dim, another chilly day, the first of February. Clouds hide the sun, casting the world in an icy gray hue. I turn the dial for the heater up a touch more, chasing away the cold.

I left the nearest city behind twenty minutes ago, and an old map navigates me far away from the rising buildings, gas stations, and all sense of familiarity. I left home nearly two hours ago, with another twenty minutes until I reach the destination that is more of a rumor than a reality; a place without even a name to the modern world.

The Appalachian Mountains loom ever closer as I cut across the landscape of West Virginia, my home state from day one, with its familiar rolling hills, dotted with endless oak, maple, and beech trees. I race toward the base of the mountains, cutting across an old highway that would certainly be considered the road less traveled.

A speed limit sign is the only indicator that I am arriving anywhere at all. A decrease from fifty-five to thirty-five. My eyes drift down to the map again and there's a note written on it to take a left in a quarter of a mile. With not another car in sight, I take the left when it arrives. The highway continues onward, just minutes from climbing the mountains, but I turn onto what looks to be an abandoned road, taking the bumps and potholes carefully in my Chevy Corvair.

Old growth trees loom over the road, blocking out most of the light. The farther I get down the road, the rougher it gets. My heart races faster the deeper from the highway I get. Considering I couldn't find the town on the map, I had to go by word-of-mouth directions.

I'm not certain I'm in the right place.

Until, finally, there's a break in the trees, letting in a rare ray of gray sun, and there's a sign.

Roselock.

Established 1762.

It's a sad sight. The wood rotten, sloping greatly to the right. Rust from the nails trails down the chipped white paint.

I roll past it.

Leaves dot the ground, stuck to the earth in wet, soggy messes. The trees only bear the last few survivors who braved the winter.

A house looms to the left. It's obviously old, with a stone exterior, a collapsed roof. No one has lived there in a century, I'd venture to guess. Another house suddenly appears on the right, not in any better shape.

Another dozen homes line the road before I hit a roundabout. Standing at the center of it are two trees, both of them dead. A crossroad branches off from the intersection, breaking to the west. Looking down that road, I see a few more homes, in various stages of disrepair, every one of them abandoned.

What are you doing here? My heart pounds. *You're crazy. You're crazy.*

But I can't stop. I won't turn around.

I continue straight and as I crest the hill, climbing in elevation to the base of the mountain, a steeple comes into view. Quickly I'm granted further view of the old church.

A cross sits atop a small steeple. An old red metal roof spans the entire building. A big broad porch sits off the very front of the building.

It's large, bigger than I think would have been necessary for this tiny failed township. From the main area jut two wings; one to the east, one to the west.

Climbing up all the sides of the building, there are vines stretching, long and massive, and despite the cold weather, despite the time of year, brilliant blood-red roses bloom all along the vines. Huge blooms, smaller buds, oblivious to the season.

A gravel parking lot sits beside the church, devoid of a single car. I pull into it and shift my Corvair into park.

I've anticipated arriving here in Roselock for two weeks now, made the necessary arrangements to get work off. But the reality of arriving leaves me questioning my sanity.

You love me, right? the voice from the past echoes.

It's all I need to toss logic aside and step out of my car.

I pull my jacket tighter around my shoulders, the moist air instantly clinging to my skin. My boots splash into a small puddle I didn't see to the side of my car.

Looking around, there's a graveyard behind the church, circling around to the sides, surrounded by a broken-down fence that can hardly hold that title any longer. Grave markers rise out of the ground here and there, each of them looking just as old as the homes that occupy the town. But there looks to be far too many graves for how few homes there are.

I look forward again, only a dim gleam catches my attention from the damp ground.

A line of pennies cuts right across my path. It stretches to my right, heading into the graveyard, and to my left, toward a house, cutting behind it.

My brows furrowed, I step over it, careful not to disturb the strange sight.

The smell of smoke brings my attention back to the church, and I look up to find a small trail of it coming from the chimney. The first sign of life I've yet seen in this place.

I stand in front of the decaying porch for a moment, taking a deep breath.

I don't want to be here. I feel crazy coming here. But I can't keep living like this.

I need closure.

One last, great pull of air, and I take the first step up the stairs. Carefully testing my weight on each one, I make it to the porch and to the front doors.

I knock.

CHAPTER TWO

SULLY

"IT'S POINTLESS REPAIRING THE ROOF WHEN NO ONE will occupy the church in just over three months," I mutter as I replace the bucket, not really caring that I slosh water onto the floor in doing so. I slide in the empty one, looking up at the slow but steady drip that falls into the Sunday School room.

"This is a house of God," my father says. "You'll not upkeep the House of the Lord?"

"He's obviously forsaken me. Why spend my last days being his caretaker?" I walk out into the hall, opening the door to the back deck and toss out the water from the rain last night into the overgrown roses.

"You've abandoned this family's duties before, Sully, don't give up now. Not on the final stretch." His tone is pleading, but resolved.

"It's been a lovely chat, father," I say, grinding my teeth as I head back to the east wing, my booted feet clomping over the uneven floorboards. As I push the bedroom door open, my fingers fist around the pendant around my neck. I rip it over my head and forcefully shove it into one of the dozens of tiny drawers that line one wall of my room.

Three days. Then two, then one. And then the real countdown begins.

"It's pointless," I mutter to myself again. The sound of dripping echoes from the far end of my room, as if screaming out loud just how much decay has overrun the church.

Decay and ruin.

The embodiment of everything here in Roselock.

Angrily, I grab the pruning sheers from the desk under the window, too forcefully. The open blade catches the fleshy part of my thumb, cutting it open.

Just at the same moment a knock sounds from within the belly of the church.

Adrenaline instantly spikes in my blood, I can almost feel my pupils constrict, and every muscle in my body tenses as I turn in the direction of the intrusion.

It's been three and a half weeks since the last morbid idiot rolled into this abandoned town and started asking questions they couldn't comprehend the answers to. My teeth grind as my jaw clenches tight. Gripping the sheers tightly, I stalk out the door and down the hall.

Dim light spills in from the windows, but I duck into shadows and pull the door open leading into the chapel. Past the massive organ that lines the front wall, past the podium. Ten rows of pews reside on either side of the massive space, though some of them are little more than broken planks of wood by this point. As I walk down the aisle, my eyes fix on the scratched and scarred wood of the front doors.

With the brutal anger of a starved jaguar, I rip it open, nearly pulling the decrepit thing from its ancient hinges.

A fawn stands there on the sagging front porch. Eyes wide, surprised, big and round. Startled, ready to run.

That's the best way I can describe the woman standing outside.

"What?" I grunt at her, looking around outside to make sure she doesn't have a camera crew with her like the last one did.

"I…" she stutters, taking a nearly imperceptible step back away from me. "I'm looking for someone. Sully? Sully Whitmore?"

The darkness on my face deepens and my fingers curl into fists. Her eyes flick down to the hand with the pruning sheers, fear creeping into them.

"You're…" she struggles for words once again. "You're bleeding. Did you know?"

I hardly register her words, but I look down automatically at my hand. A tiny puddle of blood now rests on the wooden floor, one slow drip at a time falling from my injured thumb.

"What do you want?" I say in a low voice, ignoring the injury.

"Are you Sully?" she asks, still staring at the blood dripping to the floor.

"I tell every single journalist that rolls through here the same thing," I say, grabbing the edge of the door and moving to close it. "The story here isn't one you want on the five o'clock news. I have nothing to say."

I've just about closed the door, already mentally moved on to the roses that wait for me in the back, when a tiny hand suddenly juts out and prevents it from closing.

"I'm not a reporter," she says, her voice pitched and desperate. "I'm not."

I back up slightly, my brow furrowed, every bone in me doubtful. Pulling the door open just a few inches, I look back out at her.

Those fawn eyes look at me, desperate and wide, pleading to me the request she has yet vocalized.

"Please," she says. The little quiver in her word softens something in me enough to fully face her once more. "I was told you could speak to the dead."

CHAPTER THREE

IONA

HE STARES BACK AT ME, THOSE NARROWED GREEN EYES stripping away every shred of truth. A blocky jaw covered in a thick and overgrown beard flexes. Every muscle in his body seems poised to snap me, and he could. There's no doubt about that.

I'm afraid.

Afraid of what he might do to me, this strange man who occupies an abandoned town.

But he's my only option.

"Who was it?" he asks. His voice is low, gruff. As tried and tired as the stones behind the church.

"My fiancé," I breathe. Ice crackles in my lungs as I let the words escape. Tender cracks splinter just a little wider across every surface of my insides.

Three beats become seven and eight. On ten, something lifts in his eyes, just as it falls at the same time, reflecting a broken and wild spirit.

On thirteen he pulls the door open just wide enough for my body to fit through. I don't hesitate, don't give him a second to change his mind.

I step inside, and my eyes have to take a moment to adjust to the darkness.

Dirty stained glass windows don't allow much of any light to filter into the large space. Dirt lines the walls, blown up against the pews that are semi-organized in rows, some askew, some broken. Cobwebs cling to the lanterns that hang from the walls, next to the windows.

But my eyes are instantly drawn to the majestic beast that lines the wall straight ahead.

Massive pipes and thin, tiny ones are lined up against the wall. Ornate carvings enhance their brass beauty. A keyboard and bench line up in the center of it all. I don't know much about musical instruments, but this organ is one of the most beautiful things I've ever seen.

And it's set among so much decay and ruin.

"You should know that the dead are not always happy to be brought back into our fallen and depressed world," the man says as he watches me. He stands with his thick arms folded over his massive chest.

I turn to look back at him, instinctually shying away from him, just as the lamb shies away from the wolf.

A set of heavy and thick brown boots cover his big feet. A pair of dirty and stained jeans hug his legs. A thick green Army-style jacket clings to his obviously heavily muscled body.

Distrust shades his jaded eyes. Long hair reaches past

his shoulders and down a good portion of his back. It hangs unruly and uncombed in brown locks, a slightly lighter hue of brown than my own. Small sections of it are braided, seemingly at random, and are tied back, somewhat keeping it out of his face. His beard is just as wild, nearly touching his chest.

"He'll want to talk to me," I force out around the vice in my throat. "He loved me. I know he'll talk to me."

Three seconds stretch into twelve. He just stares at me.

"Not today," he finally says. "The dead have bothered me enough this day."

He raises his thumb up to his mouth and he sucks the blood away as he turns from me. His footsteps echo through the cool and damp room. Down the aisle, around the alter, making a direct line for the door to the left of the organ. I follow him, darting across the chapel.

Something crunches underneath my boot. I look down to find a tiny skeleton, it's head now only a pile of ash beneath my weight.

"What do you mean, not today?" I say, my voice not nearly loud enough for him to hear me. I hurry along, stepping through the door after him. We enter into a dark room. A wing stretches out to my left and right, a few windows giving sparse light to the dull scene. The man walks straight forward, pushing open a door, opening into the light rain.

He tromps down one step before reaching the level ground of a deck. A pergola stretches up around us and spans the space above our heads. Intense vines wind around the beams, the white and peeling paint hardly visible any longer. Brilliant green leaves and thorns are completely outshone by vibrant red buds.

Hundreds of roses climb the structure, reaching the roofline of the church, stretching out along the edge of the gutter, before racing down another length of the building.

"How…" I gape, turning in a circle, taking in every petal, overwhelmed by the scent of the roses, strong in the gentle drizzle. It's February first. I don't understand how these roses are alive. And flourishing.

The man walks over to a section of vines, the pruning sheers in his non-bleeding hand and begins clipping stems. Two, three, five.

"You said not today," I say, taking one step forward, stuffing my hands into my pockets and hugging tight to my body to combat the chill. "It was a long drive out here. Please. I need your help."

"You've trespassed into my home," he says without looking up. He leans over, clipping some of the lower blooms, and his hair swings in front of his face, blocking it from my view. "I told you not today. I speak to the dead on my own schedule. You'll have to come back at a time when I am more in the mood."

"In the mood?" I question. Anger surges in my blood and I take three steps forward. "My fiancé is dead. I've driven two hours to come find you. You can speak to the dead. And you're telling me to come back later, because you're not in the mood?"

He gathers the roses, quite the armload at this point,

and suddenly stands, pushing his hair out of his face. His eyes instantly darken, like a storm about to unleash. "Yes."

He turns and takes a step off the deck, trekking through the rain-sodden grass, toward the little white gate that opens up into the graveyard.

When you experience pain, you're numb for a while. Eventually, when you wake up, you realize all these people who care about you have been doing so many things to help you, bending over backwards, just to try and ease some of the agony.

Perhaps you get used to their kindness. Perhaps you just expect strangers to feel the same sympathy when you tell them what you've been through.

This isn't the reaction I expected.

His anger. His bite.

His offhanded attitude about the love of my life being dead and gone.

CHAPTER FOUR

SULLY

THE FAWN FOLLOWS ME OUT INTO THE GRAVEYARD. I step through the gate, veering to the left just slightly, and turn to watch her step into the puddle she didn't know to look out for. A tiny satisfied smile crosses my lips as I look back in the direction I'm heading.

A total of one hundred twelve people rest in the ground here in Roselock. At least that's how many gravestones mark the ground. I have little doubt there are more surprises resting elsewhere, but within the township's borders. Not to mention the poor souls forever entombed in the mountainside.

I lay a rose on the grave of Lanna Perkins before moving on to Bernie and their daughter Penny. Next is the Revinski family and poor lonely Betty Simpson.

"Did you know all of these people?" the fawn asks as she quietly follows me. The rain picks up, enough to darken my shoulders and coat my hair.

"I do," I answer her, despite my desire to make her disappear. A power I don't apparently have.

"You do?" she questions of my odd-sounding reply. But maybe she isn't completely dull, because she doesn't question further when she takes a moment to piece together what I've said and the one fact she knows about me.

I move from batch to batch, leaving roses at some graves, while others remain empty. I move among the dead, the only company I've had in so long.

I try not to give the fawn's presence a second thought, but she remains so close, so observant. I've not had another living presence around in so long, she's impossible to ignore.

Careful not to let her know I'm observing in return, I take a sideways glance at her.

She looks to be a little younger than myself, maybe twenty-eight or so. She's tiny, only coming up to my shoulder and thin as a bird. Boots rise up to her knees, a black button up coat drowning her tiny frame. Dark, nearly ebony-colored hair is done up in a loose bun at the crown of her head. Thick and rich.

High cheekbones accentuate a strong chin, and those too-big eyes. Soft lips, ready to spout a million questions.

The fawn is beautiful, there's not a question about that.

But she shouldn't have come here.

Yet, like all the others, I know I won't be able to turn her away.

My curse is the one blessing I've ever been able to offer the world.

Looping through the graveyard, I last make my way to the southeast side, where the graveyard meets the tree line.

A rose for the little girl who lived too short. A rose for the woman who stayed, despite the curse. And a rose for the man who passed it on to me.

"Aaron Whitmore," the fawn reads. "Marian Whitmore. Cheyenne Whitmore."

She doesn't say it, but I know she reaches the correct conclusions.

My entire family rests here in the ground. My baby sister. My mother who outlasted the rest but still went to an early grave, and my father who couldn't escape his fate.

The clouds continue to darken, and the rain continues to pick up intensity and speed. The puddles form in the grass, the mud grows thinner. I look over my shoulder once, meeting the fawn's eyes as the day grows darker and evening stretches over the sky.

She's a pathetic sight now. Hair hanging in her eyes, shivers rocking her tiny body that offers her no padding or warmth.

I only tip my head in the direction of the door, and she immediately follows me without a word more of invitation.

Water drips all over the floor as we walk inside, though the wooden floor is so worn and old we can't cause any more real damage than it's already suffered. I cross the common room, to the wood-burning fireplace.

Crouching beside it, getting ash on my soaked jeans, I take another log round, and shove it into the roaring flames.

"You didn't seem to think too highly of my invitation to leave," I say as I push a second log into the fireplace.

"I can't give up that easily." I can almost hear her shake her head, imagine the way her big eyes widen just slightly.

I stay with one knee on the ground, my arms crossed over it, for a few moments. The exhaustion is already settling in, stealing everything I have inside of me, and we've not even begun.

"What is your name?"

"Iona," she says quietly. I hear her take three steps closer to the heat. "Iona Faye."

"Iona," I whisper to myself, quiet enough I know she won't hear me.

A perfect name for a fawn.

I climb to my feet once more, and without looking in her direction, I head toward the kitchen. "If you're hungry, you can eat. If you're cold, you can change. If you get tired, there are blankets in the basket next to the couch."

An invitation I've never extended to another.

"I'm too tired tonight," I say aloud, though it's justification aimed at myself.

"Thank you," she breathes, silently following behind me.

CHAPTER FIVE

IONA

SULLY BENDS OVER THE STOVE, WORKING CAREFULLY and with absolute focus. I'm not stupid, it's obvious he's doing it in order to ignore my presence. He takes his time browning the meat. Chopping the carrots and celery. He mixes in the stock, stirring all of the ingredients into one pot. At last he sets the lid on top and walks away.

I stand off to the side, absolutely awkward and unsure what to do with myself. I watch as he walks into the room with an empty bucket, and a few moments later he walks out with another that's completely filled with water. He opens the back door briefly and sloshes the water out and onto the deck.

I finally settle myself next to the fireplace, peeling off my coat, which is soaked through. I hang it over the back of a chair and stand on the hearth, the heat drying my backside first.

I should leave. I should return to my life in Ander. Go

in to work tomorrow. Should call those friends who keep trying to get me to go out. Should call my sister back. There are a million things I should do instead of staying here in this abandoned township. Overnight. With a complete stranger who looks like a Viking ready to go out on a raid.

We miss you, the voices call from three months ago.

You never call anymore, Viola whispered to me as she glanced over my shoulder at him.

But I'm here because none of them understood. They'd never been lucky enough to find what I had. Had never found their perfect other half.

"Did you hear me?"

Sully's deep voice rips me from my thoughts and my head jerks back in the direction of the kitchen.

"What?" I ask, my heart suddenly racing.

"I asked if you were alright?" His accusing eyes bore into me, even as he moves about his business of making dinner.

"I'm fine," I say in a short clip. "Why?"

He doesn't respond right away, just continues studying me with those intense eyes for a few moments. Finally, he looks at the bowl and the ladle he uses to fill it. "You went away for a few minutes."

My lips part to defend myself, but only lies would have come out.

He's very observant.

I did go away for a little while.

He makes a grunting noise and nods his head for me to come into the kitchen. I shiver the moment I step away from the heat of the stove, but obediently sit at the rickety table pushed up against a wall.

Sully sets a cracked and chipped bowl in front of me, followed by a slice of what looks to be homemade bread. He sets his own food out before settling into a chair that groans under his weight.

I'd guess Sully must be around six and a half feet tall.

A Goliath to my five-foot-four frame.

He soaks a huge chunk of the bread in the soup before shoving it into his mouth.

"You don't say grace in the House of the Lord?" I question him, guilt riding up my spine quickly.

"No," he answers curtly without looking up from his food.

Swallowing down the unease climbing up my throat, I grab my spoon and take a few wary bites.

Silence reigns in the church, yet suddenly I'm hyper-aware of so many different sounds. The ticking of a clock somewhere. The pounding of rain on the roof. The drips in the next room over, splashing into a bucket. The light slurp of the soup before it goes into Sully's mouth.

But not a word from him.

And I'm too scared to speak. To demand he tell me how this works. To beg him to reach into the other side and find him for me.

In silence Sully finishes his meal. I take a few small bites here and there, pick at my bread more than eat it. My nerves are too high to consume much.

As soundless as ever, Sully cleans up from dinner,

completely ignoring me when I offer to wash the dishes, placing them on a drying rack, while I silently sit at the table. He returns to the common room, where he stokes the fire. He locks the back door, and then the front. He blows out half the candles that are lit throughout the hall and room.

"Stay inside," he says without fully looking at me. "Don't go outside until…just don't go outside. The blankets are there," he points to a basket beside the couch. "Goodnight."

"Night," I mutter, though my mind is reeling, searching for a logical explanation as to why I shouldn't go outside.

I'm about to open my mouth and ask when Sully shuts a door at the end of the east wing. I hear a lock click into place.

And suddenly I'm terrified.

CHAPTER SIX

SULLY

"SHE'S OBVIOUSLY IN A LOT OF PAIN," MOTHER SAYS AS I rest my forehead against the heavy wooden door.

"They all are," I mutter, squeezing the hairpin in my hand.

"I thought I taught you better manners, Sully," she chides. "You were intentionally cruel to that poor girl."

"I just want to be left alone." I lift from the door and walk to the drawers, dropping the pin into one of them.

The rain picks up in intensity and the sound of dripping speeds up. Grabbing a bucket from the shelf by my bed, I place it under the growing puddle in the corner. I linger next to the window, straining my eyes to make out shapes in the darkness outside. Faint shadows sway back and forth, trees bending to the master of the wind. But the darkness outside is complete, the thick clouds blocking out even tiny hints of the moon or stars.

The candle lit on my bedside table flickers as a draft rushes through the room.

The church is falling apart around me. Within a year it will probably start caving in on itself.

But there will be no one left to be inconvenienced by it.

I pace back and forth, one hand rubbing over the opposite knuckles. I still now and then, my ears straining, listening for the fawn.

Iona.

But there's only silence.

Though I doubt I'd hear anything from her. She's light as a bird, she practically floats over the floor.

I watched her as she ate, or rather played with her food. She took a total of four bites of her soup, and one small nibble of her bread.

There's a reason she's so tiny.

I don't remember settling on the bed, but suddenly I realize that I'm staring up at the ceiling. Sprawled on my back, my arms above my head, a mane of hair threatening to drown me.

Suddenly I'm so aware of how long it's gotten. Halfway down my back, my beard a tangled web that touches my chest.

I don't know that I've cut my hair or had a proper shave since I left Charleston nearly nine years ago.

I close my eyes, letting the past drag me under, taking me to a warm bed, a mound of blankets, and the summer breeze blowing through the window. Mile-long legs tangle with my own, blonde hair fanning out across my chest, smiling pink lips teasing every ounce of strength I possessed.

In memories of paradise and normalcy, I drift into the darkness of sleep.

CHAPTER SEVEN

IONA

MELODIES OF BLISS AND SORROW ENTER MY consciousness. When I finally cross the line of awake and asleep into the world of the living, I find there are tears that have already saturated the pillow beneath my head.

Pulling myself into sitting position, I look around, disoriented, confused. The musty smell, the flickering candlelight throw me off balance. And the haunting music floating through the space displaces me all the further.

Pulling a blanket around my shoulders, I cautiously stand, looking around for a clock, and find one on the wall across from me.

4:23 AM.

I stared at that clock until somewhere around 1:30 before finally falling into an exhausted but restless sleep. It's still essentially the dead of night. But those sounds. They shouldn't be visiting my ears now, not at this hour.

I hesitate at the doors to the chapel, well recalling Sully's words of warning.

Don't go outside...

But he didn't finish his warning.

I don't know why I'm not supposed to leave the church. I won't, not when it's still this dark. But my curiosity...

That music. So sorrowful. So filled with pain.

Surely the player is no longer sitting at the organ in one solid piece.

This is a symphony of destruction.

Two more tears make their way down my cheek. Because this is a song I understand.

Placing my hand on the knob, I give it a twist and push.

The chapel is far brighter than it should be this time of day. A thousand candles are lit throughout the space. Along the walls, set in the broken windows. Scattered along random pews.

But most of them rest on candelabras just off to the sides of the organ.

Where Sully sits. His eyes closed, his hands rising, falling, running along the keys.

I don't think he's noticed me enter, the sound of the organ covered the alarming screech of the door opening. So I step inside, my socked feet padding soundlessly over the dirty floorboards. Hugging the blanket tighter around my shoulders, I sink into an empty spot on the second row of pews, and I listen.

Sully is talented. No. Brilliant. Gifted. No sheet music

sits before him, but he doesn't hesitate as he moves from one note to the next, pouring a lifetime of emotion into the notes. Rising and rising crescendos, and then devastating downfalls.

Lover's love and lives are ruined in his music.

I let me eyes slide closed. It rushes over me in such a wave, I can't fight it. I'm taken by the undercurrent, and tossed around to its will.

My insides quiver, more tears roll down my face, and every tiny bit of self-preservation I've managed to tape myself together with in the last two months fractures.

This is power. Sully's gift is also my demise.

The symphony suddenly comes to an end, and when I open my eyes, seven long moments later, Sully is facing me. His eyes don't meet mine, they stare at the floor somewhere along the bottom of the pew in the first row. His hands are clasped together in front of him, his shoulders slumped. He looks exhausted.

And it's no surprise, considering the life he just poured into his music.

"You should know that this isn't going to be easy," he suddenly says, and I internally flinch at his rough voice. "For either of us. It's going to open old wounds for you, bring everything back to the surface. It's going to exhaust me, finding him, holding on to someone I don't know."

I don't know what to say.

It's much I'm asking.

But I'm asking.

"I'll need something personal of his that I can hold," he

says as he finally looks up, meeting my eyes. "It needs to be something that had some kind of meaning to him, something he touched or used frequently."

I nod. The item instantly comes to mind. "I can get that."

Sully nods, the look in his eyes growing darker and more distant by the moment. "It helps, too, if you tell me about him first. It can be a little difficult to find them at first, if they aren't waiting on the other side to talk to us. If I know about him, it makes it easier to recognize him."

I nod once more. Something swirls in my stomach: anticipation, nerves, the old excitement he used to unleash in me. The aching. The longing.

Sully stands, rising his hulking form to its full height. He's dressed for the day already, wearing jeans once more and a button up blue shirt. Same boots as yesterday. A denim jacket with white fuzzy lining.

He crosses the space, and sits on the first row pew. Resting a hand along the back of the bench, he looks in my direction, though his eyes land generally in my lap, unfocused.

"What was his name?" Sully asks quietly.

I swallow once, my throat already tightening. Excitement prickles along my skin, the hair on the back of my neck standing on end.

"Jack Caraway," I breathe, and I swear the temperature in the church drops ten degrees.

"How did the two of you meet?"

"At my father's funeral."

CHAPTER EIGHT

IONA

MY FATHER WAS A POLICE OFFICER FOR TWENTY-FIVE years. He'd spent his life protecting the people of Ander and they loved him for it. So when he died in a hunting accident only one year after retiring, the entire town came to his funeral.

Mom was absolutely crushed. Some people react like that when they lose a loved one; they just completely shut down. Their brain turns off to protect themselves. That's how she handled it.

So, it fell to us—my sisters and I, and the community, the force—to find the burial plot, pick a casket, and arrange the service that we knew would be attended by over a thousand people.

It was the worst time of my life, up to that point, but finally I made it to the day of the funeral. I survived hearing all these people say all these wonderful things about the man who raised me. And there I found myself standing in a line for the final viewing.

My father, resting in uniform in the casket. My mother, with a constant stream of tears down her face, her lip quivering, unable to say anything to the people trying to offer her some tiny bit of comfort. Then my oldest sister Cressida, me, and then Viola, the youngest.

All the Faye women, in a line, on display for everyone to see our pain.

Toward the end of the viewing, my emotional energy was nearly drained. Up until about halfway through I'd been able to return the hugs and handshakes and tell everyone "thank you for coming." But now I was exhausted, each of those people took a little piece of me with them and now I was just depleted.

I'd been staring at the floor, not really responding to the individuals who walked by. But suddenly Viola elbowed me, sending a sharp pain through my ribs. I glared in her direction, prepared to chew her out, but she nodded her chin down the row of people, a twinkle in her eye, and a coy smile on her lips.

"Finally, a little reason to look alive," she said quietly.

I looked generally in that direction, and it didn't take more than two seconds to know exactly what she was referring to.

Or rather who.

Just four people down, staring down at my dead father, was the most incredible man I'd ever seen.

His face was all sharp angles, from his jawline to his

nose. His tight lips, and the drawn expression on his face. Thick dark blond hair was styled to absolute perfection. Gray eyes like a storm.

All accompanied by a body fit for a catalogue, dressed carefully in a well-tailored suit.

I could have stared at him for days.

Were I not at my father's funeral.

"You're the worst," I breathed to Viola, turning my attention back to the man shaking my hand without really looking at me. "Our father is dead, and you're looking for your next man toy?"

"I miss him too," Viola said, "but I'm certainly not dead. I think even he could probably bring the dead back for one last lookover."

Absolute horror ripped through me at her words. I turned to get physical, but a woman suddenly pulled me into her arms, tears rolling down her face.

She blubbered on and on about how my father was the most wonderful, selfless man, dampening my dress, while I glared death at my youngest sister.

But still, my heart rate spiked when the next man moved on and suddenly a warm, large hand was closing around mine.

"I'm so sorry about your father," a smooth voice said.

My eyes rose up to meet his—finding a storm and sunlight as if reflecting off a lake. His eyes were captivating.

"Thank you," I barely managed to breathe out.

"He was such a leader in our community," the man said, still holding my hand. "He will be greatly missed."

I nodded, completely stunned and dumbfounded. He offered me a sad little smile, and released my hand. I hadn't even realized for a moment that he'd moved on, politely conversing with Viola, who was smiling far too brightly.

Shaking my head and blinking three times fast, I refocused my attention on Lieutenant William's wife, who had just moved in to embrace me.

CHAPTER NINE

SULLY

"IT'S QUITE THE GRIM BEGINNING TO A LOVE STORY," I say as I stand and begin blowing some of the candles out as the sun begins to rise.

"It didn't look like it *was* going to be a love story," Iona says quietly as she looks down at the ring on her finger and twists it around. It looks far too loose for her tiny finger.

"Morning details first," I say, walking past her, back into the hallway. "We'll continue the riveting story in a little while."

The fawn scrambles to follow after me. The clock shows 5:43 as I walk into the kitchen. I pull out the ingredients needed to start the oatmeal and light the stove.

Sometime during the night it stopped raining, but now it is bitterly cold. I stoke the fireplace with more wood while the water boils, and then return to the kitchen.

"What brought you to this place?" Iona asks, leaning against the counter and watching me work.

"Birth," I respond simply. I pour in the oats and stir, staring into the mush.

I hear her nod. "I saw the family names out in the graveyard. Have you lived your entire life here, then?"

"Most of it," I tell her, but her questions are causing irritation to rise in my blood.

"Where did you live when you were away?" she asks.

"It's a Friday," I say, cutting her questions off. I look over my shoulder at her. "Don't normal people normally work on Fridays?"

Her eyes widen and she leans back from me just a touch. It's easy to startle fawns. "I, uh…" she struggles to change her line of thought. "Yeah, normally I do work Fridays. I took yesterday through the weekend off."

"What kind of work?" I ask, turning the tables.

"I'm a data analyst for a big power company." She takes a few steps back, retreating to the table as if she's afraid I'll attack. "There's a whole team of us, so it wasn't a big deal to take some time off."

"Data analyst," I repeat, not quite connecting the words with a contributing occupation. "That's a real job?"

Iona nods, only slight offense showing in her expression. "I've been doing it for six years, so yes."

I grunt and turn back to the stove.

When it's done, I scoop it into two bowls and add the brown sugar and milk. She picks at it again, not really eating. I stand at the sink, eating as I stare out the window.

Heavy fog sits low on the trees, spilling down the mountain. It only settles just higher than the church's steeple. My lungs feel tight already, just imagining how cold and damp it must be outside.

When we're finished, we leave the bowls soaking in the sink. Iona runs to her car and returns with a change of clothes and I silently wonder just how long she plans to stay here.

Dawn breaks past the trees just as we step outside the church and head down the road, pushing a wheelbarrow in front of us, gloves at the ready.

I didn't even hear the wind last night, but branches are scattered everywhere. They litter the road, and have fallen on...well, I wouldn't call them lawns anymore, but the property that surrounds the crumbling and abandoned homes. She gives me a look, but Iona follows my lead, gathering the limbs, and throwing them in the wheelbarrow.

"Is there someone who lives here?" Iona asks as we finish clearing one plot.

I shake my head. "Not in about seventy-two years," I say as we cross the road to the empty lot where I dump the branches.

"Then why are you going to all this effort?" she asks.

"Because Mrs. Granger will yell at me if I let her property turn into a mess," I say as I make my way to the house two doors down. "So will Mr. Darrok. He's a mean old bastard."

The gears turning in Iona's head are practically screaming as she turns the meaning of that over. The homes are obviously in disrepair. It's clear no one lives in them, and haven't in quite some time. Yet I'm taking this time to clean them up.

"Do you live in the church all the time?" she finally asks some time later.

"Yes," I huff as I haul a huge branch.

"Then why are you letting *it* fall apart?"

Annoyance flares in my chest as my eyes flick over to her. "Because no one will be living in it soon."

"Are you moving?" She looks back at me over her shoulder while her hands continue scraping the small twigs together.

"More like moving on," I huff and carefully step over the line of pennies that run across the sidewalk before going to gather more fallen limbs.

"You met Jack at your father's funeral," I say, tired of her endless questions. "Where did it go from there?"

She takes a moment to respond. "Downhill. At first."

CHAPTER TEN

IONA

THE WEATHER HAD BEEN SO NICE I DECIDED TO WALK to and from work that day. It was April first. I remember, because our meeting seemed like such a joke.

It was three weeks after the funeral and things were finally kind of starting to feel normal. Mom was coming back to her senses. Cressida had stopped calling every single day, going back to taking care of her husband and their three kids. Viola was back to inviting me out for drinks every weekend with her and her silly friends.

It seemed like a good day to walk in the crisp weather and clear my head. To take a breather and reset.

My work is just five blocks from my apartment, but I cut right through the middle of town. I thought I'd been paying attention to the hustle and bustle, but as I watched a fighting couple walk down the other side of the road, I suddenly ran smack into someone.

I went down to the ground, scraping my elbow

pretty bad, and twisting my knee awkwardly. The individual I walked into dropped their briefcase and was thrown off balance, but I was the only one on the sidewalk.

"I'm so sorry," a smooth, panicked voice said. A hand instantly appeared in my vision, hauling me up to my feet before I was even quite ready. Strong hands steadied me by my shoulders.

My eyes finally settled onto a face. Cut and chiseled and perfect.

"Oh," he said, the guilt and horror widening his eyes. "Hey. You're, uh, one of the Faye girls."

The devastatingly handsome man from the funeral.

"Yeah," I said, wincing against my throbbing elbow. I took half a step backward, raising it up to inspect the damage. My shirt was torn and my skin was brilliant red, but it wasn't dripping blood yet.

"I am so sorry," he said, gently cradling my elbow, inspecting it for himself. "I just stepped out of the office. I wasn't looking where I was going."

"It's okay," I said, bending to grab my bag that I'd dropped. "I wasn't looking, either."

"Don't know how I missed such a beautiful not-quite stranger," he says, pulling off a cocky smile. "You're hard to not notice, Miss Faye."

I gave him a glare as I pulled the strap of my bag back up and over my shoulder. "Really?" I questioned him. "Flirting with a girl you met at a funeral?"

I started walking down the sidewalk, back in the

direction of home. He quickly picked up his suitcase and hurried after me.

"We never even got each other's names at that… particular event," he says awkwardly, smart enough to not say *funeral*. "I consider that to be 'meeting' someone— obtaining their name. Becoming acquaintances. None of that happened before, so it doesn't count."

"You're trying really hard," I said, not looking at him, but a small smile cracking on my lips. "You realize that makes you sound pathetic, right?"

"Pathetic?" he said, sounding genuinely offended. "I'm just being polite. You're the one being nasty now."

"Nasty?" I nearly shouted, rounding on him, stopping us in our tracks. "Really? All things considered in this three-minute acquaintanceship, and you're going to call me nasty? You really know how to burn a bridge fast."

I turned and continued on my way, picking up pace.

"I'm sorry!" he called, jogging to catch up with me. "Nasty wasn't the right word. Maybe just, unpleasant."

"You're not scoring yourself any points with your varying degrees of insults," I said as I crossed the road with a small crowd of strangers.

"Then how about a do-over?" he practically begged as I continued down the road at a quick click. "I'm trying here, I really am. I'm sorry that my mouth got away from me. It happens sometimes when I'm self-conscious."

"Self conscious?" I chuckled. "You?"

"What's that supposed to mean?" he chuckled, though

the look on his face said he had a pretty good picture of what I meant.

"Don't pull that on me," I said, rolling my eyes, despite the smile on my lips.

"Okay, fine," he said. "Maybe I know a little what you're talking about. But it's true. I do get self-conscious. Are you judging me based on my looks?"

"I guess so," I said, crossing another road. One more block until I reached my apartment.

"Look," he said, gently grabbing my arm and pulling me to a stop. "I'm really sorry, for everything that just transpired in the last five minutes. Will you please accept my apology?"

I studied him, mostly because he was so nice to look at. But he did seem to mean it, at least as far as I could tell, having only known him for a few minutes.

"Fine," I said, feeling the annoyance lift from my chest. "I forgive you. For now."

A smile cocked on one side of his face and all of my resolve cracked a little. Perfectly straight, white teeth shone out, the smile all crooked and charming.

"Thank you, Miss…" he dragged out, his expression hopeful.

I bit my lower lip, debating for a moment. Stranger danger and all that, but at twenty-eight years old, I figured I was a big girl by that point. "Iona," I finally responded.

"Iona Faye," he said, settling further into his casual smile. "I'm Jack Caraway. And I wondered if I could take you to dinner Friday night?"

His audacity startled a laugh right out of me. But the look on his face told me he was dead serious. I just shook my head.

"Don't say no," he said, jumping in, like he could see that I was about to. "I promise, no more running mouth, no knocking you to the concrete again. Just a nice evening, some good food, and a perfectly pleasant conversation."

I just stared at him for a moment longer, in disbelief at the turn of events this afternoon. "Maybe," I finally said. "If I decide yes, then I'll meet you right here," I pointed to the ground at our feet, "at seven o'clock Friday night. And if I decide no—"

"You'll just leave me standing out here on the sidewalk looking like a fool?" he asked incredulously.

I smiled and nodded. And without another word, I turned back for the sidewalk and crossed the road.

"I'll see you on Friday!" he called as I walked away.

"Maybe!" I teased without looking back.

CHAPTER ELEVEN

IONA

"You met him on Friday, didn't you?" Sully asks, giving me this *look*.

"I did," I blush. "But only because Viola pestered me so much I thought I was going to kill her."

"She did sound awfully interested in Jack at the funeral," he says as he dumps the last load of branches and heads back toward the church. I follow beside him, pulling off the muddy and soaking wet gloves.

"She was. She almost didn't believe me when I told her that I'd run in to him and he'd asked me out." A smile crosses my lips, entertained by the memory.

Sully grunts, but doesn't say anything more. I can't imagine this is his favorite kind of story. He doesn't strike me as the type to enjoy silly love stories.

He heads for the shed off to the side of the church and parks the wheelbarrow in the corner, tipped up on end. Inside I also see a lawnmower, a variety of rakes, shovels, and trash bins that look like they haven't been used in a few decades.

I cup my hands together and blow, attempting to get some feeling back into them, but they're so far gone all I feel is air movement.

"You need some more meat on your bones," Sully insults as he motions for me to follow him back in through the back door of the church.

I only glare at him as he grabs more firewood from another shed.

We both kick off our muddy boots when we step inside and he immediately sets to stocking the fire once again. I instantly feel my frozen skin cells defrosting, the sensation of warming back up almost painful. When he's done putting the logs into the fireplace, he motions me over so I can thaw out.

"Don't you get lonely living here?" I blurt as I hover over the stove, holding my hands up to the heat. "I haven't seen anyone else around. It's just you, isn't it?"

Sully sinks into a wooden rocking chair close to the flames. He stacks his socked feet, one on the other, to warm them up.

"Yes, it's just me," he admits, and that's just what it feels like coming from him: an admission. "And it used to get lonely, when I returned after being gone. I thought it would drive me mad. But I'm not as alone as it seems. Being a Speaker has its benefits as well as curses."

I swallow once, studying Sully's face while he stares into the flames. This is so out of my element, so far into the strange. Yet it's his reality, and it sounds like it has been for a long time.

"They keep you company, don't they?" I ask, my voice quiet, so they don't hear me. "The dead. You talk to them when the silence gets to be too much."

Two seconds of hesitation. Five. Ten. But finally, his lips pressed tightly together, Sully nods.

It makes sense now, what he said about those people getting angry with him if he doesn't take care of their property. They might have been dead and gone long ago, but Sully still speaks to them on a regular basis.

"Do you have an item of Jack's here, or do you need to return home and get it?" he suddenly asks, still staring into the flames.

His whiplash changes keep throwing me off. It takes me a second to recover. "I need to go home and get it."

"You should go soon, then," he says as he rises to his feet. He peels his jacket off and hangs it on the back of the rocking chair. "You said you only have a few days off. We should get started soon."

"Now?" I ask, looking around, suddenly off balance. Am I really ready for this? To open the gate to the other side? To hear from Jack again? To speak to him?

"Yes," Sully says, heading down the hall, back to the door he disappeared behind last night. "I will be ready when you return tomorrow morning, but not before then."

He walks into the room, and shuts the door with a finality that makes me jump.

I look around me, suddenly hyper-aware of how empty and devoid of life this church is. This town.

Soundlessly, I gather my few things. My clothes from yesterday, balled up on the end of the couch. I slip my boots on. Awkwardly, I head for the back door, looking back toward Sully's room as I walk out.

Tomorrow morning. But not before then.

The message is clear: don't come back tonight.

CHAPTER TWELVE

SULLY

I POUR THE GASOLINE ON THE PILE OF BRANCHES AS the day grows darker. The rain has picked back up, just a light drizzle, but enough to keep everything contained. Taking the matchbox from my jacket pocket, I light one and toss it into the tangle of twigs, and the pile instantly ignites.

The mound stands as high as my head, having been added to since this morning.

Maybe the fawn made me feel guilty. Compacted with my father's words, I took the time to clear all the fallen branches and leaves from the graveyard. But not the church. I pay respect to the dead, but not the site from which so much pain has come.

The heat from the flames warm my face, sending goosebumps racing down my entire body. The moisture from the branches sends heavy plumes of smoke up into the air, the leaves crackling and sending sparks into the night.

In any other town, I'd get in a whole lot of trouble setting such a massive pile of debris on fire, so uncontrolled and big. But not here, not in Roselock. There's no police department to come ticket me, no fire department to come investigate the safety threat it might pose.

Because there's no one around to threaten. Besides myself.

A narrow two-lane highway leaves the nearest town, running for miles. The turnoff for Roselock is hardly noticeable anymore, at least last time I left. That highway just continues running onward, heading up the mountain, into recreation areas where the hunters and outdoor types enjoy a relaxing weekend away from their normal.

While I sit here, north of that highway, out of sight, far, far out of anyone's mind. With my own version of reality.

I reach into my pocket and pull out the old and ragged pink hair bow. It's dirty and faded now, but it was one of the very few items left from the young child that left this world all too soon.

"You don't look happy, Sully," her sweet voice sweeps through the night.

I look off to my left, watching as the adult version of my sister walks up. She's dressed in a long black dress, simple, with no frills or glam. Her auburn hair hangs long, lying still and flat, despite the breeze blowing through town.

"Another sad and lost soul came to ask for my help," I say, rolling the hair bow between my fingers.

"That's better than another reporter, right?" she says as she stops at my side, staring into the flames with me.

I grunt, nothing affirmative or negative.

"What about her has you so bothered?" Cheyenne asks, always far too observant. "Normally you gripe, but you talk to their dead and let them move on. Something's different."

Her question leaves me feeling unsettled. I guess that's the problem. "I don't know," I say. "Something about this just feels…"

"What?" she encourages.

"Cold," I breathe, letting a cloud of white billow from my lips. "Dark."

She looks over at me and without looking back, I can feel her studying me. She's always been so observant. Maybe that's why I speak to her most often. She knows me better than I know myself.

"She seems so functional," my sister moves on. "Some of them are so broken when they come to see you, sobbing, shaking messes. She's so composed."

"I think maybe that's a sign that she's the most broken of them all." I bend down and pick up a twig at my feet, tossing it on the flames. It gives a tiny pop. "It's all hiding under the surface, waiting to manifest in some explosive way."

"Is that why you're so scared of her, Sully?"

My head whips in her direction, my brows furrowed, sharp words on my lips. But this is Cheyenne, and I can never be too harsh with her. Not when I can still recall holding her tiny, lifeless body.

49

"You treat her different," she says, raising her eyebrows just slightly. "You're unnecessarily harsh with her, but you're constantly studying her. And you keep this…distance. It's…peculiar."

I reflect back to our encounters, and I didn't realize I was doing any of that, not consciously. But she's not wrong.

"It's getting dark, brother," she says, looking toward the horizon. "You shouldn't be out here when the sun goes down. It's too close to the anniversary."

I look to the sky, as well. A deep red, laced with gold saturates the cloudy sky to the east. The clouds to the west are too thick to allow any color. It means darkness will fall earlier than normal.

"The fire will be fine," Cheyenne says, giving me a tiny smile. "You should head in."

"Walk with me?" I ask, taking one step back from the bonfire.

"Of course."

CHAPTER THIRTEEN

IONA

THE WORDS OF THE ARTICLE ARE DIFFICULT TO READ in the pre-dawn light, but my eyes strain to read them nonetheless, one more time.

A little research at the library yielded far more information than I expected.

Roselock, West Virginia: an abandoned mystery

A hopeful new American family, excited about mining prospects, and a new life.

When John Whitmore and his wife Ronella arrived in West Virginia in 1761, they had big dreams. Coming from an old mining family, the young man had every confidence in striking out on his own. Hearing rumors of coal in the mountains, he and his young wife settled and began the process of creating their mine and founding a town.

But only five months after the settlement and work in the mountain began, war struck.

The Shawnee Indians migrated back to the area and found Roselock built upon their burial grounds. John Whitmore and his people had disturbed their ancestors.

It was a bloody battle to an ugly finish that left four newcomers dead, and an entire tribe eliminated.

Most don't claim to believe in curses, but learn the fate of the family Whitmore, and you'll be a believer.

On the anniversary of the battle in 1762, the town's new church was dedicated. But in the same moment the bell tolled, there was an explosion in the mine that was heard throughout the entire town.

Several support structures were later found with saw marks, indicating someone intentionally cut the beams. Thirty-three poor souls were crushed that day, forever trapped in the mountain.

A series of unexplainable events occurred following the mine collapse. Untimely deaths seemed to be a common occurrence. Cases of madness were high within the borders, with residents claiming to hear screams at night and to find pools of blood leaking out from beneath the church.

Few residents remain in the borders of Roselock, and who can blame them, when misfortune seems to be synonymous to the town name?

The article is dated from eleven years ago.

So sometime between then and now is when the last remaining residents left—or died—leaving Sully alone, as sole keeper of a dead town.

And no wonder he's stayed. It was his family that founded the entire town.

Noise from the apartment below me pulls me back into the present. Gray morning light begins to dance outside the window.

I didn't sleep last night. After my trip to the library, I spent most of the night pouring over the articles. Reading so many strange and unexplainable things about the town of Roselock. Here and there I found mention of the strange and reclusive man who still inhabited the town, but I got the impression he'd refused to talk to each and every one of them, just like he'd first tried to close the door in my face when he thought I was a reporter.

Placing the last article in the folder, I set it on the kitchen table and continue gathering up the last of my things I plan to take with me.

I walk back into my bedroom for my scarf when a knock sounds from the front door. Scrambling to get back to it, my heart in my throat, I pull it open.

"Viola?" I say in confusion as I step aside for her to walk in. "What are you doing here? It's still so early."

"You hadn't been in to work in two days and your car wasn't here, and neither were you!" she says, her voice hurried and panicked. "Where have you been?"

I can almost feel all of the color drain out of my face.

And my panic must be just as visible from the outside, because Viola's expression grows very grim and angry.

"Please tell me this has nothing to do with Jack," she says quietly. I see her fingers roll into fists.

"It's really none of your business," I say through clenched teeth as I turn back for the table, throwing all of my things into an oversized bag.

"Where are you going?" she demands as she follows me across the apartment. "Why does it look like you're packed for a trip away?"

"I'll be fine, Vi," I growl, throwing in some snacks, though hunger is the furthest thing from my mind right now. "I just need... I just need some answers."

"Getting those answers isn't going to bring him back, Iona," Viola pleads, grabbing my arm and forcing me to stop and look at her. "Damnit Iona. Just look at yourself. You're a mess. You're falling apart. And you have been since long before he died."

"Don't," I hiss, closing my eyes and forcing control into my willpower. "Don't go there."

"I can't stop," she whispers. "Not until you realize. You stopped being you. You stopped being part of the family. You stopped caring, about *everything*, except Jack."

My hand flies up, but she must have been anticipating my retaliation, because she just as quickly snaps her fingers around my wrist, stopping my slap.

"See?" she breathes, her eyes wide and studying me. "This isn't you."

"You don't understand," I say through quivering control. "None of you ever understood."

I yank out of her grasp and shoot for the door. I don't even bother with instructions to lock up before I storm out into the hallway, my youngest sister yelling my name as I walk away.

She never understood. Cressida never understood. None of them ever understood.

CHAPTER FOURTEEN

SULLY

I TELL MYSELF THAT I'M ONLY CLEANING THE SUNDAY School room out because we need a space, not because I feel guilty for letting the church fall apart. We need a space that is distraction free, not too overwhelming for the dead when he returns temporarily to our world.

I sweep the floor. Hang a curtain over the window. Carry in two chairs. Set out a dozen candles. Even burn a lavender scented one to clear out the musty smell.

I've just finished when there's a soft knock from the back door. I glance at the clock as I go to answer it. 9:22.

Iona stands on the deck, layered in so much clothing she actually looks like a human being with meat on her. In her hands she holds an oversized bag.

"Morning," she says softly as I take the bag from her.

I grunt something back, not entirely a greeting. I cross the hall, back into the common room, setting her bag on the couch. She follows behind me, looking around the space with fresh eyes.

"You brought something?" I ask unnecessarily.

She nods, swallowing hard. "I brought some pictures, too. I thought it might be helpful."

I nod, indicating for her to retrieve them. As I watch her dig through the bag, I notice the tension in her shoulders. The angry set to her jaw. The clipped movements.

She's upset about something.

But then everyone who comes to see me is upset about many things.

"Is something wrong?" I finally ask.

"It's nothing," she answers a little too quickly, a hard edge to her words. Forcefully, she digs through her bag, clothing spilling out onto the couch. Apparently, she is planning on staying for some time.

I'm fairly sure it's not nothing, but I'm about the last person who's going to press about it.

Finally, she produces a bound book, and something gold and shiny slips down a chain. Iona holds them both up, nodding for me to join her on the couch.

She smells like roses and fall as I sit beside her. She slides closer to me, her thigh resting against mine, her shoulder pressing into my own. Looking at us, side by side, we seem comical opposites. My leg is literally double the thickness of hers. She seems a tiny child next to Goliath.

She pulls the book into her lap and I realize it's a photo

album. And the flash of gold I find is a pocket watch that she tucks into one hand.

Inexplicably, she opens the photo album to the back, not the front. First to greet us is a picture of Iona from behind. In front of her kneels a man, holding open a ring box, a look of pure joy and hopefulness upon his face.

"How long had the two of you been engaged?" I ask, being witness to his proposal.

"Two and a half months," she answers quietly. Gently, she reaches out and brushes her fingers over his face. I look up at her, and I was right when I spoke to Cheyenne. She'd called Iona so calm and composed. But it's there, hidden deep in her eyes.

This is the most broken woman I've met, yet.

She smiles sadly and turns the page. The next image is of the two of them, dressed in costumes, some kind of medieval getup.

"Where is Jack buried?"

Iona's head jerks up, and she fixes me with a look of shock or offense, I'm not sure which, but she slowly relaxes when she realizes that this is the type of question someone like me will ask.

"Jack was cremated," she says, looking back down at the photo album. "His will requested that his ashes be scattered in Central Park, his favorite place when he lived in New York."

Perhaps this is part of the problem. Iona has nowhere to go visit a grave, nowhere to go mourn and visit.

I study the two of them as she continues to flip through pages of pictures.

Jack is how Iona described him. The perfect all-American handsome boy. Dark blond hair, defined features, athletic looking. The two of them look so happy together.

"How old was Jack?" I ask when she turns to a picture of him standing in front of an office door that has his name on it. He's wearing a button up shirt and khaki slacks, a briefcase held in one hand.

"Thirty-one," Iona says, smiling at the image of Jack. "He was exactly three years and three months older than me."

I was right on. That would make Iona twenty-eight.

"And what did he do for a living?"

She taps the picture, where his name is on the door, just above the height of his head. There are words beneath that, but his head is blocking them. "He was a psychologist. A really good one. He had so many clients."

"People must have really liked him," I mutter, feeling itchy and impatient. There's something too tragic, too surface love-sick about Iona and Jack. They make me want to puke.

Iona nods. "He specialized in helping people with self-conscious issues, people who struggled with identity anxiety. I'd say that's about half our population these days." She does this little chuckle, but there's a hitch to it that makes me look at her face, and I see the cracks beginning to show.

She doesn't say anything else. She flips more pages, showing me more photographs.

The two of them at dinner. Jack lying on a couch. A peaceful shot of Iona sleeping. A trip to Florida. Countless images that reflect a perfect and happy start to a lifelong relationship.

The fall pictures slip into summer, and eventually into spring. I remember Iona telling me their first official meeting happened on April Fool's Day.

Something unsettling sinks into me as we work our way backwards in time over the last eight months. It takes me a few more dozen pictures to realize what it is.

I glance at Iona once more, taking in the bird thin arms, the stick skinny legs.

And I look at the woman posing with Jack in front of some spring tulips.

It's Iona. But the woman in the pictures has been steadily gaining weight as we flip back in time. The woman in front of the tulips has curves. She has hips, an hourglass figure beneath that thin jacket.

They almost look like two completely different people.

I'd wager the Iona sitting beside me is at least thirty pounds smaller than the Iona in the pictures. The one in the pictures from last spring is stunning, amazingly attractive. The one sitting beside me is certainly beautiful, but not healthy looking.

I've seen grief change people physically, when they're too weighed down to eat. But that isn't what this is. She started losing weight before Jack died.

I look at Iona's face again, and something disturbing settles into my stomach. She only smiles wistfully at the images. She doesn't see anything wrong like I do. It's as if she doesn't see the physical change playing out in the images.

The page turns once again, and this time I find an image taken from what looks to be down the hall from a front door. Iona stands sheepishly inside, a faint smile on her lips. Jack smiles at her, his forearm braced in the doorway, the other hand on his hip.

Both of them are dripping wet.

"Our first date," Iona says with a smile.

CHAPTER FIFTEEN

IONA

"Why are you acting like this is such a bad thing that Jack asked you out?" Viola teased as she helped put the finishing touches on my hair while I finished applying my lipstick. "Have you not looked at the man?"

"Looks aren't everything, Vi," I said, glaring at her in the mirror, even though a smile was cracking on my lips. "You realize you have this habit of only looking skin deep?"

"But when it's beautiful skin..." she trails off, letting me out of the bathroom to go find my shoes.

I look at the clock and realize it's already 6:57. I swear under my breath and search around my room. Finally, I find the pink pumps half under the dresser.

"Want me to go stay with Cressida tonight, just in case you need a little...privacy later on?"

I grab a book from the dresser and throw it at my baby sister, hitting her in the shoulder. She laughs as she tries to dance out of the way, too late. "You need to stop! I really will kick you out if you don't let up! You know I'm not like that!"

Viola held her hands up in surrender, laughing hysterically. "Fine, I relent, I'll stop!"

"Thank you," I said, annoyed, but not too deeply. She is my baby sister, after all.

"I promise I really am looking for a place," she said as she followed me to the front door. "I actually have an apartment I'm going to look at tomorrow. Maybe I won't be on your couch forever."

I smiled as I turned back to her, for just a second. "You're welcome as long as you need." I pressed a kiss to her cheek before she shooed me out the door.

The weather was just as beautiful and warm as the day before. I stepped out onto the sidewalk, not even a chill in the air as the sun began to lower below the horizon. I waited for the crosswalk to change to go, and walked in my lightweight white dress with a pink cardigan to match my heels.

Just as I stepped back onto the sidewalk, I spotted him down the block.

A smile immediately pulled his face into a brilliant wonder as his eyes met mine. And I couldn't help but admire him right back. He wore a black suit, perfectly tailored to fit him, his hair just as flawless as it had been the last two times we'd crossed paths.

"I can't tell you how excited I am to not look like a fool tonight," he said with a smile as I finished my walk to the spot where I'd told him to meet me.

"You may still end up looking like a fool," I told him. "But at least you won't be on your own looking like one."

"You can be a feisty one, Iona Faye," Jack said, extending an arm for me. I smiled as I looped my arm through his.

We ended up walking just two blocks before Jack ushered me into a fancy restaurant where he'd made reservations.

Casual conversations were easy for the first thirty minutes, talking about family and work. Jack had been born and raised in Toronto, Canada. His father had been a founder of the psychology program at some university there. But Jack decided he wanted to forge his own path, his own way, and decided to go to New York University to study, instead. He'd gotten his masters degree in psychology, just like his father. He was an only child, and then he lost both of his parents just after he graduated, and now he lived here, in West Virginia, with his own practice.

Easy and casual.

"Now, tell me something true," he said as we were nearly finished with our main course. "Something deep and real. We can talk all night about the surface stuff. But I guess I kind of like to jumpstart things whenever possible. Tell me something real, Iona Faye."

I looked up from my plate, thrown off by his deep and thought-prying question. I wiped the corner of my mouth with a napkin before setting it back in my lap. "Something real. Like everything I've told you about myself tonight hasn't been?"

Jack shook his head. "That's not what I mean," he said, his eyes growing sincere. "Facts are simple. I want to know something hard. Because you have captured me, Iona."

His serious confession threw me all the more. But there was a depth to his expression that hooked me and didn't let go.

So I took a moment, reaching deep inside me, looking for something hard and true.

"I feel like the clock is ticking," I finally said to him, leaning forward, resting my chin on my hand folded over the other. "Like everyone is watching me, wondering what is taking so long."

"So long to what?" Jack asked, leaning forward so our faces were only a foot apart.

"To find 'the one.' To settle down and get married. I feel like everyone thinks I'm so old now and that they all think I'm two seconds away from missing the train."

"Why?" he asks.

I shrug, leaning back in my seat. "My sister got married when she was twenty. Her kids are already nine, six and almost one. All my friends from school are married too, with at least a couple of kids. And here I am."

Jack studied me for a moment, his eyes boring into mine. And suddenly I'm sure I can't do this. Get involved with someone who picks people apart for a living.

"Do you want to get married? Is that the life you really want for yourself?" he finally asked.

I didn't answer right away. My eyes fell to my lap, searching for the answer. There's the one I think I should give, the one everyone expects me to produce. And the one that's buried deep down. And the one that meets the middle ground.

"Someday," I say. "I think that urge is going to hit me sometime. But right now…"

"Right now, what?" he encourages.

"Right now I'm happy just being me," I confess. "Right now I'm happy to have spontaneity spring up at any moment."

A smile cracked on Jack's face and I could just feel it, the energy building in the air around him.

"*That's* the real and the hard," he said as he reached into his pocket, producing a wallet. He laid down some money and stood, reaching for my hand.

"Are we done eating?" I asked, thrown by his sudden move to depart.

"Unless you're still hungry," he said. There was a spark in his eye, begging me to go live up to that spontaneous desire I just confessed to.

A smile crossed my lips, and I finally laid my hand in his, letting him pull me up to my feet. Without looking back, he hauled us out of the restaurant.

"Where are we going?" I laughed as he started running down the road.

"If I told you, it would ruin the surprise!" He laughed as we raced down the street.

Darkness had fully fallen on the night, but light from the businesses in the heart of town cast us in a dim glow. We raced past the ice cream parlor, alongside the library.

Past my work. The sound of the train next to the river cut out into the night. And finally, we hit the far end of town, coming up to the intersection of Main and Alder Avenue.

A huge park sprawled out to the east, with a playground and a massive gazebo. Picnic benches sat along the pathway that meanders around the border. And here, at the edge, next to the road, there was a huge water fountain. A big round pool held a massive sculpture of a town founder with mountains sculpted around him, water cascading from them into the pool.

It's an ugly sculpture, really.

"What are we doing?" I laughed, out of breath from our run through town. Concluding that this must have been his destination, I reached down and pulled my shoes off, my feet killing me from the dash on heels.

Jack reached into his pocket, and a moment later produced a small handful of change. He took a penny and placed it in my waiting palm. "Make a wish."

I looked up into his face, and found excitement and wonder there. A smile crossed my face. Turning to the water, I closed my eyes for a moment.

I wished for something magical to happen that night.

Opening my eyes, I tossed my penny into the pool. I looked to my side to see Jack throw one in just a moment later.

"What did you wish for?" I teased him, taking one step closer.

"I'll never tell." He shook his head. Suddenly he reached out, grasping me around the waist and lifted me until my feet were touching the rim that ran around the edge of the pool. I wobbled, but he grasped my hand tightly so I wouldn't fall.

"Tell me, Jack Caraway," I said as I began walking the rim, Jack holding my hand. "What's your true and dark and real?"

He looked up at me, the fun of the night growing heavy with my question of reflection. And the longer I looked at him, the heavier it grew.

"You told me about your future and your romantic life, so I guess here's mine," he said with a deep breath. "I'm a little afraid I might be cursed."

My brows furrowed. "What do you mean?"

He looked away, his expression growing distant. "I was engaged once," he said. "Thought I knew exactly how the rest of my life was going to be, and it was a pretty damn perfect picture."

"What happened?" I asked, my heart already breaking for him.

"She died," he responded. "About a year and a half ago. We had been engaged for nearly a month."

"Jack," I breathed. "I'm so sorry. That's so tragic."

He shrugged and looked up at me. "Guess that's all we can do when we think we're cursed, right? Either accept it and be miserable, or look for a way to break it."

There was a sudden glimmer in his eye, a mischievous flash. And suddenly he let go of my hand.

My footing immediately slipped, and one leg slid down

and into the pool. With enough speed that I lost my balance and stumbled fully into the pool.

Immediately springing to my side, suddenly Jack was in the pool too, catching me before I fully tripped and immersed myself.

"You did that on purpose!" I bellowed, trying to get myself fully upright, my mouth wide with shock.

"A spontaneous slip of the hand!" he defended himself with a laugh, dodging out of the way as I sent a wave of water in his direction. Only he was the one to misstep this time, slipping on the slick tiles beneath our feet. He went slipping backward, falling completely into the water, a wave washing over his head.

Suddenly a hand wrapped around my ankle, pulling me, and instantly I was falling forward, landing right on top of Jack.

Sputtering and shivering, we half pulled each other up, half shoved and wrestled playfully.

"Now look what you've done," he teased as he carefully helped me step over the wall and back out onto dry ground.

"You can pretend all you like," I said, shaking my head, my wet and ruined hair sloshing trails of water all over the place. "But we all know that was every bit you."

Jack squeezed my hand tight, pulling me closer to him. With his other hand, he reached up and tucked a wet strand of hair behind my ear. "Could you ever forgive me?" he asked quietly.

I looked into those gray eyes of his, searching for every intention there, and finding many things that pulled unexpected reactions from my body. The grip he had on my hand loosened and shifted to the small of my back. The fingertips at my ear slid down to my neck, and every nerve ending in my body sparked to life.

"I'll think about it," I breathed.

He leaned in just a little closer, and my eyes began to slide closed.

"I'll walk you home," he whispered instead. And my eyes flew open to see a soft smile on his lips.

He slipped his hand back into mine, and slowly, the conversation returned to light and easy, and we walked back to my apartment.

CHAPTER SIXTEEN

SULLY

"Here's how this works."

Iona's eyes snap up to my face, the focus there taking a moment to return. She's shaken, and I mean that literally. The hand that holds the pocket watch trembles.

"We are going to go into a quiet room," I continue as I stand. Nervous energy is spiking in my blood and I'm too on edge to sit at the moment. "Sometimes the dead are overwhelmed by the world of the living, it's best if we don't over stimulate them."

I crouch, swinging open the glass-faced door to the wood-burning fireplace. I grab some more wood, shoving it in. Ash falls to the hearth as I close the door once more. I stay down, crouched, my forearm resting against my knee. "I'll take the personal item, all I need to do is touch and hold it. That opens the gate between me and the other side. As I told you, sometimes it takes some time to find them, especially depending on their willingness to communicate. Considering your…" I hesitate, "circumstances before he died, it shouldn't be too difficult."

Iona nods, and despite my stoking the fire, the temperature in the church dips.

It always does right before the gate is opened.

"Where is he going to be coming from?" Iona asks quietly. Fear has begun creeping into her eyes. Her skin is pale, she holds unnaturally still.

"They all say it is the same thing," I explain as I stand. I tuck my hands into my pockets and walk to the window that looks out over the graveyard. "The afterlife looks just like our world. Everything is familiar to them, all the same landmarks, same buildings. Depending how strong their ties to individuals still living on the earth, they can still see us. Though…it's hard to describe…but they're separate. They say it feels different, disconnected from us. But they're alone over there. The dead seem to each exist in their own world."

"They don't see each other?" Iona asks.

I shake my head.

"That's awful," Iona protests.

Once more, I shake my head. "None of them have seemed to mind. I think time doesn't mean the same to them, so they don't begin to feel lonely. But they do seem to be aware that they're waiting."

"Waiting for what?"

"None of us know," I breathe, creating a foggy cloud on

the window. "Judgment. To be reunited with loved ones. Something grand and epic. But they all say the same: they're waiting for *something*."

The silence in the room is deafening. For myself, this is the hardest part to swallow about death. Knowing there is some kind of afterlife, but even I only know so much about it. Every dead person I've spoken to tells the same tale. Even they don't know what lies beyond limbo.

"The connection to the dead will stay stronger if you are touching me," I continue. "You won't be able to hear them, but I will relay everything said."

I look over my shoulder. Iona stares at the floor, and nods her head. She's still statue still, and looks as if she's about to be sick.

"Are you sure you want to do this?" I ask. "Sometimes it is better that we leave the gate shut."

Anger flashes into her eyes and they flick upward to meet mine. "No," she says with hardness. "I need this. I have to speak with him."

We hold one another's gaze for a long moment, and that feeling of wrongness builds in my chest. It tightens my throat. Clams my hands.

"Let's get started, then," I say. I cross the room, down the hall as Iona stands to follow me. I open the door, watching her as she follows, the golden pocket watch swinging through the air.

She steps into the dark room, standing awkwardly in a corner. I step inside, hesitating before closing the door.

"One more question," I say, fighting the rising dread that swims in my blood. "How did he die?"

Iona's eyes jump to mine once more, and something changes in her expression. "He was murdered."

CHAPTER SEVENTEEN

IONA

THERE'S BEEN THIS LOOK OF DREAD AND apprehension in Sully's eyes since the moment he opened the church doors to find me. It's been growing into something hard and cold moment by moment. But with my revelation, it solidifies into something heavy as the world.

"Sit down," he says in something very close to a growl. He points to one of the two chairs set in the middle of the room.

I sit, dread and fear and anticipation climbing in my throat.

Sully closes the door, and locks it.

The huge man stalks around the room, lighting a match to first one candle, then taking it to light the others. The room gradually grows lighter until a dozen of them are lit, and I can finally see more than a foot in front of me.

I rub my hands over my arms, because suddenly I

realize that it is freezing in here, despite the roaring fire Sully has kept in the other room.

Deep, slow breathing pulls my attention back to the man.

He stands in one corner, before a solitary, lit candle. His back is turned to me, his hulking shoulders blocking out most of the light, casting him in an eerie glow. His long hair hangs around his face. He breathes, slow, deep. But there's a quiver to it. Something unsteady.

I want to ask him if he's okay. To ask what is the matter, because everything in me screams that there is.

But I'm too petrified to open my mouth.

A draft pushes through the edges of the covered window, sending the flames dancing atop the candles. A shiver works its way down my spine.

Sully suddenly steps back from the corner and drops down into the seat across from me. He holds his hands out.

"The watch," he says nodding to his right hand. "Your hand." He indicates the left.

I can't stop shaking. I set the pocket watch in his hand, and trembling, I rest my hand in his other. He closes his fingers around mine, fully engulfing it with his size.

Sully's eyes slide closed. I watch his face, seeing something come over it. Like he's slipping underwater, preparing to hold his breath against certain death. His breathing becomes very light and shallow. His entire body becomes very still. The temperature of his hand drops.

The pain in my chest comes to a peak and I realize just how hard my heart is beating. My hands are slick with sweat. I lean forward in my seat, far too close to Sully's face for comfort.

My breath is held.

"Jack," Sully says, his voice low and deep. I jump when he speaks, startled, a bent twig on the verge of snapping. "I know you've moved on, but I have someone here who wishes to speak to you. If you want to speak to her, please show yourself."

Sully is quiet for a long moment afterward, one that seems to roll into an eternity of anticipation.

"What's happening?" I whisper, a cloud of breath billowing out from me.

Sully lets out a slow, long *shh*, his face suddenly going peaceful.

All the blood in my body drops into my feet.

"Iona," Sully says. There's something breathy in the way he says my name, something disbelieving and hopeful and so full of everything.

"Jack?" I breathe as tears spring into my eyes.

"Yes," Sully says, and he suddenly opens his eyes. But they only meet mine for a moment. They shift off to the right, next to the window, by his shoulder.

Goosebumps flash onto my skin as my eyes follow Sully's.

"Can you see him?" I whisper. I want to shy back, to put some distance between myself and the ghost only he can see. But I'm also dying inside, knowing he is hidden from my eyes.

"Yes," Sully says, not looking away from that place in

the corner. "He looks just like he did in the pictures you showed me. He seems very happy to see you."

A laugh escapes my lips as tears break free onto my face. My lower lip quivers, in time with the rest of me.

"Jack," I whisper, looking into that corner Sully indicates. "I've missed you so much."

"I've missed you, too," Sully communicates. It's amazing. Every syllable, every enunciation is just how Jack sounded. Sully relays it with nearly perfect replication. "But what is happening? Why are you here? And who is this?"

I shake my head, biting my lower lip. "I couldn't…" I try to speak, but my words catch in my throat. "It was all just too sudden. I needed to get more… I needed you and you were gone."

"I know, baby," he says through Sully. I close my eyes, smiling, my chest swelling at his pet name for me. "It got so crazy. I don't even really remember what happened."

My jaw clenches, hot acid rising in my blood. My fingers roll into fists, folded into my lap.

"What happened, Iona?"

I shake my head, the memories instantly sucking me back to that horrific night.

"Do you remember us being at your office?" I ask, looking up and staring into one of the flames, my eyes losing focus.

"Yes," he responds. "You'd come to help me close up. We were going to go somewhere."

I nod. "We were about to head to the movies. You'd worked an extra long day, had a client call in last minute who said he had a crisis, so you stayed to help him. I'd been waiting for you for over an hour, so finally I just showed up at your office."

"You brought me dinner," he recalls. "Fried chicken and cornbread."

I smile, just a tiny and brief reflection of how happy he was when I walked through the door with food. "You ate it down like it was your last meal." The dam breaks free as I realize the truth in my words.

It was indeed his last meal.

My eyes rise to Sully's, and they tell me he didn't miss what I said. The breath catches in my throat, the oddness to this situation so overwhelming. This stranger, this man who is shrouded in his own mystery, communicating with my dead fiancé, talking just like he's Jack.

"We had just finished cleaning up dinner when the bell to the door rang," I press on. I can feel Jack's warm hands on my hips, feel the hard wall at my back as he took charge of my lips as a thank you for bringing him food. Feel myself jump in surprise at the unexpected noise.

Hear the footsteps walking into the reception area. The way it ripped through the otherwise silent night.

"You walked out of your office, stepped out to the secretary's desk." My words feel so cold as I say them. "I followed you. There was a man there. Dressed just like he was about to head into the grocery store or out for a casual drive. But his face." I shake my head, squeezing my eyes closed, recalling every tiny detail. "He was so angry."

"He had a gun," Jack says.

I nod. "Only a second could have passed since I walked out to see what was going on. He had it ready, pointed. He pulled the trigger."

Bang. Bang. Bang.

Three quick shots to the chest.

The screams that poured from my chest must have been heard across town. I lunged forward, catching Jack as he fell back. But his weight was too much, and instead we both fell to the ground. Blood instantly coated my hands, my lap, the floor. Everywhere.

Jack took a labored breath, but as he exhaled, blood spilled onto his lips.

His eyes wide, they searched wildly, landing on the intruder.

"I had to stop it," the man had said, shaking his head. The look in his eyes turned from angry and crazed to peaceful and accomplished. "I couldn't let him keep doing what he did to her. You'll thank me someday."

"He killed you in cold blood," I say, pulling back into the present. "The sick thing was that he waited outside on the sidewalk until the police arrived. Calm and so..." I struggle for words. "Composed. He confessed to everything, even as the paramedics were loading you into the back of the ambulance."

My hand trembles where it's held tightly in Sully's massive one. I can smell the scent of Jack's blood as I climbed into the ambulance behind him and the paramedics. Watched in panic as they hooked all kinds of things up to him, pressing so hard into his chest to stop the bleeding I was sure they'd crush his ribcage.

I reached for his hand, squeezing it tight, praying that everything would be okay.

But only two minutes into that ride, Jack's hand went limp.

"You died on the way to the hospital," I breathe, feeling myself go slack, as well. I slump back into the chair. My connection to Sully only remains because he holds on tight.

"Iona," Jack whispers. "I'm so sorry you had to witness that."

I shake my head, the anger once again rising in me. "The sick thing is that he never gave a real reason why he did it. He's only ever insisted that you had to be stopped. Jack, why? I don't understand why he would do what he did?"

My head falls, and sobs consume me.

It's quiet for a moment as my brain shuts out everything. The pain and the grief roll through me like a tidal wave. Just like the night he died. Just like the days of pain and confusion that followed.

A hand rests on my shoulder before gently moving to run down my hair. "He says he wishes he could hold you right now." Sully's voice is guarded, unsure. "He's kneeling beside you."

The sob rips harder from my lungs as I look to my side, so clearly able to picture Jack kneeling there. His beautiful face broken with pain. Those soulful eyes locked on my face. His strong hands pulling me to his chest.

I recall every impression of his body, so acutely aware of every way my body fits against his.

But I'll never touch him again.

"I need you back, Jack," I whisper as my eyes squeeze closed. "I can't live without you."

"I'm always with you, baby," Sully translates. "You might not be able to see me anymore, but I'm always with you. Always within you. I would never leave you abandoned."

I cry harder. "It hurts too bad," I'm nearly frantic. "I'm consumed in pain, every second. Every day. I can't function. I can't breathe. I can't do this without you, Jack."

"I'm right here," Jack whispers. "Always."

Something shifts in the air, and suddenly the room feels ten degrees warmer. I feel the change as a physical thing, my body instantly reacting. I sit up straighter, filled with panic, looking around the room.

"He's gone," Sully says. He lets go of my hand, setting the pocket watch on the floor, and slumping back into his chair.

"What do you mean, he's gone?" I ask, panicked. "I wasn't finished. I need so much more!"

His eyes narrow at me, annoyed at my frantic state. But they shift away as he brings his hands up to rub his eyes. "It takes time to condition the dead to stay present in the world of the living again. They can't handle staying long. The first talk is always short."

My insides quake, like a drug-addicted leech, craving its next fix. "How soon until we can speak to him again?"

"Maybe tonight," he says, leaning his head back in the chair, letting his eyes slide closed. He suddenly looks exhausted. "But he might not be able to return again until tomorrow. We will find out later."

I feel a bit like I did the night Jack was shot. Like everything happened too fast and I'm left searching for answers to what happened.

But it's just done. Like that.

A soft snore sounds from Sully not a minute later.

CHAPTER EIGHTEEN

SULLY

SCREAMS AND SHOUTS AND GUNFIRE RING THROUGH the night. A full moon casts a hazy glow on the bloody site. Women and children cower in half-destroyed homes. Slaughtered men lie in the streets.

Who's innocent and who's right is a matter of debate with no clear answers.

A pool of blood lies on the ground, saturating into Whitmore ground that never really belonged to us.

John. Patrick. Nicholas. Neal. Steven. Lee. Aaron.

Their faces flash before me. Always followed by black.

I bolt upright with a gasp, my hands reaching for something in the dark.

But it's pitch black, and I'm alone.

A single candle burns near the door. I'm still in the Sunday School room, still resting in the chair. But the night feels cooler, day clearly long past.

Pushing my hair out of my face, I rise and walk out of

the room. I find a fire still glowing in the wood stove, though it's burned down. Iona lies on the couch, her eyes closed, her expression peaceful in sleep.

Lying half on her chest, half on the couch, is the photo album. Held loosely in one hand is Jack's watch.

Her angle is slightly awkward, and the shoulder of her shirt has been pulled down, exposing her rail thin shoulder.

She has a tattoo almost to her shoulder, just to the left of her heart. It's some kind of symbol, an infinity sign of some sort. I wouldn't have pegged her as the type to go under the needle.

Her hair is a mess and her face seems puffy, as if she's been crying. I wonder if she'll stop until she gets her closure here and leaves.

I restock the fire and head down the hall. The clock on the wall reads 3:49. Dawn is still far off, but there will be no more sleep for me, not after sleeping most of yesterday away. The floorboards creek slightly as I cross them, heading into my bedroom.

I light a candle, and silently, I sink onto my bed, facing the wall across.

The oversized sorting unit lines most of the wall, composed of over a hundred little drawers, each containing some little trinket. Some personal possession of someone who once lived in this town.

On the wall above the unit, hangs a calendar.

Today is circled in red pen. February fourth.

I stand, pulling open three drawers, removing their contents.

"Happy birthday, son," a sweet voice says just moments after I sit back on the bed.

"You're getting so old."

I try to smile for Cheyenne's sake, but I don't think I do it very successfully. I look up to see my family, all standing there, watching me. My sister with a twinkle in her eye, a mischievous smile. My mother wears a sad smile, trying so very hard to act like everything is okay.

But the look in my father's eye tells the truth.

He knows what this day means.

"Think that pretty girl out there will make you a cake when she finds out it's your birthday?" my sister says when no one seems to know what to say on this heavy morning.

"I doubt it," I say, actually managing to crack half a smile. "I don't think I've been nice enough to her for that."

"I'm proud of you, though," Mother says, walking forward. She sits on the bed beside me, but doesn't depress it one millimeter. "You're helping her be able to move on."

I shrug. "I don't think she'll leave until I Speak for her. It's an act of convenience."

"Don't do that, Sully," she says. She moves as if to push my hair back, but remembers last second. "Don't harden yourself. You used to be happy. Can't you find just a small grain of that again?"

"Leave him be, Marian," Father cuts in. I look up at him and the agony on his face is undeniable.

"There's still time, though," Mother says, the hope and wishful thinking so evident in her voice. "He still has three months and three days. Why not make the fullest of it?"

She looks back at me, and I turn to meet her eyes. A soft brown, matching her hair, which is tied up in a bun at the back of her head. "Who says you have to finish out these days in misery and loneliness? You deserve to have some happiness, Sully."

"I tried that once," I say. My chest aches. I want to say words that will make her happy, give her hope. But this day destroys all of that. "But Roselock is in our blood. What happened here is almost over, Mother. I just want to get through it."

I look over at Cheyenne. Tears brim in her eyes and she bites her lower lip.

"What?" I ask, wishing I could reach out and comfort her. "You can't mourn this. You've always known it was coming."

She shakes her head. "It's not about that," she breathes. "It's just…I'm going to miss you. I've been gone for so long, but once the time comes, I won't see you anymore. You're the only reason we get to be together as a family anymore. I'm not ready for that to be over."

"There's still time," I say as the weight on my chest grows by a thousand pounds. "Three months, three days."

CHAPTER NINETEEN

IONA

THE QUIET VOICE DOWN THE HALL PULLS ME FROM sleep. Sitting up, the photo album hits the pillow on the floor. I rub my eyes, searching for Sully. But his voice drifts down from his bedroom.

I pull the blanket around my shoulders, glancing at the clock as I pass. 5:03. Quietly, I walk toward his voice.

The door sits most of the way closed, only a thin sliver still opened, just enough for me to see through.

Sully sits on the edge of his bed, still dressed in yesterday's clothes. He holds something in his hands, though I can't tell what.

"I see no point in ever leaving again," he suddenly says. I jump, hard. His eyes are turned to just the side of him, fixed on one certain point. "I tried that once. Roselock called me back in a very unpleasant way."

He says nothing for a long minute, his eyes still fixed on

one certain point. They then flick to the right, and he remains quiet.

He's talking to the dead. More than just one person if I had to guess.

"Can we please stop having this argument?" he says, sounding worn out. "Words change nothing. They don't turn back the clock."

Sully suddenly stands and walks out of my view.

"I think you know that in this family we have never celebrated on a birthday," he says grimly. "Certainly never on mine."

I hear something clank, a soft sound, repeated twice more. And then it is silent.

Only for three seconds, before the door is pulled open, and I find myself nose to chest with a very startled Sully.

"What are you doing?" he demands, sucking in a deep breath and taking a step back from me. His eyes narrow and his lips form into a thin line that disappear into his beard.

"I…" I scramble, my heart hammering in my chest, stepping out of his doorway, as if I can run and hide my embarrassment. "I heard your voice, it…it woke me up."

He looks down at me again, studying my expression as if to see if I am lying.

"It's your birthday?" I ask timidly.

His expression only darkens all the more. He leans his shoulder against the doorjamb and gives an almost imperceptible nod.

"Can I ask how old you are?" I say as I pull the blanket tighter around my shoulders. "It's…it's kind of hard to tell."

His eyes jump over to mine once more, disapproval and bad attitude spread all over his face. "Thirty-three."

I bite my lower lip and nod, unsure of what to say now. In my family growing up, birthdays were always a big deal, but the look on Sully's face tells me he's not too happy about the day.

"How about I make you a special breakfast?" I ask, because it's the only thing that comes to mind.

A little something changes when I say this. A tiny chip in the angry and rough façade. Maybe a little weight lifts from his shoulders.

"Fine," he says. No *thank you*. No show of appreciation. He pulls away from the door and walks past me.

I follow behind, so very unsure of how to step when it comes to Sully Whitmore. I don't know what to say, or how bold to be. I'm terrified of the large man who speaks to the dead.

He takes a look at the clock on the wall, and without a word, steps into the chapel, closing the door most of the way behind him. Just a moment later, hauntingly beautiful notes drift through the air.

I take my time. Breakfast is a challenge to make in this rudimentary kitchen. Ingredients are varied but the options are an odd selection. I silently wonder where it comes from. If some brave soul dares come into Roselock to deliver food, or if Sully actually leaves the town in quest of modern grocery stores and conveniences.

Considering the conversation I overheard just minutes ago, I don't think it's the latter.

Fifteen minutes later, I've fully enjoyed a masterful concert and concocted a breakfast of scrambled eggs, canned sausages, and apple slices. Balancing the two plates, I walk through the kitchen, into the common room, and push the door to the chapel open with the heel of my foot.

Sully doesn't stop playing when I enter, though the way his back stiffens tells me he at least noticed me walk in. I take my place once more on the second row of pews, setting the plates on the wooden bench to my side.

The song Sully plays is so mournful. It echoes like a lone whisper at the bottom of the darkest lake. Like an ending with no promise of another beginning.

And indeed, when he reaches the end of it, he does not start another.

His motions stiff, he turns on the bench, and walks to the first pew, just like he did the other day.

I hand him his breakfast, which he immediately starts eating.

I pick up my own plate and stab at a sausage. I take a nibble as I watch him.

"Why do you not eat more?" he suddenly asks, minutes later. His plate is nearly empty. "Every meal so far, you take two or three bites and that's it."

I look down at my fork and realize I've been using it to push the food around on my plate. I look up at Sully, a little surprised by his sudden probing question. "I guess I've just been nervous ever since I got here. My appetite isn't too strong when my nerves get the best of me."

He shakes his head, his look deepening. "It can't just be that. I saw the pictures, Iona. This is obviously habitual."

I set my plate down on the bench, my appetite disappearing altogether. "What is that supposed to mean?"

He looks at me for a moment, as if he's willing the correct response out of me. But something in his expression breaks, and I see unwilling acceptance fall into place. "Did Jack ever say anything about your weight soon after the two of you started dating?"

"What?" I balk, my own eyes narrowing. "No, of course not!"

"Iona," Sully says, setting his plate aside, fully cleared of all food. "Do you not think you've changed? Do you think you look the same as you did eleven months ago?"

I blink four times fast, shaking my head. Where did this discussion come from?

"You never eat anything, and the sick thing is that I don't think you even notice," Sully says, looking down at my virtually untouched plate. "Go look at those pictures. Tell me you haven't changed. Tell me it has nothing to do with Jack."

"Tell me why you're so angry it's your birthday," I spit back. Aggression and violence spike in my blood. I clench my teeth tightly, my hands rolled into fists. The same anger I felt yesterday when Viola said the things she said.

Sully is quiet for a long time, staring back at me. It's a tug of war and it's clear: neither of us is going to back down and let the other win.

"Get your boots and a coat on," he says, standing. He

grabs his plate and is gone in a second. Frustrated and annoyed at his constant whiplashing, I take my own plate to the kitchen, where I dump all of the food in the garbage.

I retrieve my coat and boots and go to where Sully waits for me at the back door. Together, we walk out onto the deck and step down into the grass. Morning mist sits heavy in the air, quickly freezing my lungs and clinging to all the tiny hairs on my face. I shove my hands deep down into my pockets.

Sully opens the gate to the graveyard, and we wind our way through the different headstones. I realize where we are going when we aim for the back corner of the area.

His family plot sits there, well taken care of, and fairly full. The name Whitmore is splashed across so many headstones.

"John, Patrick, Nicholas, Neal, Lee, Steven, and Aaron," Sully says when he stops where we can see them all. "Do you notice anything peculiar about their headstones?"

I can only read four of the names, the other headstones too worn to make out. They're all in various stages of antiquity, with John's being the most weatherworn, and Aaron's looking the newest. Their death years reveal Sully listed them off in order.

I shrug my shoulders, shaking my head. "Not really. I assume these are your relatives."

"My father," he says, pointing to Aaron's headstone. "My grandfather." Steven. "His father, and his father before him."

"John founded Roselock." I state the fact that I read.

Sully nods his head, though my statement seems to have nothing to do with the point he's getting at. "Simple math, Iona. Look at their birth and death dates." His voice grows harder as the day grows fractionally lighter as dawn breaks. "Simple math."

I look at the dates on his father's headstone first. Born September fourth and died December seventh. At the age of thirty-three.

Steven was thirty-three, as well.

My eyes dart between each of the dates and I see the same horrifying pattern.

"They all died when they were thirty-three," I say as understanding dawns on me.

Sully nods. "Not just when they were thirty-three," he says. "Look a little closer."

September fourth to December seventh. June fifteenth to September eighteenth. November tenth to February thirteenth. April twenty-second to July twenty-fifth.

"Thirty-three years, three months, and three days," I whisper. My eyes flick from date to date, double-checking that my math is correct.

It is.

"Yes," Sully breathes. "Every one of them met a strange and seemingly random death three months and three days after they turned thirty-three."

I look back over at the eighth generation Whitmore male. And my mind counts out the days.

"So, May seventh…"

"I'm going to die," he says in a breath.

CHAPTER TWENTY

SULLY

"Why?" Iona asks. I turn back around, making my way through the graveyard. "How?"

"Doesn't really matter at this point," I say as I step around Dot Hannely's crumbling headstone. "It's a proven system. I've had my entire life to prepare for its execution."

"Sully," she says as she hurries to catch up to me. "There has to be something that can be done about it. No one is supposed to know when death will come for them. How can you...how can you just accept it with such ease?"

I sigh. I should have known better than to go where I just did. "Iona, in two days you're going to leave. And I'm sorry that I reminded you that while you are dealing with grief and so love sick you can't move on with your life, others are dealing with real issues, as well. The world continues to move on, problems and pain and all."

She's quiet for a moment, but I don't look in her direction. I'm certain there's yet another taken aback

95

expression on her pretty little face. She's getting very practiced in them. Apparently, I'm quite a jarring person.

"Okay, so what is it then?" she moves on, expertly ignoring my previous honesty. "Is it a curse or something? I mean, it's so specific. I just—"

I round on her and she nearly crashes right into me. "Look," I say, my voice sharp and low. "You will be leaving very soon. You do not know me. You do not know the Whitmores or Roselock. You do not need to feel sorry for me or feel guilt or whatever emotions are rushing through you."

I take half a step closer to her, which is impressive considering our proximity. "You still have a long life before you. I will speak to Jack for you twice more. And then you will return home. You will eat one whole chocolate cake a day until you don't look like a skeleton anymore, and get healthy and human. And then you're going to live your life. You're going to learn to be happy and eventually you will find someone else to love."

Tears spring into her eyes and she leans away from me, a scared little fawn.

"And in a few months, you won't think of me for one moment," I say, feeling the rabid monster in me calming. "You'll separate from this cursed place the minute your tires hit the highway. You're going to move on, from all of this."

Three tears roll out onto her cheeks.

But I don't offer comfort.

It's what I needed to say and what she needed to hear.

I turn and head back to the church. I push open the

gate and cross the soggy lawn before stepping up onto the deck.

Half a step into the warmth of shelter, an absence of color catches my eye.

Hundreds of roses climb all over the church. Red and brilliant as blood against the white siding.

But there, just above the window to my right, grows a new bud. Its petals have only just begun to peel open.

Red. White.

A perfectly formed rose with red petals.

But within the center of it, a snowy white one is just barely visible.

An omen of the approaching end.

Footsteps on the deck pull my attention away from the rose and I see Iona looking very solemn and quiet. I step aside, letting her into the church and then I close the door behind the two of us.

"You said you'd speak to Jack two more times," she says through a thick throat. "Give me an hour. I need to figure out what I want to say to him."

I nod once. Leaving her alone next to the fire, I walk through the door into the chapel.

CHAPTER TWENTY-ONE

IONA

"Cressida, I'm sorry," I said into the telephone, wrapping the cord around my finger. "I just can't afford to take time off work."

"We need this, Iona," she said, the frustration and annoyance heavy in her voice. "Harold is...well, things have been tense between us. A vacation would do us so much good. And mom, I just can't leave the kids with her when she gets like this."

"I know," I say, squeezing my eyes closed. I lean my forehead against the wall. "I really am sorry. You know I love spending time with the kids, but we have all this stuff going on at work, and if I take time off I'm afraid they'll fire me."

"Fine," my older sister clipped. "Do what you've got to do. It's only my marriage on the line."

She hung up on me.

I sat the phone back on the hook and ran my hands

down my face, frustration seeping into my bones. I loved my sister, I really did, but sometimes she got a little unrealistic with her expectations.

A knock echoed through the apartment from the front door.

Cursing under my breath, I headed to it and pulled it open.

"I'm so sorry," I said, ushering Jack inside, unable to even pull off a little smile. "My sister called and I completely forgot about dinner. Want to re-schedule for tomorrow?"

"Hey, hey," he said gently, running his hands down the back of my arms, pulling me a few steps closer to him. "I'm not here just because you said you'd feed me." He chuckled. "How about I help you make everything, and you tell me what's wrong?"

I sighed, squeezing my eyes closed as I let myself fall forward into his arms, hugging myself to his chest.

Four weeks had passed since our first date and dip in the fountain. Numerous dates had taken place, and a Thursday night tradition quickly formed where I would make dinner for the two of us after work.

I lifted my chin, my lips quickly finding his, feeling so much comfort sink into every crack in me.

Dozens of kisses. Endless walks, hand in hand.

Jack Caraway had very quickly become the highlight of my life.

"I don't really want to talk about Cressida and her drama," I said as I turned for the refrigerator, pulling out the ingredients. I pull out the cutting board and put Jack to work on the tomatoes. It was just the two of us for dinner. Viola was at work. "How was work today?"

"Fine," he said, dutifully setting to cutting them up once he took his jacket off and loosened his tie. "We both agreed one of my patients didn't need to see me again for the next two months."

"That's good," I said hopefully as I put the noodles in the big pot.

"Yeah," he said with a smile in his voice. "I think she's going to be just fine."

I moved on to the next stage of dinner, but I found my mind drifting back to Cressida and her kids.

Guilt was eating me alive.

"Iona," a soft voice suddenly said from behind me, at the same time a strong pair of hands wrapped around my waist. He pulled me back, nestling my body against his, a perfect fit. "Something is obviously bothering you. Talk to me."

"Don't you get tired of people talking to you?" I said, trying to push off the seriousness with a playful tone, and failing.

"Never you," he whispered against my cheek, his lips brushing my skin. Instantly my eyes fluttered closed, every hormone in my body going crazy. "I never get sick of you, baby."

I turned in his grasp and he stepped closer, pinning me between the counter and his body. His hands rose up to my hair, guiding my face to his. Placing my lips on his, exactly where I wanted them.

I tugged at his tie, pulling it from around his neck, my fingers getting forceful with the buttons on his shirt. Jack's hands went from my back, down to my hips, pulling them closer to him.

"I need you, Iona," he breathed into my mouth. "I need you like oxygen. Like a vice I can't break. You're my drug habit I can't and don't want to break."

"Jack," I moaned as his hands wrapped around to my behind, and he pressed his hips all the harder into mine.

"Say you'll be mine," he whispered against my skin as his lips moved to the hollow beneath my ear. "I want you to be mine. Only mine."

My eyes fluttered once before sliding closed once more, my head lolling back as he kissed a line across my throat. "I'm yours."

His hands hoisted me up, my legs wrapping around his waist. My fingers fought to free him from the buttons with more vigor as he took possession of my lips once more. One slow step at a time, he took us back to the bedroom and pushed the door closed behind him.

I DON'T REMEMBER FALLING ASLEEP AFTER WE MADE love. But at some point, late at night, I woke up. I was lying on my stomach, facing the door. My eyes fluttered open, feeling groggy and heavy. Our clothes were scattered all over the floor. A sock there. My skirt pushed up against the closet. A scattering of Jack's things on the bedside table. Some change. A set of keys. His grandfather's pocket watch.

I heard Jack shift in the bed beside me and rolled over to find myself nose to nose with him.

"Hi," he breathed as he ran his knuckles down my cheek.

"Hey," I smiled. "Sorry, I didn't mean to fall asleep."

"It's okay," he said with a smile in return. "Guess my talking afterward lulled you right into sleep."

I chuckled, a happy sigh escaping me. I snuggled myself tighter into his side.

The look in Jack's eyes grew deeper. He propped himself up on his elbow, looking down at me. I let my hands rise up, tracing them down his defined, bare chest.

"You know I adore you, right?" he said, low but firm. "I adore you, Iona Faye."

And something clicked inside of me. I'd never felt this way for another person. So right and connected and centered.

I lifted one hand to place it on the back of his neck, bringing his face closer to mine.

"I love you," I said, firm and true.

And I had no doubt he felt the same way. Something solidified in Jack's eyes, something that promised to never, ever let me go.

I had no doubt about it.

This was it.

"I love you, too."

CHAPTER TWENTY-TWO

SULLY

"COME ON."

Iona stands in the doorway, not meeting my eye. My fingers are still on the organ keys. I look up at her. It's hard to describe her demeanor right now. Tense. Tight. Locked up.

I had shut her down earlier, called her out. And then she had time to go and prepare herself for what is to come.

I'm not sure if it's a sign of strength, or her further fracturing.

The two of us walk out of the chapel and down the hall to the darkened room. I pick up the matches and begin lighting the candles. Iona closes the door behind us. And instantly, the room grows colder.

I look over my shoulder to see Iona standing before her chair. She lets out a big billow of breath, forming a cloud. But she doesn't look afraid. She looks ready.

"The second time is always easier," I say as I finish lighting the last candle. "The first time is overwhelming for the both of you. The second time you are more prepared and know what to expect."

Iona nods, still not looking me in the eye. We both lower into our seats, and I hold out my hands. Determined, she sets the watch in my right hand, and lays her hand in my left.

I let my eyes slide closed, letting the darkness open in my chest. Probing, searching.

"Jack," I say just once.

A shift in the air, a drop in temperature.

I open my eyes, and there he stands just to the right of Iona.

"Thanks for bringing me back," he says, looking me in the eye.

"He's here," I tell Iona.

Her head immediately perks up, looking all around the room. Something the living always do when I open the gate. I nod my head to where Jack stands, and her eyes settle a little off to his right.

"I'm sorry I left so suddenly last time," Jack says and I relay his words. "It got too difficult to stay."

"It's okay," she says, a smile beginning to pull onto her lips. "I understand. Sully explained things."

Jacks eyes flick up to mine, and there's something difficult to read in them. There's something about him that crawls under my skin, like a hundred starved beetles.

"So that's what you do?" Jack asks me. "You act as a portal between the dead and the living."

"Yes," I respond.

Iona looks from Jack to me, confusion on her face.

"He's just asking how this works," I tell her, suddenly wanting to protect her from any more distress. Jacks presence and absence are doing enough of that on their own. I look back to Jack. "I can communicate, summon you through a personal object." I nod to his watch in my hand. "And relay what you say to the living. She can't see you, can't hear you, herself."

There's a little flick of something that sparks in his eyes, but I can't quite tell if it's surprise or fear.

"Jack, I can't stay here forever, so we have now, and Sully has agreed to open the gate once more after this," Iona cuts in, as if she can feel the clock ticking. Which it is. "I just have some things I need to say. Some things I have to put out there between the two of us so maybe I can finally start to piece myself back together."

"I didn't mean to leave you broken, baby," Jack says. He kneels at her side, his hand hovering just over her arm, but he hesitates. He doesn't touch her.

"I know," she says as her voice cracks and tears well up in her eyes. "It wasn't your fault."

"What do you need to say?" he asks.

I shift uncomfortably, Jack too close for comfort, even though I know he can't touch me. I'm ready to send him back to limbo and we've only just begun.

"I need to get all of the plans I had for us out of my head," Iona says, shifting her gaze to where I indicate. "Our engagement was only three weeks long and I know we didn't have much time to talk about wedding and life details, but I've spent the last two months thinking about it all, over and over and over again."

"Tell me, baby," Jack says, scooting all the closer, and if he's not careful, he's going to fall right through her. "Tell me every single detail."

She smiles, despite the tears that break out onto her cheeks. "I wanted to get married on May first," she begins. "When all the flowers are out and the air is fresh and warm. I wanted to do it at the park in town, because that's where so much of this started."

"It's perfect," Jack says with a smile, nodding his head. "We could have even taken an unexpected dip in the fountain."

Iona laughs, squeezing more tears out onto her cheeks. She nods. "And danced on the pavilion, even if there was no music."

There's some memory to that comment I don't know about, just like another million details to their relationship.

"Any night you felt spontaneous," Jack says, reaching out as if to caress her cheek. But he stops himself just in time.

She nods. "I picked out this dress from the shop on Third. I tried it on and everything, two weeks after…" She doesn't say the word, and they rarely do. If they come to me, they haven't gotten to the acceptance part of the grief cycle. "I would have bought it if I'd had the money."

"I wish I could have seen you in it," Jack says. "I know you looked spectacular."

Iona bites her lower trembling lip. Her hand that rests in mine shakes terribly. She's about five minutes away from crumbling to rubble.

"We would have gone to Spain for our honeymoon," she continues painting the painful picture she can never make a reality. "I know how badly you'd always wanted to travel there."

"Would you have let me run with the bulls?" Jacks asks with a smile.

"Not a chance," she laughs. "But we would have done that hike you kept talking about."

She's quiet for a long moment, and Jack doesn't say anything, either. Her eyes have fallen into her lap, a slow stream of tears tracing their way down her face. Jack just silently watches her, poised so close, yet so unable to connect.

"You know that little white house on Pine Street?" she finally says. She looks up, her eyes searching for his face, only she'll never find it again.

"Yes," he says.

"It went for sale two days before everything happened. I don't know if you noticed. But I wanted to buy it. I wanted us to start a life there, so bad."

I watch Iona as she speaks, and it's so difficult. Seeing the way her lip trembles. The red splotches forming around her eyes. Feeling the quivers that rip through her hand. And I know she doesn't deserve to feel the way she's feeling. I look at Jack, and something just isn't...

Just isn't...

"Four kids," she says with a smile. "Because three growing up was always such a way to start fights. Someone is always left out."

Something in Jack's expression tells me that perhaps their future desire for kids might have differed.

Not that it matters now.

"But that would have had to wait for a few years," she says, a playful smile perking on her face. "Because I wasn't ready to give up being spontaneous. I just wanted to do it with you."

"Always." There's a quiver in the air, just small, nearly imperceptible, but I know it's going to grow quickly. Jack looks over his shoulder at me, and I know he can feel his time is short.

"Listen, baby," he says, his words suddenly hurried. "I know this is hard for you. So hard. But I promise, I will never really leave you. You can never liberate yourself from me."

She laughs at that, though the tears freely stream down her face now. She can hear the urgency in his words, and she knows time is short.

"We would have had a robust and exciting life together. Don't let go of that dream." Jack moves to sit on the arm of the chair, leaning in closer, his face only an inch from hers.

"You know I adore you." At his words, Iona's eyes slide closed, as if fully absorbing them.

The air quakes, shifting and vibrating violently. Darkness creeps into every one of my limbs.

"I love you."

And Jack disappears back into limbo.

CHAPTER TWENTY-THREE

IONA

EVENING TWILIGHT CASTS ROSELOCK IN VIOLENT shades of red and gold. The sky is laced with random clouds, but it's the most I've seen of the sky in a week.

I walk down the one road that leads to the church, my hands pushed deep into my coat pockets.

Back behind me, I can feel Sully's presence, standing on the porch, feel his eyes watching me.

I need some space. Some air to breathe. Some room to stretch and feel once more that the world is real.

Because I feel like it keeps disconnecting. It's become this small ball of pain and grief and obsession and not caring one bit.

I *open* my eyes as I walk down the road.

Leaves not blown elsewhere from fall are pushed up against the steps of one house. A frozen puddle fills the left side of the road before another house. The trees moan on the edge of town where the wind pushes its way through them.

At the roundabout, I veer onto the road that cuts to the right instead of keeping straight where it leads back to the highway.

Be back before dark, Sully had said as I walked out the front doors.

I should question that. But I don't.

Not a chance I will be out here after dark.

Half a mile down the road and I only see two more houses. One is tiny and hardly stands. Most of the siding has been ripped off from the wind. The other is built of stone and looks intact except for the broken windows. Behind it stands the remains of a barn.

I continue down the road another half mile, over the gravel that crunches beneath my boots.

The landscape has been growing flatter and flatter the farther I walk. The mist starts creeping in, so slowly I don't even realize it's there until it's fairly thick.

So I don't notice the trees that suddenly crop up when the road dissolves into a field.

Planted in perfect rows, stretching out at least two dozen deep, stand some variety of tree I don't have a name for. Some of them seem to have since died, branches hanging to the ground, their trunks black and in various stages of decay.

But the trunk of every single one of them takes a sharp curve, right where it comes out of the ground. Like a reaper's scythe. It rounds wide, and finally climbs up, stretching up to the sky, finally straight.

The sounds of nature grow quieter as I walk into the grove, checking over my shoulder in every direction. A twig snaps far off to my left, and for a moment, I'm about to loose a scream, when I turn to see a deer darting off into the distance.

Despite the non-threatening animal, my heart rate can't seem to calm down. But my feet can't seem to stop, either.

The colors fade from red to gold, slipping slowly to bluish gray.

The trees stretch on for at least half a mile before I can make out familiar oak and scrub in the distance.

But all of these crooked trees, bent, as if someone punched out their bases and they shaped like clay... They cocoon me into their nest.

My foot suddenly slips, and I nearly topple over, scrambling back and barely catching myself.

A hole rests just to the side of me, leaves and roots tangling into the walls of it, making it difficult to notice, at first. But it stretches four feet across, six feet long.

And six feet deep.

My hands shake as through the dark, I put what I'm seeing together.

Two skeletons, perfectly white and crisp and clean, lie together at the bottom of the grave. Their hands are clenched together, their heads tilted toward one another.

A small little gasp erupts from my throat and I scramble back from it, only to crash into something warm and solid.

A scream rips from me as I whip around, prepared to run from a bear or a moose or some other deadly wildlife.

But the only wildlife present is Sully and his mane.

"It's okay," he says, holding his hands up, and I realize I've got my fists raised. "It's just me."

"What are you doing?" I ask, not dropping them, the adrenaline still burning too hot through my veins. "Are... are you following me?"

His eyes dart to the grave and he nods. "It's getting too dark. We need to get inside."

"What?" I ask, looking around, trying to figure out which direction I came from. But I'm completely turned around. "Why are they there? Why aren't they in the graveyard?"

I turn back, staring down at their skeletons. Clinging to one another so tenderly, so desperate to not be parted, even in death.

Sully grabs the back of my coat and pulls me in the opposite direction. I stumble, still staring at the grave, but follow him through the quickly darkening evening.

"The Lovers, as they've always been called," Sully explains. His words fall flat, unable to travel far in the dense grove. "They've been there since before Roselock was founded, the trees too. The grave was filled in several times. But it was always re-exhumed by the next morning."

"Who keeps digging them out?" I ask as a cold drop of fear slips down my spine.

"It's Roselock," Sully says as we break out of the grove

and back onto the road. "There are a lot of questions with no answers here."

My heart won't calm down as we quickly walk down the road. So many questions are racing through my mind, but none of them slow down enough to form into words.

The abandoned nature of Roselock. The trail of pennies that runs all through town. The curse Sully's family suffers from.

I come from the *real* world. Of work and families and mundane boring days. None of this makes sense to me. None of it feels real.

"How long has it been since anyone else lived here, Sully?" I finally find my words.

He looks over his shoulder back at me. He walks at a much faster pace than I do with his long legs. I scramble to catch up, afraid of being left behind as the light fails by the moment.

"Six years," he says. He pushes his hands deep into the pockets of his coat. "Carl Henderson was the last of the old timers. He passed away, and then it was just me."

We walk around the roundabout, past the dead trees that sit in the center of it. Just a few dozen yards until the safety of the church.

Some kind of yelping noise sounds from the trees. My hand instantly darts out, clinging to Sully's arm. A second later, I swear I hear a laugh over the sound of the wind.

Sully's hand engulfs mine, and he pulls the two of us forward at a faster pace.

The air grows colder, the wind picking up speed. Just five yards from the front steps, my feet catch something wet and slick, and I slip.

Sully grabs me before I go down, picking me up like I'm a rag doll. I look back over his shoulder, searching through the dark for what I slipped in.

Something dark saturates the ground, growing and spreading out from beneath the church.

A rush of air rises like a howling wolf. The stairs protest as Sully's hulking form hauls the both of us up, yanking the door open, and slamming it behind us, locking it.

"Something…" I say, breathless, as he sets me back on my feet. "Something isn't right in this town, Sully." Sharp claws bite at the back of my eyes, threatening to make tears pool. "You shouldn't be here. Why…why do you stay?"

Cast in candlelight, I pace, trying to make my mind process what started just outside those doors.

But as I round to retrace my steps, I still in horror.

Following up to me, the same shape and size as my boots, is a set of red footprints.

"Is that…" I gasp, my hands coming to my mouth. The dark red, smeared with mud.

"It is," Sully says. He stands beside one of the arched windows, hands on his hips, his back turned to me. "It'll be gone by morning."

"Sully, that doesn't make any sense," I say, shaking my head. I sink onto a pew, violently attempting to remove my boots and the blood I can't explain. "This whole town, it doesn't make any sense. This place is dangerous. There is a reason no one lives here, anymore."

"Yes, there is," he says without turning back to me. "My family cursed the land."

CHAPTER TWENTY-FOUR

SULLY

"What is that supposed to mean?" Iona says.

I turn to see her sitting on a pew, her knees tucked up into her chest, looking so small and so shaken.

"I told you to be back inside before dark," I say with annoyance and frustration. "You didn't need to see that."

I turn and head through the chapel, passing the organ and through the doors. The embers in the fireplace are just enough to not have to re-start a brand new fire. I stuff three logs inside, opening the air vent to give it oxygen and make it roar.

"Please," Iona says as she follows me in her socks. "Don't do that to me, Sully. Don't just brush me off. Don't treat me like I'm just some fragile idiot. I can't take any more of that."

I turn to face her. She stands there, so small and so fragile and yes, a love struck idiot. But there's a spark in her eyes, something determined and fierce.

"It doesn't matter," I say despite her surprising show of inner strength. "You'll leave tomorrow and I told you, you're never to think of Roselock again."

"And how do you think that is possible?" she says as she takes three steps closer to me. "What I've seen here. You? How do you ever expect me to just never think of all of this again?"

Her eyes are so sincere and fierce.

I see something of myself reflected there. Something lonely and isolated.

"Please, just talk to me," she begs, taking another step forward. She stands only a foot away. "I don't have anyone else right now. No one has understood for so long. They…" she shakes her head. "I feel so isolated these days. Please, Sully," she looks up at me. "Just talk to me like I'm a human being again."

Something cracks in my chest when she says my name. Reaches out and holds a mirror to my own empty soul that's been isolated for so long. Who hasn't had another soul to talk to in ages.

"John Whitmore showed up in the valley in 1761," I say without looking away from Iona. I don't move. And neither does she. "He brought with him five other families and his wife and daughter, and their unborn son."

The journals, detailing the entire story sit on a shelf in my bedroom. John's handwriting is nearly illegible. But it tells a grim tale.

"He'd heard rumor there was coal in the mountains," I continue the tale. Iona grabs my hand and leads the two of us to the kitchen. She starts digging through the pantry, pulling out seemingly random ingredients. "My ancestors have a long history in mining, so he was well prepared to begin his own. Had investments and financial backing to get started."

I sit at the table. "They arrived in the fall, barely surviving the coming winter as they worked, started the mine, and slowly began building homes for the five families. But as they dug into the ground, they kept finding bodies."

The wooden spoon in Iona's hand slips, clattering to the counter. She looks over her shoulder at me, her brows furrowed.

"All the graves were unmarked, but there were dozens of bodies, scattered around the valley. But by this point they were too far into the development of the mine. And they were already finding coal. John decided they couldn't move, despite the disturbing things they kept finding."

Iona turns back to the food she is preparing, chopping something before dumping it into a pot.

"But come spring, after the first five houses were done, two more in process as others heard about the job opportunities, a tribe showed up."

"Roselock was their burial ground," Iona says, understanding coming into her voice.

I nod. "They'd brought the remains of their loved ones with them, intending to bury them on what was their holy ground. Instead, they found strangers who had built homes right on top of their ancestors."

"How terrible," Iona says as she stirs whatever is in the pot. "For everyone. John didn't know. And the tribe must have been devastated."

I nod. "You can imagine it didn't end well. They fought. It was a small tribe, and even though there were only a few families in the township, they had guns. After two days, four of John's people were dead, but every one of the tribe was, as well."

The screams. The blood.

I close my eyes, and I can see it all. Played out over and over in my nightmares.

"All of them?" Iona breathes.

I nod, my eyes still closed. "No one had been willing to compromise. John and his people buried the tribe in a mass grave, tried to do the Christian thing. And they tried to move on, despite having killed thirty-three innocent people."

She looks over her shoulder at the number and I know she hasn't missed its significance.

"More and more settlers came to Roselock over the next year and the mine was producing well. More homes were built. Talk of a train being brought in was heavily discussed."

I place my hands flat on the table, rubbing them back and forth across the rough surface, letting my eyes trace the grain of the wood. "But strange things kept happening. The children sleepwalked. Women would forget what they were doing half way through dinner and catch their skirts on fire. Tools were constantly breaking."

Iona puts a lid on the pot and comes to sit at the table. I don't look up at her, I just study the table, but I'm seeing an entirely different picture.

"The population rose to one hundred and twelve. They brought in a pastor and started building this very church."

The wind picks up outside and the building moans under the pressure and age.

"Construction was completed in the spring of 1762. It was dedicated on March third, the anniversary of that bloody battle one year prior. The very same moment the bell first rang, there was an explosion in the mine."

Iona takes in a sharp breath.

"Thirty-three men and boys were killed in the mine that day," I say, able to list off every one of their names. "Forever trapped inside the mountain."

"That's awful," she whispers. She reaches forth a hand, resting it over one of mine. "So, the land was cursed?"

I nod. "Everyone believed it after the mine incident. Most decided it was too unsafe to stay, and half of the town moved away over the next few weeks. Including the pastor."

"But your family stayed." She squeezes my hand, trying to be comforting.

"No," I correct her. My chest tightens, making it harder to breathe. "They moved to Carmack with the first wave. John was ruined financially, he had no choice but to try to find a way to survive elsewhere."

I look up to see the confusion on her face.

"But his family had only been gone for one year when John began having nightmares about that night the tribe returned to their holy ground. Intense, penetrating nightmares. It nearly drove him mad. Finally, he visited Roselock, stayed one night, and the nightmares ceased. He moved his family back the following week, right back into their old house."

"How old was he when they moved back?" she asks, knowing what is eventually coming for poor John Whitmore.

"Thirty-one. He died two years later, collapsed, just dead, while helping a neighbor with his cows."

"A heart attack, maybe?" she asks.

"Maybe," I say. And maybe it's true, but maybe this ice in my chest says it was something else. "His son, Patrick, was eight years old when he died. Patrick also tried to leave Roselock, met his wife while working in Baltimore, only to nearly go mad from the nightmares of a scene he wasn't even alive to see."

"What?" Iona gasps. "Patrick wasn't even born, but he saw the same war?"

I nod. "And so did every one of the Whitmore men, on down to my grandfather Steven, who only ventured out of town for two months. By the time my father came along, he knew better than to try and leave. He lived his entire life in this decaying town, and never once left its borders."

"And each of them died at thirty-three, three months and three days," she states as she sits back in her chair like she's borne too much weight just saying the words.

"Patrick got sick two days before his death date. It just progressed, and when the day came, by supper, he was dead. Steven was pushed down a well, though none of the witnesses were able to identify the woman who pushed him. She simply vanished the moment after.

"Over and over, the Whitmore men met strange, early ends," I say. "And then my father simply sat in his bedroom the entire day, under the careful, watchful eye of my mother," I said, remembering the weight of that day. "She was determined that my father could beat this curse, that if he could only make it to the next day that he could break it for good. So he sat in his bed, staring at the walls, waiting for the hours to count down."

Iona suddenly yelps and pulls her hand away. I didn't realize I'd been squeezing it.

"I'm sorry," I say, blinking quickly, trying to pull myself out of the memory of that day. I'm unsuccessful. I shake my head. "At ten o'clock, my mother started to breathe a little easier. At eleven she brought out a bottle of champagne. But at 11:52, my father dropped his glass, reached into the bedside table, produced his handgun, and shot himself in the head."

A small squeak slips past Iona's lips and I look up at her once more. Tears have welled up in her eyes, fat and heavy, threatening to break free.

"And that is the legacy of the name Whitmore," I whisper. "The town of Roselock is always strange at night. There are always voices, always moans that slither between the trees. But for a month before, and a month after the anniversary of that bloody battle, the spirits are stronger."

The air is so, so cold. The silence is deafening, as if

those dead have gathered round, leaning in, listening to their bloody tale. "The battle replays every night, for sixty days. You'll not see the dead, never catch them with your eye. But the town, it replays the echo of that night. Over and over."

The nighttime echoes began two days ago. Now there is less than a month until the anniversary of that battle.

"*That* is why you shouldn't go outside when it's dark," I whisper.

Iona shakes her head, loosing a tear. She doesn't ask more questions, though. I'm certain she's too afraid, as she should be.

"Your food is burning," I interrupt the maddening silence as the smell wafts into the air.

She looks relieved for the change of conversation and instantly leaps up. She turns down the heat and sets to stirring the food before it's ruined.

"I hope you're hungry," she says as she pulls two bowls down from the shelf with shaking hands.

CHAPTER TWENTY-FIVE

IONA

I draw a bath when it's nearly eleven. The water steams, hot and fogging the windows which I'm too terrified to look outside of. Stripping off my clothes, which feel cursed themselves after everything I've learned today, I sink down into the water.

Tiny flecks of rust swirl in the claw foot tub, just five of them. Like everything else in this church, it's suffering from neglect and disuse. A single candle burns on the counter, casting me in shadows.

My eyes slide closed and my muscles relax. Suddenly, I'm exhausted. I hadn't realized how much the mystery of Roselock and Sully's past had taken out of me.

How terrible. How unfair. The way his fate is sealed.

I'm sure he can't wait for this day to be over.

Yet it just speeds up the countdown.

Come on, Jack said, aiming that irresistible smile at me. *It's my birthday. I've been dying to take you on this trip.*

"I don't know," I said, shrugging as Jack walked me home from work. "I mean, we always made Mom's birthday a big deal. It was kind of Dad's thing. And with this being the first one since he died, I just don't know that I can miss it."

"I want you to think about it," Jack said, slipping his briefcase into the other hand before taking mine in his. "I swear, if I'd known your mom's birthday was the day after mine, I wouldn't have gone ahead and booked the trip."

I look over at him, somewhat annoyed, but also entirely flattered at his grand gesture. I'd walked home from work, meeting him at his office as he was closing up, where he sprang the news on me that he'd booked us a surprise trip to Florida for his birthday.

But complications made this not as easy as he'd hoped.

"I'll think about it," I said, offering him a small smile. Something tugged in my chest, a war battling for my desires. The loyalty to my family, knowing I'd be needed, and knowing how very badly I wanted to travel to Florida, where I'd never been, to spend time with the man I love.

"Do what you feel is best for you inside," Jack said with a smile as he hesitated on the corner across from my apartment. He pressed a quick kiss to my lips and we said our goodbyes.

I wipe my wet hands down my face, pressing hard, trying to block out the past. The familiar pain is seeping up through my veins, climbing its way into my heart. My breathing picks up as the panic settles into my chest.

Jack is gone.

Jack isn't coming back.

He's really dead.

Water splashes everywhere as I lunge forward, reaching down through the water for the plug. I rip it up, tossing it across the bathroom. My breaths rip in and out of my chest, all too quick. My head spins, the heat of the water letting my blood travel through my body all to easily.

Slowly pulling myself to my feet, I step out and grab the towel on the counter, the one Sully gave me before I came in. But looking around, I realize I forgot to bring in clean clothes.

I listen at the door for a long moment, but it's silent. It has to be close to midnight, it seems safe to assume Sully has gone to sleep.

Cracking the door, I peer out, and when I see no signs of Sully, I creep out and down the hallway.

I rummage through my bag and begin pulling clothing out.

And nearly jump out of my skin when a small creak sounds through the space.

My head whips up, meeting Sully's eyes as he steps from the chapel into the main hall.

"I, uh…" he struggles for words. And I don't miss it as his eyes travel down and back up, quickly, because I do stand here in just a tiny towel. He looks away uncomfortably. "Sorry, I was trying not to wake you. I didn't expect you to still be up."

"It's alright," I say quietly, standing with my sleeping clothes clutched in one hand, the other holding my towel, trying to pull it higher up on my chest. "I was just getting ready for bed."

He nods, turning toward his room. He takes a few steps in that direction, when he falters before turning back. "Your tattoo," he says, his eyes darting momentarily to it. "What does it mean?"

My own eyes look down at it, where it hesitates so close to my shoulder. "Infinity times infinity," I say, looking down at the two infinity signs intersecting. "Jack had one, too."

Sully nods. "How long have you had it?"

I bite my lower lip, holding in the smile. "We got them in June," I tell him. "We'd been out all night. I'll admit, I don't remember going to get it, I was so drunk that night."

Sully smiles too, though it doesn't look genuine. He nods once. "Okay. Goodnight, then."

"Goodnight," I breathe, raising my clothes to cover up the tattoo.

Without another word, Sully stalks down the hall toward his bedroom, his shoulders tense in that animalistic way.

CHAPTER TWENTY-SIX

SULLY

"She's entirely fixated on this man," I say. Steam billows from my mouth in the cold air. "Everything about it just screams…unhealthy."

I sit on a dusty chair in a broken and dilapidated house down the road. There's a hole in the ceiling the size of a bowling ball. An abandoned bird's nest rests at the top of the wardrobe. Dirt and debris are blown into every corner.

In my hand, I clutch a pair of spectacles.

And in front of me stands a man with wild white hair, his clothes always disheveled, his eyes a little too bright for his own sanity.

"Love makes you do strange things," Alfred Carakos says, slowly walking around his old home, a look of sadness in his eyes at its pitiful state. "Just look at most teenagers. Their hormones and feelings control their every thought. They let it control their entire lives."

I shake my head. "This feels different. She's a grown

woman. Smart. Independent. She had her own life before Jack Caraway came into it. But now she's…"

A shell is what comes to mind, but the word feels too harsh.

"You never knew the woman before this Jack died," Alfred says as he finally stops his tour of his past life and settles onto the old, very broken rocking chair in the corner. But he isn't a tangible being, and it doesn't disturb the old piece of furniture. "I'd wager she only seems worse now. She suffered a great loss. She saw the man she was going to marry be murdered. Trauma can leave deep scars that can have scary aftereffects."

I shake my head. "And what about this feeling in my bones? The one setting off warning bells? The feeling that makes my skin crawl? Do I just ignore my basic human instinct that something isn't right?"

Alfred leans forward, fixing me with his gray eyes. "What does it matter now if there was something wrong? The man is dead."

I lean back at those words. And relief floats up in my chest.

Jack *is* dead.

He can't touch Iona. Can't do anything to her ever again.

My eyes slide back to Alfred's. They study me, reading down into my core, and I know he's slipped into professional-opinion mode. "I think the question you should be asking yourself, Sully Whitmore, is why do you care so much?"

I don't have an answer right away. My brain is turning, over and over, trying to find an answer, because the long dead crazy psychologist, who came to Roselock to live out the rest of his days studying the supernatural, is right.

I do care.

"Because pain and loneliness recognizes pain and loneliness," I say as I stand. "It's a basic part of human nature to bond together to remedy those things."

I look back at Alfred when I reach the door.

He shakes his head. "But in bonding together, you know you're only going to cause more of it in three months and two days."

I nod, looking out at the sun dawning over the trees. "I know. I won't let it go that far. She'll leave either tonight or in the morning, and we will never see one another again."

I slip the spectacles into my pocket, and the presence of Alfred evaporates.

Down the steps I go. Something crunches as I step off the last rickety stair and I look down to see the crushed skull of a crow beneath my boot, and it's skeleton extending beyond it, tiny feet sticking straight up in the air.

The day is surprisingly warm as I slowly walk back in the direction of the church. With the sun rising, the temperature is rapidly warming. An unexpected, pleasant surprise on this early February morning.

Carefully, I step over the trail of pennies that cuts across the road, placed there the year after I was born by a child afflicted with madness, a product of this cursed town.

When I come into view of the church, I see Iona standing on the sagging porch, just watching me.

Her hair is twisted up in a bun atop her head. Those dark eyes watch me with all the emptiness of a deep grave. Her shoulders are tensed up to her ears, holding all of the sadness and regret bottled inside so she looks like a human being on the outside.

I nod my head for her, and a moment later, she steps off the porch at my invitation and works her way down the drive toward me.

"What time is it safe to leave the church?" she asks as we head south.

"Ten minutes before dawn, things settle down," I answer her. "So the time changes with the year."

She's quiet. I look over and her face is pale. She swallows, and I can see the tightness of her throat.

"What is it?"

She doesn't respond immediately. She pushes her hands further down in her coat, staring at the road ahead. "You weren't there when I woke up. After last night..." She pauses, steam blowing out from her lips. "I was scared."

I don't know if she realizes she does it, but she takes a step closer to me, walking side by side. I can feel her body heat through our coats.

"You're a smart woman, then," I say, ignoring the tug in my chest that I can't quite explain. "Roselock is dangerous. Those who don't have to be here shouldn't stay."

Iona nods her head, but I can tell from the distant look in her eyes that my words didn't connect.

"I will speak to Jack tonight for the last time, if you like," I say when she doesn't say anything. "Or tomorrow morning."

She doesn't respond. Doesn't make a sound. Doesn't look my way.

I am walking beside a shell.

"What will you do, once you leave Roselock?"

I stop suddenly, looking at her as she takes three more steps before she realizes that our walk is over. She looks back at me, her brows furrowing together slightly.

"Once you get your closure, once you say goodbye to Jack," I continue. "What will you do with your life?"

She looks at me. And at first, it's confusion on her face. As if she doesn't understand. Can't comprehend that there is a life outside of mourning her dead fiancé. And then, it's almost as if there's fear in her eyes.

She shakes her head.

"I…" she says, her very voice sounding lost. "I don't know. I'm…" Her lip begins to quiver. "I'm not sure I'm going to be done after today. If one more time will be enough."

I slide my hands into my pockets, and the wariness in me grows deeper roots. "I've given you more time than I've ever given anyone else, Iona. You can still live. Still find happiness. You don't have to stay an eternal prisoner to this grief."

She takes a step toward me, her eyes fixed on mine. "Tell me how you do it, Sully. You've lost people you love, more than once. Tell me how you deal with it."

And I know she's backed me into a corner. Because I don't have an answer for her. Not a good one. The ways I've dealt with death and loss aren't necessarily good, healthy advice. The look in Iona's eyes tells me she knows it.

"Take the day to decide what you'd like to say as your goodbye," I change directions. "We will open the gate tonight."

I turn and walk back toward the graveyard.

CHAPTER TWENTY-SEVEN

IONA

"I HOPE YOU TAKE TODAY AND THINK ABOUT WHY THIS is so wrong." Cressida followed me to the door, venom burning in her eyes. "You've only known Jack for a few weeks. This is your *mother* you're abandoning. You're a Faye, Iona. Don't forget that."

She slammed the door in my face, and I just stood there, stunned, for a moment.

I knew it wasn't going to be received well, but I didn't expect her full-on meltdown.

"Hey," Jack's voice cooed into my ear from behind. I felt his hand on my hip, one on my arm, pulling me back toward the car. "It'll be okay. It's just a little fresh right now."

I nodded my head and stepped back to the car, though my eyes stayed fixed on the house.

The drive to the airport was long, and I should have felt anxious about the upcoming flight, but my mind was back home, thinking of the way my mother's face crumpled, the tears that fell down her face, when I told her I wouldn't be there for her birthday, but I'd take her out when I got back.

I think I broke her, then.

Jack took care of all the details, checking us in for the flight, getting our baggage to the right area for drop off. He guided me through the busy airport and the next thing I knew, I was in my seat.

"Hey," Jack said, leaning in. "Where's that head of yours?"

I blinked five times fast, dragging myself back into the moment. I looked around, confused for a moment, and then Jack's face came into focus.

Those concerned brows. That strong jawline. His beautiful green eyes.

A smile curled on my lips and my heart instantly warmed. I leaned forward and pressed my lips to his.

I felt him smile against my own lips and he brought a hand to the back of my head.

"This is exactly where I want to be," he said. "Right here with you."

His words sank into my heart, wrapped around my lungs, took root in the soles of my feet. "Me, too."

Soon, we were in the air, and I watched in wonder as the earth grew smaller and smaller. Jack stayed at my side, his hand laced with mine, as he pointed out the barely recognizable landmarks below us, before everything disappeared behind a cover of clouds.

Touching down on the Miami soil, I held the arms of

my chair with white knuckles. Jack just smiled and gave a little laugh as he watched me. Together, we exited the plane, collected our luggage, and I about melted to the hot concrete as we walked out, and a driver was waiting beside a limousine, holding a sign that said *Caraway/Faye.*

He drove us to our hotel, a sky-high building right at the edge of the place where the sea met the land.

I sighed in contentment as we entered the room and I set my bag beside the bed. Outside our window stretched the endless ocean.

"Jack," I breathed as I walked to it, taking it all in. "This is amazing."

He came up behind me, placing his hands on my hips, tucking his chin into my neck. "You're amazing. Thank you for coming with me."

I reached a hand back, lacing my fingers into his hair. "Can we always go on adventures like this, on every birthday?"

"We can have as robust of a travel life as you want, baby," he whispered into my ear. "Wherever you want to go."

I smiled, leaning back into his chest, imagining all the adventures we could have together.

"You want to go get some dinner before we explore that beach?" he asked.

I smiled and shook my head. "I'm not hungry. Let's go see what those waves are all about."

CHAPTER TWENTY-EIGHT

IONA

I WALK INTO THE ROOM BEFORE SULLY DOES AND GO straight to the box of matches sitting on the floor. I strike one and light the candles around the room. Not looking at Sully, I sit on the chair, and wait for him.

The sound of his heavy boots warns me he's moved. His tall form casts a long shadow against the wall. The scent of pine and cotton and dust envelops me as he sits in his chair.

I can't meet his eyes.

Because for the past twenty-four hours, he's been studying. Digging with that gaze of his, looking to unearth something.

I think I'm guarding that something. I don't know why. But a little viper sits coiled in my stomach, waiting to strike if he digs too deep.

I pull the watch out from my coat pocket and drop it in Sully's hand.

"You've never mentioned why the pocket watch is so significant to Jack," Sully says.

I'm frustrated. Ready to begin.

But I take in how Sully intentionally avoids taking my hand, filling the time instead with words.

"Why this?" he asks, raising it in his hand briefly.

"Because it belonged to his grandfather," I say. My eyes fix on it. It's nothing special to look at. Plain, with no adornments. Gold, real gold, yes. But simple. "It came from Toronto, where Jack grew up. His grandfather gave it to Jack's father when he went off to college. And then Jack's father gave it to him once he was a freshman."

I smile, a memory surfacing, of me running my finger up the gold chain, wrapping my finger around it. Of the proud way Jack looked at it as he told me the same story.

"He carried it with him everywhere," I continue. "He got some strange looks because of it. It's beyond old-fashioned. But he was proud of it."

Sully depresses the catch and the face of it pops open. There is no picture inside, as some old watches had. Jack said he intended to put our wedding picture inside, someday. But for now, it's just the gold surface, and the now-still hands of the clock.

Frozen forever at three-thirty-three.

My blood goes chill.

I look up at Sully, and his eyes are locked on the time, as well.

It seems significant. That it died at that particular time.

My heart jumps to a tripping race. My palms sweat. My breathing feels lodged and stuck in my throat.

But Sully only looks at it, his brows furrowed together.

"I…" I stutter. "I-"

"Some things are purely coincidence, Iona," he cuts me off. He closes his fingers, shutting the watch. It entirely disappears into his giant hand. "Are you ready?"

I look up from his hand to his eyes. There's something resolved in them. Maybe relief. This is the last time he has to Speak for me, and then I will be out of his way, and he will never have to see me again.

I nod.

I place my hand in Sully's.

And the air grows frigid.

"Iona," Jack speaks through Sully.

"Jack," I whisper. All the air leaves my chest, and I sag forward.

"Iona, I know we don't have much time, so I just wanted to tell you a few things," Jack says.

My eyes wander the room and Sully nods his head just to the right of me, his line of sight low, as if he's kneeling next to me. I angle that direction, my eyes straining, as if I look hard enough, I can pick him out of the air, make him materialize and become tangible.

"Things are going to be hard, and the way up to the surface might not be clear, but I want you to remember that I adore you," Jack says. It's amazing, the inflections and tones Sully uses, it's Jack's voice, only slightly deeper.

A tear breaks free from my lashes, rolling down my face.

I see Sully's eyes slide from my right, to me, watch as they move slightly to my cheek. And I wonder, is Jack trying to wipe away my tears?

"I love you, Jack," I breathe out. "I don't know how to move on. I feel like my life is ruined. Tossed upside down, and nothing is as it should be, and now I'm just alone and drowning."

"Don't drown, baby," he says. "I wish I could still be there. Wish I could be your safe harbor. But you have to be strong. Can you do that for me?"

My hands shake. Sully tightens his grip on me so we don't lose the connection. I squeeze my eyes closed, forcing out more tears. I bite my lower lip because it quivers.

I shake my head.

"You have to," Jack says. "It's almost over. You can make it."

"Over?" I question, my eyes flying back open.

"It can't hurt this bad forever," he says.

There's a hesitation in Sully's voice that I don't think is repeated from Jack. My eyes slide up to his, but he's looking just beyond my shoulder.

His eyes are narrowed just slightly.

"But what if it doesn't end, Jack?" I say, turning in my seat, looking where the speaker for the dead looks. "What if I don't ever get over this?"

"You will," Jack says. "Because you're my girl. I believe in you."

I let my eyes slide closed once more. I reach a hand out,

searching for something solid and physical. But there isn't anything.

I take a deep breath in, slowly letting it out.

I want the effort to make me feel better. To suddenly feel the spark of relief and the ability to move on.

But I just feel exactly the same.

Still, I nod.

For Jack.

"And are you…happy?" I ask, raising my eyes to where I think he is. "Where you are? On the other side?"

There's a moment of pause. "I…" Sully hesitates. "It's not what I thought there would be. The emptiness. The waiting. There was still so much I wanted to accomplish in life."

I nod as another tear breaks free. "It's not fair. You were doing such incredible work."

"You were my greatest," Jack says, tugging my heart.

A little sob doesn't quite escape my lips, when suddenly Sully jerks back just slightly, though he doesn't sever the touch between us.

I blink three times fast. "What is it?"

Sully looks around, his lips forming a thin line. "He's gone." He releases my hand, and instantly it's cold. Even though the room immediately warms.

"What…" I stumble, confusion stunting my speech. "What do you mean, gone? Last time…last time you could tell he was about to go. Why didn't you give me any kind of warning?"

Sully stands and goes to one of the candles. He blows it

out harshly. A little curl of smoke rises into the air, and he stares at it for a moment.

"Sometimes it happens quickly. The dead can't handle it anymore, and suddenly, they're just gone."

I sit, frozen on my chair, looking around the room for signs of the wormhole Jack was sucked into. "Can we call him back? Will you give me one more chance? That wasn't...that wasn't enough."

Sully goes to the door, opens it, but stands there. "Our deal was for three."

"But that was cut off!" I argue. I stand to my feet, adrenaline and anger coursing through my veins. "That was only...only a half. It can't count."

"What more would you say?" Sully says, and his volume increases. There's a razor sharpness that makes me retreat half a step. "You told him you love him, he said the same. You got an opportunity no one else does. Take your closure, and move on with your life, Iona."

He stalks out of the room, and I hear his booted feet stalk to the back door. It slams closed behind him a moment later.

Panic creeps into my chest, and I dart out of the room to the window that looks out over the graveyard.

It's twilight outside. A light drizzle makes the world even darker. I see Sully's form retreat down a small path in the woods beyond where the dead rest, and he disappears.

It will be dark within minutes.

CHAPTER TWENTY-NINE

SULLY

THE LAST OF THE SUN'S RAYS DISAPPEAR IN THE woods. A canopy of leafless branches stretch over me in a cage, locking me down next to the dirt and decaying leaves as the fog creeps in.

A beating drum sounds in the back of my brain. Pounding, over and over, a thump of war and heartless echoes. With every step I take, deeper into the woods, it grows more and more steady.

A chirping howl sounds out into the night, a sound made deep in a feral throat. It's a warning. An alarm.

I shouldn't be out here, and the entire forests of Roselock know it.

But I have to put some distance between me and that woman. Between me and that gate I opened.

There is no longer a path that leads to my destination. Thick mud mixed with leaves and broken twigs that were not strong enough to survive the winter litters the ground, making the way slick and nearly impossible to see. I brace my hand on the trunk of an oak tree, narrowly avoiding landing face first in the filth.

In my head, the look on Iona's face as she heard Jack's words replays over and over in my head. The brokenness. The hollowness in her eyes. The quivering lip. The tears.

I'd been wrong before. I thought she was the most broken person yet to seek me out.

I'm fairly sure she's the most broken person on the entire continent.

And it's all caused by this Jack Caraway.

I grit my teeth tighter, fingers curling into fists, and walk a little faster through the nearly black night.

Just before I arrive, the clouds shift, and a sliver of moonlight peeks through, illuminating the true color of the ground at my feet.

Red.

Blood.

It's been dark long enough now that it's spread from the church, all around to the entire town borders.

Ahead, I see my destination, and my feet slow slightly.

There's a well up ahead. The stones lining its edge rise up out of the ground three feet. They're chipped. Some of them missing. The mortar crumbles. But the general structure of it still exists, even after a hundred years of disuse.

The house beyond it is unrecognizable by this point. Merely a pile of stones in a general rectangular shape.

But erected over the well, stands a winged angel.

Slowly, I cross to the well, standing just before it, and look up into the angel's face.

Those who once lived in that demolished house called her Santa Muerte.

She stands at least ten feet tall. A peaceful face is carved into the stone. Her eyes are downcast, looking directly down into the well. Her hands are outstretched, palms facing downward, as if warding off something inside the well. A great set of wings is outstretched at her back.

And at her feet, a great wolf is carved as her companion.

I blink as I look down from her face, down the empty well.

I place my hands on the stones.

Blood fills the walls that plunge down into the earth. It rises, coating the stones. Twelve feet down, ten feet.

I watch it rise, even as the noises around me increase. That yipping call grows louder and more frantic. A whispering breeze rattles through the bare branches above me, warning. Telling me I should not be out here.

But I have to know. Have to ask my question.

The blood reaches the lip of the well, and rises no further.

I can barely make out my reflection on its still surface. The moonlight comes and goes in brightness as the clouds are quickly blown through the sky.

Once upon a time, I came here to the well and asked a question of my fate.

Can I ever fight it?

Now I ask another. But not for myself.

"Did I do the right thing?" My voice cuts into the dark, and suddenly, all that howling, the rustling wind, dies away.

The entire town of Roselock waits in silence for the answer.

I pull the sleeve of my jacket up to my elbow. My lips set in a thin line, I hover my hand above the surface for a moment.

A bubble rises. Pops, sending little sputters of blood flying. It's followed by two more.

Slowly, I sink my hand into the ice cold red, submerging it halfway up my forearm.

It's impossible to breathe when your arm is submerged in a well of blood. Impossible to think outside of this very small circle of curse and dread.

Impossible to feel anything at all except the ice-cold liquid. And the anticipation.

Something reaches up from below and touches the palm of my hand.

My eyes squeeze closed. My stomach tightens.

Slowly, it traces the shape of a circle onto my skin.

Yes.

My eyes still sealed shut, I nod my head.

"Thank you," I offer.

Three more bubbles rise up around my arm, splattering me with more red.

I pull my arm out. Red, brilliant and bright, runs off of it as I drop it at my side. Instantly, the blood is soaked back into the already saturated ground.

Years ago, my answer was not the same. I reached my

hand into the well, and a straight line was drawn across my palm. A clear *no*.

No, I couldn't fight it.

I tried anyway.

But the truth was brought to pass, regardless.

My answer received, the wind picks back up. The dead project their muffled screams through it. Men yell and women cry. Shots are fired, bodies fall to the ground. And the wind carries the truth of the battle through the town, never letting it forget what happened here.

The trees moan, and I know it's time to go.

Shadows stalk through the trees, always just out of view, disappearing when a straight eye tries to pin them down. The animals protest at my presence. The fog grows thicker by the moment, freezing onto my hair, my beard, my eyebrows.

The night does not want me here.

The graveyard welcomes me back, and whispers slither through the cold air. Each of those individuals that I know telling me not to be a fool.

I heed their warnings to move indoors.

My feet can't move fast enough as I cross the graveyard. I cross the rotting deck in three long strides and, at last, step back inside the church.

Barely visible embers glow in the fireplace and the building is already significantly cooler. And because of past experience, I know to look at the clock hanging above the door.

What felt like only thirty minutes to me has actually been three hours.

Three hours I spent out in the woods, my hand soaked in blood. Three hours walking the living, vengeful dark of Roselock.

Time has a different meaning in this town when the last of the sunlight disappears.

Gently, I step forward, my eyes searching the space. I hear her before my vision can adjust to the darkness.

A soft breath drawn in pulls my attention to the couch. Stepping further into the room, attempting to not let the floorboards squeal, I make out the shape of Iona.

She lies on the couch, curled into a little ball, facing the back of the couch. She wears only a thin nightgown, her shoulders exposed. The blankets have slumped to the floor, and her balled position tells me she must be cold.

The gown does not cover much. The rises and falls of her ribs are visible under it. Bony hips poke out from beneath her panties. Her legs are bird-thin. I could snap them with the flick of my finger. Her knees and anklebones are knobby and protruding.

Iona Faye is incredibly beautiful.

But she is withering away.

My eyes slide to the side, to the folded stack of clothes. Her purse lies beside it. Her big bag also waits, packed.

Just to the side of her bag, rests her engagement ring.

As my eyes slide over to Iona's sleeping face, my gut tightens.

The well was right.

I know I made the right call.

I lied to her earlier.

Jack didn't get sucked back into limbo. It didn't become too difficult for him to stay in our world.

I cut him off.

Shoved him back into that world of isolation and waiting. And slammed the door closed behind me.

Because with every word Jack spoke, the truth in my soul grew clearer.

There's something not right about Jack Caraway.

And even in death, he's still got a vice-tight grip on the woman before me.

CHAPTER THIRTY

IONA

My car slips in the mud as I pull out of the neglected parking lot. I grip the steering wheel tighter, adrenaline spiking in my blood.

Finally, I clear the lot, and my tires hit the crumbling road. I press on the gas, picking up a little speed.

My eyes flick to the rearview mirror.

The church still sits there, forlorn and decrepit, housing a man with the ability to reach through the veil and find the dead.

He doesn't stand on the porch, doesn't watch me leave.

I only looked at him this morning, watching his face, reading his eyes, interpreting the set of his shoulders and clench of his jaw.

He'd told me three times he would open the gate. There would be no bargaining for a fourth.

So I didn't say a word.

I dressed. I packed my things.

And I left.

Leaving behind a little sliver of my soul.

The second my tires hit the highway, I step on the gas, throwing myself back into my seat, burning rubber to burn away the hollow cavern in my chest.

I SHOULD HAVE GOTTEN HOME TO ANDER LAST NIGHT. It's now Tuesday and I certainly do not have the day off. So, through the pre-dawn light, I drove like a maniac. Around sharp turns, blowing through stop signs. I narrowly missed hitting the tail end of a truck.

Despite my efforts, I'm still forty-five minutes late to work.

My boss heckles me for it. Gives me the stink eye about my disheveled appearance. I'm not properly put together. There are bags under my eyes, I know it. My hair hasn't had any real attention in days.

But I sit at my desk, pull the stack of papers that await me there, and set to the work.

And it only takes a few minutes, before my mind has drifted off, going back to a much happier day, one from six months ago.

I was digging through my bag, trying to find my lipstick, so I wasn't watching where I was going, and suddenly, there was a body and mine, falling back to the ground.

"Whoa, whoa!"

Strong hands grabbed my arms, knocking my bag to the ground, but keeping me from landing on my backside.

"Jack," I laughed in surprise. "What...what are you doing here?"

"What?" he asked in innocence. "I can't surprise my girl with a date after work?"

A smile curled on my lips and my heart warmed. Jack bent to grab my bag from the ground, sweeping its contents back into it. He held it out, a smile on his face.

"You certainly can," I said, taking a step toward him. I leaned into his chest, smiling as I brought my face closer to his.

His eyes burned with intensity, a mischievous glint to them. His hands gripped my hips, clinging to them possessively. He ducked his head, bringing his mouth to mine.

Jack kissed like the Devil and he wanted me to be his Queen of Hell. He was fire and power and amazing grace.

I'd never kissed anyone who kissed like Jack did.

"This must be the new man."

A playful voice from behind dragged me back to reality.

My co-worker and friend, Beverly, stood there watching us with a coy smile. She takes five steps forward, extending her hand.

"Guilty as charged," Jack said, shaking her hand, flashing her that devilishly charming smile of his. He could get away with murder with that smile. "Jack Caraway."

"Beverly Buhler," she said with a charmed look. "My, my. I see why Miss Iona has had her head in the clouds all this time, now." Beverly raised an eyebrow and actually winked at me.

"Okay, Miss Flirt," I said, taking Jack's hand and pulling him away from the front doors. "I better take him away before you steal him right from under my nose."

Beverly only smiled and winked as we walked away.

"I like her," Jack teased as he started leading me.

I gasped in mock horror and playfully smacked his shoulder. I shook my head, but really, I couldn't stop smiling. "So, what's your big surprise for tonight, womanizer?"

He laughed at my name-calling, but he pulled me a little closer, warming my body against his.

We went to the zoo. Slowly, hand in hand, we walked down the trails. Ooh-ing and ah-ing over all the exotic animals. I squealed in delight at the petting zoo, running my hand over the wiry hair of a four-hundred-pound pig. Jack bought me ice cream.

We kissed in front of the elephants. He whispered he loved me next to the tiger. He wrapped his hands around my waist at the primate exhibit.

It was the best date ever.

As the sun was setting, we headed home. Laughing and joking about our childhoods on the drive. I felt myself sink even deeper in love with Jack that day.

I'd never been so happy.

When we pulled up to my building, I saw Viola's car parked out front.

She'd found her own apartment three weeks ago, living

with four other girls in a three bedroom, fifth floor walk-up.

"Haven't seen your sister since I helped her move out," Jack said as he opened my car door for me. He slipped his hand into mine and we walked to the building. Just as we got to the main front door, she walked out, nearly running right into us.

"Iona!" she said excitedly as she wrapped her arms around me. "I thought I was going to miss you." She takes a momentary studying look and smiles. "You two must have been somewhere fun. You're both glowing."

I smiled and looked up into Jack's face. "He's always surprising me with fun little adventures."

Jack smiled back. "It was just the zoo," he says to Viola with a little shrug, but a proud grin.

"Well, why end the fun now?" Viola said. She wedged herself between the two of us, taking one of each of our hands in hers, tugging us back to Jack's car. "A bunch of us are going to Chucker's, and the both of you are coming!"

I glanced over at Jack and shook my head.

Once Viola got something into her head, it didn't leave easily.

We were going with her and her friends to the bar across town.

The place was crowded and noisy and full of energy. I actually smiled, getting excited as I walked in. I wasn't much of a drinker, at all, really. But after an amazing day like today, I was ready to let loose.

"You prepared for this?" Viola asked with a little wag of her eyebrows.

And I knew I was in for it. A night of her shenanigans.

Sure enough, after two hours, I'd drank more gin and lime Gimlets than I ever had in my life. I'd sung a duet karaoke with her. Danced like no one was watching. And in general, acted very drunk and inebriated.

"I'm so glad you came tonight!" Viola called over the loud music. She held my hands, bouncing up and down with me. "I miss you!"

"I miss you, too!" I said, feeling instantly sappy.

"You and Jack seem to be doing really good though!" she said, sounding so happy.

I nodded. "It's amazing, Vi. I've never been so happy."

My younger sister smiled, pulling me into a hug.

"You've lost weight lately," she chuckled. "Forgetting to eat in the midst of all that happiness?" She winked at me suggestively and danced off to join one of her male friends.

A set of hands wrapped around my waist from behind. I turned to see Jack looking down at me, a coy smile curling on his mouth.

"I think I like watching you dance," he purred in a low voice.

"Oh, yeah?" I said, my vision slightly foggy.

He nodded. "It's nice to see you liberate yourself from your inhibitions."

He leaned down, slowly, taking one...two breaths. Before he touched his lips lightly to mine. And he let them slide to my cheek. To my jaw. Down to my neck.

And instantly there were far too many people around.

All I wanted was Jack and I.

"Should we get out of here?" I breathed into the space between his neck and shoulder.

Jack only nodded.

I was more drunk than I thought that night. I didn't remember leaving the bar. Didn't remember the short conversation we had outside the tattoo parlor that was on the way from the bar to his car. Certainly didn't remember the sting of the needle inking my skin permanently.

But the next morning, I woke up naked in bed, Jack beside me, a tender spot between my chest and shoulder, and a new tattoo.

Jack bore a matching one, in the same location.

"You almost done with the report?"

My head snaps up, my heart instantly in my throat. My supervisor, the one who is already annoyed with me, stands in front of my desk.

"It will be ready in about ten minutes," I quickly explain, swallowing.

He only gives me a stern look, and walks back to his office.

I watch him walk away, my hands trembling.

It's a cruel thing, being able to recall the details so vividly. Able to relive one of the best days of my life in such detail.

Only to be forced back into reality.

The one where everything is so broken and dark.

The hole in my chest opens back up, and threatens to suck me into the void.

I finish the report, and five minutes later, the workday is over. I clean up my desk and head out the doors.

In my car I sit alone, gripping the steering wheel tightly, forcing breaths in and out.

It's hard to breathe.

The anxiety claws its way around my stomach, gnawing on my liver, my left lung. Wreaking havoc.

A tear works its way out onto my cheek. But as my hands tighten around the steering wheel, a new emotion surfaces.

Anger.

I was well on my way to the happily-ever-after I wanted. I had it, right there.

And one man took that all away.

I start the engine and put the car into first gear, and then second.

I never got any answers before.

I'm going to get them now.

The drive takes twenty-five minutes. I go through the gate, which takes a few minutes to gain clearance. I park in the lot.

My hands shake as I walk to the doors. But I'm ready. A raging storm. An angry mob. The crimson-beaked eagle.

I give my name, and it takes several more minutes as permissions are granted. Another ten minutes later and they buzz me through a dozen locked doors, a guard leading the way.

Finally, they lead me to a large room. Cinderblock walls cage me in. Four large round tables dominate the space. There's the door I just came through, and one other.

I wait for two minutes. And then there's a buzzing sound, and that other door slides open.

A man in a black and white striped jumpsuit shuffles into the room. His hands are cuffed, his feet, too. He's immediately followed by an armed guard.

Raymond Douglas settles across the table from me, his eyes dark and wary. He sits, his back ramrod-straight, his hands in his lap. But his eyes are searching, studying me, looking me over.

I look up at the prison guard, who watches Raymond with hawk-like eyes, his hand on his gun.

Looking back at Raymond, I catch his eyes.

There's something like relief in them. Resolve. And there's absolutely no guilt in them. Or regret.

I lean forward, resting my arms on the cold surface of the table.

"You never said," I begin. "Never gave any real, legitimate reason." My stomach tightens. The blast of the gun firing sounds in my ears. The feel of Jack's blood smearing all over me creeps down my skin. "I need answers. Now."

Raymond leans forward, his eyes fixed on me.

"Why did you kill Jack Caraway?" I ask.

Raymond doesn't say anything for a moment. He only studies, looking for something deep in my soul.

"Because he killed my sister," his answer comes with the surprise strike of a rattlesnake in the bushes. "And he was going to kill you, too."

CHAPTER THIRTY-ONE

SULLY

Through the window of my bedroom, I watched Iona leave.

I'd crushed her. Dashed her hope, ripped the rug out from beneath her feet. She'd been right when she said I'd only given her half an opening that last time.

But that gate had to be closed.

She was gone. And I could only hope that she would try to move on with her life now that she'd gotten a chance at closure.

And now I can return to my solitude and wait out my days alone.

I grab the pruning sheers from the table in my room and go to the west side of the church. The roses are in various stages of bloom. Some fully open, soaking up the faint sun's rays. Others are buds, still a week from opening.

They eternally bloom, warmed and fed by the blood of innocent lives.

An hour later, my hands cut and bleeding from the thorns, I carry an armload of red roses to the graveyard. One by one, I visit the graves. I place their rose on their final resting place. Give a mutter of greeting.

I am the keeper of the dead.

The reacher beyond the veil.

But it remains a mystery as to why.

My father could not speak to the dead.

My grandfather and his father and his father before him could not reach them, either.

But for some reason, I can.

Perhaps it is because every bit of me was bred in Roselock. The eighth generation to be born here. This cursed, wicked town entirely engrained in my skin, my bones, my soul.

My mother claimed it was because I was made extra special.

The reality was that I had to be extra cursed.

When, at four years old, you wander into one of the abandoned houses, find an old, forgotten doll, and become friends with the young girl who I couldn't touch, that doesn't make you special. It makes you a creature that terrified your parents.

I talked about my friend Agatha to my family. And soon she was joined by the teenage boy James, and then the old, kind woman, Emma.

My parents assumed they were imaginary friends. Children I dreamed up to combat the loneliness of growing up in a dying town.

It wasn't until I touched my grandfather's cufflinks, made his acquaintance, and relayed details about him to my father that their faces grew cold. Their expressions slack.

I'd never been scared of the dead. Not until then. Not until I saw their reaction.

And then my baby sister passed away of disease. Only two years old, and Cheyenne was dead, like so many others.

I'd taken her hair bow. And when she returned to me, she had the face of a child my own age.

My parents were horrified.

For a year they tried to prevent me from touching anything that had belonged to the dead. They were terrified their ghosts would hurt me. Would drag me to an early grave. Would turn my mind mad.

But I missed my friends. They were the only ones I had. So I snuck Cheyenne, Agatha, James, and Emma's possessions beneath my bed, and visited them every night after I was tucked in.

I came to learn that after months of this, my parents overheard me talking to them. They listened at the door. Peered through the crack in the walls. They watched and observed, and when they knew I wasn't in any danger, they talked to me about it. They tentatively told me if it made me happy, I could speak to them again.

As I grew older, the desire to gain more friends, more people to talk to, grew.

I went into every abandoned house in town, and that was ninety percent of them, and found belongings. I got to know every deceased resident of this town.

Soon, I had over a hundred friends.

They helped combat the sadness I was consumed with when my father died. I was ten years old. And then my mother realized we could still have a family, in a twisted and supernatural way. I could still speak to my father and my sister. And I could speak for them to my mother.

For a few years, we were happy. We spent every day together, and I relayed day- long conversations between my father and mother. The more I summoned them from beyond, the longer they were able to stay in my world.

I spent hours with my father next to Roselock Pond, discussing the fate that was going to come for me, once I was old enough to understand and accept it.

I was sixteen, then.

And then it was only my mother, who was dying of an incurable disease, and four other residents of Roselock left in town.

I was angry. In denial.

When I turned eighteen, my mother finally succumbed to her illness and then I buried her next to my father.

And I left Roselock.

I look down at my parents' headstones now. My father's in a line with all the other Whitmore men, and my mother buried above him, in line with all my grandmothers.

The past is the heaviest weight of all and it pulls me under in my loneliest moments.

And suddenly the lack of life here in Roselock, which has so often been my saving sanctuary in my supernatural cursed life, feels suffocating.

I wasn't kind to Iona.

But I now realize how her presence was a breath of fresh oxygen, when I've been surviving off of stale air for years.

She was so different from the others. Unlike the reporters or thrill seekers who wander through town.

She was broken enough to tug an emotion out of me.

To make me care, even just a little bit.

Mentally, I'm not hungry in the least, but my body tells me it's time for nourishment. Wrapping up the last of the rose placements for my friends and family, I head inside.

Crusty bread and scrambled eggs tame the hunger and I shove two more logs into the fireplace.

I wonder if I'll live long enough to feel the weather warm.

The beginning of May is questionable territory. It could reach temperatures in the eighties, or get a cold spell and get a dusting of snow on the ground.

I wipe the bark from my hands against my dirtied pants and turn to go clear out the Sunday School room.

I do a double take at the little glint of light.

There, pushed almost underneath the couch, Iona's engagement ring catches the faint light that filters in through the dirty windows.

I swear under my breath.

This means she'll be coming back, probably by tonight, to retrieve it.

I cross the room and squat down, reaching out for the white gold band with three diamonds set into it.

"You have to go warn her."

"This isn't over."

"You have to help her figure out how he did it."

I fall back, my rear hitting the wood floor before tipping right over onto my back with a startled huff. My eyes go bug wide, my shoulders shrugging up to my ears as I scramble back across the floor.

Away from the three women who just stormed through the gate to the other side.

I clutch the ring into my fist, the diamonds cutting into my palm, not feeling an ounce of the pain through my shock.

"Who are you?" I ask with a slight shake to my voice. "And why are you all tied to Iona's ring?"

One of the women steps forward. Her darker skin is smooth as butter. Her curly hair frames a perfectly balanced face. "Because that ring once sat on my finger. Placed there by the man who asked me to marry him."

My eyes slide to the other two women. One short and blonde. One with dark ebony hair that stretches all the way down her back.

"The both of you, as well?" I ask in a quiet breath.

They both nod their heads.

My hands shake, but I push myself to my feet, rising without taking my eyes off them. "And your fiancé's name?" I ask of the woman closest, the first who spoke.

Her eyes harden. "Jack Caraway."

I swallow once.

I look to the blonde.

"Jack Caraway," she echoes, her face pale, a look of horror and disbelief in her expression.

"Jack Caraway," the raven-haired woman confirms when I look at her.

My fingers curl around the ring. A vice tightens around my throat.

"You have to help her," the first woman says, stepping forward. "Just because he's dead doesn't mean Jack is finished with her."

My stomach knots. "I opened the gate to him for her. Three times."

"Then you better hurry," she says. The other women step forward. "Before it's too late."

"Is she really still in danger?" I ask, even though I can feel the answer down to my marrow. "Jack is dead."

The first woman takes one more step toward me. "He never touched me. But he knows how to get in your head. And destroy you from the inside out."

"He's still alive in her mind," the blonde says. "And he'll obliterate her."

I look at the three of them, and then hold the ring out in my hand, palm up.

The well told me I did the right thing by cutting Jack off.

But maybe the mistake had already been made.

Chill sinks under my skin.

I never should have opened up the gate for the fawn.

I turn in the room and stalk to the back door. Across

the deck. Across the lawn. And to the shed that waits at the edge of the parking lot.

The locks protest with rust as I tug at them. But they squeal and finally swing open.

The long unused Cadillac Series 62 sits there. Waiting.

I've probably only got minutes before the gate will close on these women.

And this car hasn't been started in two years.

"Start talking," I say as I push my sleeves up.

CHAPTER THIRTY-TWO

IONA

RAYMOND LOOKS FROM THE PRISON GUARD, WHO stares at a blank wall to the side of us, and then back at me.

There's a foreign darkness in his eyes, one of utter hatred and anger. But something in my core tells me it isn't directed at me.

"He's all you think about, isn't he?" Raymond finally speaks. His eyes rise back up to mine.

I don't answer immediately. Because I've had this fight before. With my sisters. With my mother. They all accused me of becoming obsessed with Jack. Of letting him take over my life.

"I love him with my whole heart," I say in response. "Of course he's what I think about."

Raymond places his hands on the table, the chains clanking. "But he's filled every crack in your head. Taken over everything that used to give you joy and replaced it. Like he's got clawed talons around your heart, isn't it?"

I swallow, pulling my hands back on the table, slipping them into my lap. My cheeks instantly go cold.

I won't think the thoughts. Confess to myself.

Raymond nods, and the look in my eyes must be confirmation enough.

"I read her journal after," he continues. "It was so easy to see when it started. His name suddenly popped up. Within days, there wasn't a single sentence that didn't have his name in it. Jack was there, in every breath she took."

Raymond's hands curl into fists and I lean back just a little.

"It isn't hard for him," he says. "Think of what he does for a living. He gets inside people's heads. He unravels them. Helps them piece their lives together. He knows how the mind works. So, of course he knows how to shape you into something he can control."

I lace my fingers together and shake my head. I don't say anything for a moment, because my thoughts are racing but not making any logical connections.

"Jack was a brilliant psychologist, but he only ever helped people," I whisper, a little anger lacing into the syllables.

"On the surface, yes," Raymond says, leaning forward onto his forearms, the storm in his eyes darkening. "But he has special pet projects. Like my sister. Like you."

I shake my head almost imperceptibly. My hand twitches. The urge to slap him across the face is nearly impossible to suppress.

"Did he ever tell you about her?" Raymond asks. "About my sister, Simone? About how she died?"

And the finale of his sentence, it jolts me a little straighter.

"He was engaged once before," I say, my voice sounding hoarse. "Jack told me she died. He said he thought he was cursed. But I don't know how it happened."

Raymond gives a short, huff laugh, looking away. He shakes his head. "He said *he* was cursed?"

I nod, recalling his words, from that very first date we went on.

Raymond shakes his head once more. "Should have been five shots to the head. The bastard deserved a thousand times worse."

I lunge across the table, my fingers outstretched, and claw across his face. My fingernails sink deep, cutting into his flesh.

He scrambles back, tipping right over in his seat onto his back. The prison guard yells, rushing forward, his hand on his gun, the other outstretched toward me.

"Back away!" he yells. "Back up!"

I sit back in my seat, my breathing harsh, my vision red. I hold my hands up, surrendering.

The guard pulls Raymond to his feet. Three deep claw marks mar his face, running from just above his left eyebrow, down over his nose, onto his right cheek.

He doesn't look angry. Just shocked.

"Back to your cell," the guard growls. "Visit is over.

Don't expect to be allowed back." He glowers in my direction.

"I don't know how he does it," Raymond says in a hurry as the guard begins steering him back toward the gate. "He gets in your head. He makes you do things. Simone didn't want to kill herself."

All of my organs—my lungs, my kidneys, my heart —turn cold.

"Jack somehow made her do it," Raymond says, pushing back against the guard at the gate. "I pray now that he's dead he doesn't do the same to you."

The guard shoves Raymond through the gate. I get to my feet, crossing the room, watching through the bars as the guard pushes him down a long hall.

"All the same signs are there," Raymond calls over his shoulder to me. "The obsessive love. The weight loss. I'd guess you've cut yourself off from everyone you care about. Once the dangerous behavior starts, it won't be long."

They turn down another hall, and my view is cut off.

"Look for records!" Raymond yells from somewhere in the prison walls. "Find a way to fix yourself. Don't let him win!"

His voice fades away, and he's gone.

I stand there in the visiting room, trembling from head to toe.

CHAPTER THIRTY-THREE

SULLY

I HAVE NO IDEA WHERE TO LOOK.

Iona told me she lived in Ander, but I know next to nothing about her, in reality. Where she works. Her sister's names. Her mother's.

So, I've been driving all around town the entire afternoon. Passed the post office. By the banks. Around the grocery stores.

My eyes burn from looking so hard. My arms and shoulders are stiff and sore.

I haven't driven anywhere in two years.

I ride alone. Iona's ring sits in the passenger seat. I'd been right, just as I finally got the engine to turn over, the gate slammed shut. And then off I went.

Finally, I park next to the school. The lot is empty, everyone long since gone home. My eyes sweep the town, but I turn inward mentally.

I wrack my brain.

Iona told me several stories about her life here in this town. About how she met Jack.

Instantly a light bulb goes off.

I put the car into drive, and head back the opposite direction.

Earlier that day, I drove past the police station. The one where Iona's father once worked for twenty-five years. Parked in one of the narrow spots out front, I climb out. Up the stairs, and through the front doors.

Only two police officers occupy the building at this hour. One sits at his desk, going over papers. He looks young, much younger than myself. The other stands across the room, leaned against a desk, on the phone, sporting snow white hair and a well-manicured mustache.

"Excuse me," I say, suddenly nervous. I haven't had any natural human interaction in years.

The young cop's head snaps up suddenly, his eyes wide.

"Apologies," I say. "I didn't mean to startle you. I…" I glance over at the older cop. He's still speaking on the phone, but his eyes are fixed on me, taking me in, analyzing. "I was hoping you could help me find someone."

"Name?" the young cop asks, and I notice his nametag. Tilton.

"Iona," I say. And the effect saying her name has on me, I don't like its strength. "Faye. The daughter of…I think it was Mason and Willa."

Officer Tilton's eyes narrow slightly at me. He looks me up and then down. From my mud crusted boots, to the dirty jeans. To my calloused hands. My mane of hair, overgrown beard. My six-foot-five frame.

"How do you know her?" he asks doubtfully.

I pause.

That's an answer I can never give.

"I was a friend of her fiancé's," I lie. One that makes me sick.

I drove by a business part of town earlier. And saw an office with his name on the door. Just waiting there like he would return any day.

The older officer hangs up and walks across the room, hands on his hips. I don't miss how close one of them is to his gun. "You were friends with Jack?"

I'm sweating. My throat feels tight. I haven't talked to anyone by my own choice in so long now, much less lied to someone, and well.

I nod.

"If you're a friend of Jack's, why don't you know where to find Iona?" he questions, his eyes narrowing on me.

"I'd never met Iona until last week," I say. "She wanted to talk about Jack, so she looked me up and found me. She took some time off of work this last weekend and spent a few days at my...house."

Partial truth, big lies.

I read the officer's nametag: Langford.

"Did you work with her father?" I ask.

Langford looks at me for a long time, deciding if he trusts me or not.

He nods. "We worked in the force together for over

twenty years. Best man I ever knew. Raised some amazing daughters."

I nod my head, like I really know. "I'm trying to find Iona," I say. "She left her engagement ring at my house when she left, and I know she's going to want it back."

Tilton and Langford both study me.

I don't blame them.

I'm more beast than man right now. Looking for the fragile police department princess.

"Poor thing hasn't gotten any peace since that man killed Jack," Langford says. His eyes lower for a moment, his gaze drifting inward. "Though I think just about everyone close to her is relieved Jack's gone. But Iona…"

I nod. "I know. That's the reason she came to see me. I was trying to help her."

Langford looks up at me, his lips pressed into a thin line. Finally, he nods. "She will want that ring back. She lives over on Second. Building on the corner of Center. I think she's somewhere on the third floor."

"Thank you," I offer, backing toward the door.

"Sir," Langford calls out as I begin pushing it open.

I look back, my heart pounding, desperate to get back out there.

"Iona's an amazing girl," he says, sadness lacing every corner of his face. "What she's gone through… If you can help her, please, don't give up on her."

His words lock cement around my heart. Make me too heavy. Fill me with a sense of dread.

But still, I nod.

Putting the car into drive, I point the car in the right direction, and set down the road.

Watching the street signs, I pass road after road. I roll down Center, my heart pounding. And there, Second comes into view.

Cars are all parked parallel on the side of the building. Lights glow from windows here and there. Three floors of apartments make up the building.

I find a parking space across the street, and climb out.

The sounds of the city grow quieter, the hour creeping toward nine. The air is chill, a wind picking up, reminding all that it is February, and winter will not go quietly.

The clouds shift above me, only the movement is too sharp, and my head whips up.

A figure stands at the ledge of the building. A blanket is pulled around their shoulders.

Stark still, they stand, staring out over the city.

"Iona?" I breathe, the word barely formed. I take a step closer. Squinting against the dark. "Iona!"

She shifts, looking down at me. Only she loses her balance slightly, and stumbles.

"No!" I yell, holding my hands up, as if I can keep her from slipping off the edge of the roof. "Iona! Back up. Get down from there. Please."

She rights herself, still standing at the edge of the roof. "Sully. What…what are you doing here?"

"Please," I plead with her. "We'll talk in a minute. Can you please just get down from there?"

She just stares at me, that vacant and distant look in her eyes.

"Stay…" I huff in the cold night. "I'm coming up."

I dart forward, across the street. I yank the front door open, searching around for the stairs. Down the hall I find them, and I take them two at a time, climbing to the second floor, the third. I yank a door open that says *roof access*, and climb the final flight.

The wind blows harder this high up. The cold steals my breath as I search for her.

And there she still stands, her back to me. The blanket pulled around her shoulders. Just staring out over the city.

"Iona," I breathe her name. I cross the roof, my footsteps cautious so I don't startle her. "Let's go inside. It's freezing out here."

She looks over her shoulder at me. And there's little to no life in her eyes.

I stop at her side, looking up at her, standing on the ledge. I reach a hand up. And she just stares at it.

"Iona, please," I beg her.

And something sparks there. For just a brief moment. But it's enough.

She takes my hand, and I grip her tightly as I half lift her down.

Internally, I curse. She's light as a feather. Easily under a hundred pounds. Made of bones and skin.

I tuck the blanket tighter around her, wrapping an arm around her shoulders, and pull her into my side. She doesn't say anything, just stares ahead emptily.

I'm genuinely scared.

Without a word, I guide her back to the stairs, and I half carry her down the flight of stairs back to the third floor. I'm not sure if she knows where she's going as her feet shuffle once we reach her floor, but finally, she stops outside the door that reads 308.

Hoping and praying this is it, I twist the knob, and push the door open.

I don't pretend to keep the church clean in any way shape or form. But compared to the place we enter, it's as fresh as a hospital.

Dirt coats the floor. Garbage is strewn about everywhere. There are clothes lying around. Books lie about. The small kitchen just off the entry is caked with a layer of dust. The garbage can is overflowing with what looks to be boxes and old food—the smell confirms it.

I cover my nose with a hand, fighting the urge to gag at the reek of spoiled food.

But Iona doesn't seem to notice any of it. She shuffles forward like the walking dead. She turns left, through a small living room. She aims for the door at the far side of it, and pushes it open.

The bedroom is just as much of a disaster. Clothes everywhere. Garbage. Two of the four light bulbs in the fixture on the ceiling are out.

Iona climbs into the bed, and she's swallowed up by the mound of pillows and blankets there.

I notice there are little white circles on her dark blue bedding. Tear stains. All over the place.

This is far, far worse than I expected.

"Why were you up on the roof, Iona?" I ask, because I have to start somewhere. "It's below freezing and the wind… You could have easily fallen."

She looks over at the window, but it's dark outside, pitch black, and there's nothing but a few city lights here and there. "Because it's quieter up there."

I sit on the side of her bed. "Iona, there's no one else here. It seems pretty quiet in this apartment to me."

She shakes her head. Again. Again. But she doesn't say anything.

"Please," I say. "Don't go on the roof again."

She doesn't agree. Doesn't nod.

"I learned some things today," she says quietly. "And I don't know what's true. None of it seems real."

My head lifts slightly. "Oh?"

She nods. And finally, she looks up. "I went to see Jack's killer today."

Her words rip a knife from my navel up to my throat.

"He said things," she continues, still staring at the window. "All these things. And how can I believe them when I watched him murder Jack in cold blood? But…" Her voice quivers. "How can I not, when he knew so many things about me?"

A well exists inside myself, and it fills with thick, black ink. It ripples out through the highway of my veins. Spreading dread.

"What did he say, Iona?"

"He killed Jack because Jack killed his sister." She says the words so clearly. "Not with his own hands. He thinks Jack got in her head, twisted her all around. And in the end, somehow made her kill herself."

"Was it Sharon, Simone, or Joanne?" That ink begins to crystalize into ice.

Finally, Iona's eyes flick to mine. Wide.

"Simone," she says. "His sister was Simone."

She studies me for a long moment. And finally, she raises her hand, looking down at the left one. "I left my ring at the church."

I nod.

She looks back up at me. "He knew exactly what is happening to me. He said…" Her voice falters, and a tear slips out onto her cheek. Her eyes grow distant again, glassy. And she looks scared. "He said it's exactly what his sister went through, before she killed herself."

A magnet draws me closer to her on the bed. I breathe deep, growing myself. The instinct to protect this tiny fawn from the echoes beyond the veil cause the beast in me to grow.

I reach into my pocket and grip the cloth. I draw it out, letting the cloth fall open in my palm to reveal the ring.

"I found it beneath the couch at the church," I explain. "I grabbed it. And *three* other women stormed through the gate like the horsemen of the apocalypse."

Iona's eyes fix on the ring. She looks ill. And confused. And lost.

"Sharon, Joanne, and Simone," I say. "In the few moments they were able to stay in our world, they told me their stories. Each of them loved Jack. Each of them said yes to his proposal. And each of them took their own life."

A sharp breath is sucked into Iona's throat. She actually pushes herself further back against the headboard, trying to put a little more distance between herself and the ring.

"I know you loved Jack, Iona," I say. My body wants to be physically ill at the words I know are coming. "But I don't know that you actually chose to do so."

She presses her lips tightly together, squeezing her eyes closed, forcing out a stream of tears. She turns her head away from me.

"This is dangerous," I breathe, closing the cloth around the ring again, placing it back in my pocket. "There is something…not right going on. We have to stop it."

"Jack is dead," she says, the words harsh and angry. "It has already been stopped."

"Be honest with yourself, Iona," I say, my volume increasing slightly. "Look inside yourself. Do you really think it's over?"

Her breath hitches. Like she can't properly suck it in. She shakes her head again, but it's more of a denial than an admission.

"You need rest," I say, drawing energy from a well inside of myself that is diminished. "Sleep. We'll figure things out in the morning."

She stares off at the wall for a moment longer. But she sniffs, wiping the blanket over her nose. And she nods.

Gently, as if she's in physical pain, she slides herself further down into the bed until she's lying down. She curls onto her left side, her back turned to me.

CHAPTER THIRTY-FOUR

IONA

A VOID. THAT'S WHAT IS INSIDE OF ME.

Big.

Dark.

Consuming.

Somewhere at the bottom of it is doubt and confusion.

Raymond's words beat against the back of my brain. Sully's information sinks claws into my flesh and drags them down my back.

Truth.

What is the truth?

What is reality?

And a voice keeps trying to whisper in my ear, *they were right.*

They were right.

CHAPTER THIRTY-FIVE

SULLY

I PULL THE DOOR MOSTLY CLOSED, BUT LEAVE A ONE-inch sliver open so that I can peek in on her if I need to.

I know she isn't asleep. There's a good chance she won't be able to.

But she needs to think things over. And being here, watching the doors, I can give her a safe space to do that right now.

I cover my nose again at the smell. Holding my breath, I stalk over to the garbage. I tie off the bag and carry it out to the hall. I'll take it down to the outside bin later.

Opening the fridge, I find more spoiled food. As I dump one thing after another out, I find that every single item in here has expired and begun to rot. I fill another garbage bag full, and put it out in the hall, as well.

I check all the cupboards, and I'm not surprised one bit when there is very little food filling them. Iona's self-starvation tendencies are here on full display.

I open the windows, despite the outside freezing temperatures, just to air the space out and get rid of the decaying smell.

I wander around with another trash bag, filling it with the random garbage just left here and there. I fill two bags. I next make a pile of all the dirty laundry and start a load in the washer I find in a closet. Sweeping is immediately followed by mopping.

Well into the wee hours of the night, I scrub and clean.

All the while, the thread at the back of my brain tightens just a little.

That tug that connects me to Roselock.

I'm ever aware of its exact location in relation to where I am. North. South. On the other side of the continent.

Slowly, so gradually, each fiber of that thread grows thicker. Pulling me tighter.

"You okay?" a concerned voice asked.

I looked up, and realized I'd been gripping the table tightly, my knuckles white.

Roselock was calling. The pull at my brain was agonizing. The screams in my ears were so loud. The ground at my feet felt slick with blood.

"Yeah, sorry," I apologized, squaring my shoulders, shoving the anchor back.

Bobbi looked at me with worry in her blue-green eyes. "You look like you could use some sleep. Should we call it a night?"

I reached across the table, placing my hand over hers, totally enveloping it. "You're always too understanding." I smiled, taking in her angelic features. The bright eyes. The narrow nose. Lips stained pink by color. Her blonde hair. "As much as I want to say no, I have to admit I'm exhausted."

She smiled, leaning forward, and pressed a gentle kiss to my cheek. "I'll take care of you."

She stood, pulling me behind her. I dropped the money on the table, and the two of us walked outside into the late summer evening.

It had been a perfect summer here in Charleston. Once the semester ended, my graduation finally over, I spent as much time as I could at the water. It was there I met Bobbi, waitressing at my favorite café. After a dozen muted smiles, blush from her cheeks, I asked her to go to the movies with me, and she said yes.

It had been bliss. Her hand in mine, the sand between our toes. The sun on our backs as she looked up and kissed her lips to mine.

That was the way it was. Light, summer.

Hand in hand, we walked back to my apartment. She would stay for the weekend, before she had to head further inland to return to school for her sophomore year at Charleston Southern University.

Bobbi talked on and on about some party her cousin had tomorrow, casually inviting me to it, while I got ready for bed. The woman could talk. About nothing and everything. If I paid attention to every single detail she spoke, I was fairly sure I would know every single detail about her.

But it sometimes became difficult to absorb all her words.

Especially when she was so beautiful to behold.

It was distracting.

I lay on the bed, she in the bathroom, talking while even brushing her teeth.

I smiled in amusement, lacing my fingers across my chest, letting my eyes slip closed. I grew heavier.

Heavier.

People milled about, doing their daily activities. Beating the dirt out of rugs. Harvesting vegetables from their side gardens. Shouting at the children to stay within sight.

And then there was the beating of drums.

And screams. The horrified looks on darker skinned faces.

Women hid with their children. Men went for their guns.

Arrows were fired. Tomahawks thrown.

Gunpowder filled the air.

Blood.

Blood poured onto the soil. Splattered against the houses.

It bubbled up from beneath the church.

Bubbled.

Gurgled.

"Sully!"

The screaming grew louder, morphed into my own name.

"Sully!"

Hands shook my shoulders, violent.

I was suffocating.

I rolled over, coughing violently. Blood splattered from my mouth, spraying onto the wall, all over the floor. I pushed myself up on an elbow, coughing more blood up. Gasping to catch my breath.

"Sully," Bobbi cried in horror. "Keep breathing, I'm going to call 911."

I gasped, finally sucking down air. I flung out a hand, grabbing her arm. "No. Don't."

"Sully!" she cried in horror. "You start suffocating on blood in the middle of the night, you need a hospital!"

I gripped her arm tighter. Darkness made it near impossible to see. I shook my head, though. "No," I repeated.

I didn't need a hospital.

Roselock wanted me back. And it was going to do anything it took to bring me back.

Three nights in a row now, I'd had the nightmares. Last night I woke up with the taste of blood in my mouth.

The stories of my grandfathers were true.

And it was my time.

Pulling back to the present, I lean over the sink and spit, clearing the faint taste of blood from my mouth.

In the window above the sink, I can barely make out my own reflection.

Wild hair. Overgrown beard. Dark eyes.

Savage man.

The product of Roselock, and all its madness.

I glance over at the clock above the stove, reading five in the morning.

It has taken me seven hours to clean Iona's apartment. But I turn and observe my work.

It's habitable again.

The floors are clean. The surfaces have been wiped. The fridge has been sanitized. All smells have evaporated.

Tired and sore, I head toward the bathroom next to the bedroom. Starting the water, I strip my filthy clothes off. Wrapping a towel around my waist, I cut back to the washer, throwing my clothes in. I return to the steaming hot shower.

It's been a long time since I had to worry if I was actually clean or not. But I remember the look on Officer Langford and Tilton's faces yesterday. It is likely I will have to interact with others before I return to Roselock. And I shouldn't look like a savage.

When I'm finished showering, I find a brush under the sink, and drag it through the mass of hair. Tame my beard as much as I can.

Looking at myself in the mirror, I seem a little more civilized.

Walking out of the bathroom, towel wrapped around my hips, I aim for the laundry closet, when a figure next to the dining table freezes me.

The woman stares at me, horror and shock pinning her features.

I look around, feeling panicked for a moment.

An explanation. I have to give some kind of explanation.

"Who…" the woman stumbles. "Who are you and why are you in my sister's apartment?"

Sister.

Looking at her now, it's obvious. Put about thirty pounds on her, and Iona would look just like this woman, perhaps a little older.

"Viola?" I guess, feeling bare and exposed. Literally, considering I'm wearing only a towel.

"Yes," she confirms. "I'd say you're a maid, considering," she looks around the now clean apartment. "But you don't look like a maid, and it's six in the morning, and you're not wearing any clothes."

My awkward discomfort growing by the moment, I inch toward the washer, grab my clothes, and stuff them in the dryer.

"I'm uh, a friend of your sister." Lie.

Viola raises one eyebrow, a little smirk tugging on one side of her mouth. "Wow," she says. "I didn't think she was even close to being ready for…that. But I'm happy she's finally moving on."

"No," I shake my head, feeling my face heat. "Not like that. I, yes, I spent the night cleaning up. It was dirty work." I indicate the running dryer.

We whisper, so as to not wake Iona, who I'm fairly

certain did actually fall asleep somewhere just after midnight.

"Oh," she says, seeming a little confused. "Well, I...I was on my way to work, I'm a nurse at the hospital, and I saw her light on and got worried."

I want to tell her that she *should* be worried. That there is far too much to be worried about right now.

"She's not been the same, you know," Viola says, her eyes fixed on the bedroom door. "Not in a really, really long time. I assume you know about Jack?"

I nod.

She does, too. "I encouraged them to be together at first. He was good looking, and for the first little while, he seemed so good for her. Did and said everything just right. But I was wrong."

She looks back over at me. "Whoever you are, thank you for helping her. This..." she looks around the apartment. "It's a big step. Her letting you inside her apartment, it's something. So, thank you."

"Sully," I offer.

"Thank you, Sully," she says with a smile, and steps for the door. She offers a sad little smile before letting herself out the door.

"Mom and Viola and Cressida told me our relationship was getting unhealthy."

I startle, turning to find Iona standing in the doorway of the bedroom. She wears clothes I'm guessing are from yesterday, wrinkled and rumpled.

"I'm starting to think they were right," she croaks.

CHAPTER THIRTY-SIX

IONA

SULLY PUTS A BOWL OF OATMEAL WITH BROWN SUGAR before me, and watches as I eat.

One spoonful. My throat tightens against it.

Two spoonsful. My stomach knots.

On the third bite, I actually gag.

Sully shakes his head, a hard look in his eyes. He places his hands on the counter top, staring at me. "Again," he says, nodding at the bowl.

I'm not hungry. But I look down at my hand, the one holding the spoon, and it looks so breakable. The bones are so obvious.

I just keep staring at it.

When did this happen?

My eyes move up my arm, which is just as withered. I actually reach up and feel my face. My cheekbones are protruding. My jawline is sharp.

"Take another bite, Iona," Sully says.

My eyes rise up to his. A dozen emotions rest in them. He nods at the bowl once more.

I grab the spoon. My hand shakes. I raise it up to my lips, and put the mush in my mouth.

Every muscle in me quakes, my stomach tightens.

I clamp a hand over my mouth, forcing myself to make it go down. To not wretch up the few bites I got down earlier.

"You are physically unable to eat more than a few bites." Sully says it so matter-of-factly. He keeps looking at me. Like a scientist studying a lab rat. "You're eating only just enough to keep you from dying."

I nod, even though tears sting the back of my eyes. I think back, to the past few months. To really, the past six or so of them. I'm never hungry. Food has held no interest for me.

"Everyone kept telling me I was losing too much weight," I say, my gaze blurring as I stare at nothing. "But it's been like…like I didn't even hear them. The words, they didn't connect."

"You need to start connecting again, Iona," Sully says, leaning forward slightly. "You need to see the damage that has been done."

I look up, meeting his eyes. But it's hard to keep him in focus.

I get to my feet and head into my bedroom. I pull my shirt up over my head. Unbutton my slacks. My clothes fall to the floor.

I step in front of the mirror that hangs next to the closet.

And the tears burn my eyes. A sob gets caught in my throat.

My collarbones cut sharp lines across my chest. My rib bones are so visible I can count every one of them. My hipbones jut out sharply against my panties. There is a wide gap between my thighs.

My skin looks a little loose on my own body.

"This is dangerous, Iona."

I look to the side to see Sully standing in the doorway. He turns away sheepishly, but there's that look in his eyes, like he can't help but look at the sad sight. Can't help but stare at the horror.

"You're literally wasting away," he says.

I look back in the mirror, and my lower lip trembles.

The woman I see is not me.

I don't know when I morphed into this…this thing. It took time to get here, but I don't remember the effort it took to become this.

"I…" I shake my head, and words fail me. "How? How could this be because of Jack? This is *my* body. I have control over it. How could he have anything to do with it?"

Sully takes another step into the room. "The mind can do powerful things to the body. The body has to obey."

There's a dark echo in his voice that tells me he knows from experience.

A tear breaks free from my lashes and slips down my

cheek. "I..." I can't accept it, that someone I loved so fiercely could do anything like this to me.

"Would you have ever chosen to do this to yourself?"

But there it is. The brutally honest question.

I have to answer truthfully.

"No," I breathe. "Never."

I more sense than see Sully nod. "Get dressed. Let's go find some answers."

"Jack had no family or relatives left," I say as we walk down the street. I pull my coat tighter around me, slush washing over my boots. "So everything of his went to me. Not that he had much."

We cross the last street and Sully and I walk up to his office. I should be at work. But it is the very last thing I care about today. Sully called in sick for me.

"I've been paying the lease since he died," I say as I fish the keys out of my purse. "Though I'm not going to be able to afford it next month. I'll have to clear all of his stuff out in the next few weeks."

The door opens and the bell above it chimes.

I have to take in a deep, steadying breath when we step inside. I'm washed in the scent of him, and the ache in my chest is enough to bury me six feet under.

"You can do this."

Sully's deep voice billows against my back, standing me straight again, reminding me to look at myself in each individual moment.

I stand a little straighter, rolling back my shoulders.

"He only had a part-time secretary," I say, indicating the desk immediately inside the lobby. "I haven't heard a word from her since he died. I think she got a new job with Dr. Sparrow, across town."

I walk past her desk. There's a small restroom just beyond it, a set of stairs beside that, and then off to the right, is Jack's office.

I push open the door, and the two of us step inside. His desk is pushed under the window. Filing cabinets sit to either side of it, filled with his notes, medical records, secrets he was sworn to keep as a psychologist.

There's a comfortable chair to one side, where he spent hours and hours listening to the problems of his patients.

And then a big, overstuffed, leather couch. Where his patients could sit, or slump, or lie down if they wanted.

Jack's diploma hangs on one wall. There are various soothing-looking paintings hung on the walls here and there.

And on his desk sits a framed picture of him and me.

I reach for it, studying our faces.

We'd been dating for about five weeks. We'd gone for a walk through the park in town and then laid out on a blanket to watch the sunset and the stars wink into view. It had been awkward and difficult for Jack to take the picture of the two of us with the new camera he'd just gotten a week prior.

Our faces were too close. But we were both smiling, looking so joyful and happy.

"Viola was right," I say as I study the two of us. "We were so happy, and Jack did always say and do the right things. All the way until the very end."

"I understand why it's hard to have others question the authenticity of it all," Sully offers sympathetically. "When you were so happy."

I nod, and I feel it again. This questioning of words. Just like my mother's, and Cressida's and Viola's. The words don't quite connect. Don't sink in.

"Why couldn't I ever really hear them?" I say. "Their warnings? When they told me something wasn't right. It was almost like they were speaking another language. I got the general message, but the root of it all? It was lost, somehow."

"It sounds like obsession," Sully says as he begins a slow walk around the office. His eyes take it all in, looking at the things on Jack's desk. Opening the top drawer. "When something occupies your mind so thoroughly, nothing else really matters."

That turns on a little light bulb.

Because I have to be honest with myself.

That's exactly what it was.

Nothing else mattered after a while.

Nothing, but Jack.

"I have the keys to those filing cabinets," I say, pulling a set from my purse and dropping them on Jack's desk. "Raymond said to look for files. If they exist, maybe they'll be in there. He kept all his patient records in there."

Maybe I was one of them all along, and just didn't know it.

The very thought makes me ill and I shove it out of my mind.

I turn, walk out of the office, and head up the stairs.

Jack's apartment rests right above his office. It's a loft style. A kitchen occupies the far wall. A bathroom is walled off to the side of it. His bed and a closet dominate the left side, and a couch and chair are off to the right.

My knees quake. Because this is Jack up here.

There's still a coffee mug next to the sink. One of his jackets is slung over a chair at the dining table. The bed is unmade, as if just waiting for him to climb back into it.

And the smell of him doubles.

"I don't know if I can do this," I breathe when I hear Sully's heavy boots step beside me. "I don't know if I can go through his things, looking for incriminating evidence. Looking for proof to damn what I felt for him."

Sully shifts, as if to put an arm around my shoulders. But he stops, and takes a deep breath.

"Then you tell me where to look," he says. "And you watch me do it."

CHAPTER THIRTY-SEVEN

SULLY

BESIDES MORE TIES THAN ANY MAN SHOULD EVER possess, there's nothing strange in Jack's apartment.

I start in the kitchen, the least likely place to find anything. Boxes of crackers, snacks, pasta occupy the cupboards. Exactly four plates, bowls, and cups. I run my hand along the drawers, the cabinets, searching for anything hidden. All I come away with is two splinters from the old wood.

There is nothing suspicious or hidden in the dining table or the chairs. The bathroom yielded nothing strange. I pull apart all of the couch cushions, ransack the chair. I go through the cabinet against the wall and find it to be completely empty.

"How long had Jack lived here?" I ask as I move on to his bedroom area. I rip the blanket, pillows, and sheets off.

"He moved to Ander a few months before we met," Iona says. "January, I think. So, just over a year." She stands by the stairs, watching me. She hasn't moved once since I started going through everything.

"And before that, where did Jack live?" I ask as I lift the mattress, looking between it and the box spring.

"In New York," she explains. "He went to school at NYU. It's where he got his degree."

"In psychology?" I say. I get on all fours and look under the bed. There's a single box underneath it. I pull it out.

"Yes," Iona confirms.

The box rattles. I lift the lid off.

Inside I find four keys.

They seem simple enough. Normal house keys. Gold or silver colored. Sharp ridges and indents.

Iona walks over, peering into the box.

"Any idea what this is about?" I ask, reaching in and picking up two of the keys. I lay them one on top of another. They're all different cuts.

"No," she says, shaking her head. She kneels down on the ground beside me, studying them. But her eyes narrow.

She gets up, reaching for her bag on the floor by the stairs, and pulls out her keys. Crawling back over, she kneels beside me again, and takes the key with the biggest head.

Holding it on top of the mystery key, we both look at the cuts.

They're the same.

"It's a key to the office," Iona says. She turns them over, double-checking, and I can tell, they are in fact identical.

"But the other three are different," I say out loud.

Iona compares the other three keys to her own house key, but they don't match.

"Maybe they're just old keys," she muses, sitting beside me, leaning her back against the wall. "They could be to his parents' house back in Toronto, before they died. They could be to his old apartment back in New York."

An idea sparks and my hand goes to my pocket, and I feel the ring wrapped up in it.

"Did Jack only recently graduate from university?" I ask, climbing to my feet.

Iona looks up in confusion, and I extend a hand, pulling her up.

"No, he's been done for…eight years," she calculates.

"But he had only been here in Ander for just over a year," I say, walking back downstairs to the office. Iona quickly follows me. I turn into his office, going to look at the diploma. Sure enough, the date is from eight years ago. "What was Jack doing before he came here?"

Iona stands at my side, looking at the diploma, as well. "He was still in New York, working at the public library. He only started his practice when he moved here."

I shake my head. "You said Jack was good. If he was so good, why would he wait so many years before practicing what he studied?"

Iona looks over at me and I see the wheels turning behind her eyes. She doesn't respond.

"Where was Raymond Douglas from?" I ask, turning, my eyes sweeping the room, looking for answers.

"Pittsburg," she answers.

I nod. A map hangs on one wall above the client couch and I cross the room to it. I place my finger on this town. Trace over to New York, and then over to Pittsburg, forming a triangle.

Iona crosses the room and reaches into the box I hold. She lifts out the keys. "You said there were three other women tied to my ring," she says, her voice holding a little quiver. She holds up a key, one, two, three. "And then me." She holds up the last key, the duplicate of the one that unlocks that front door.

"Maybe Jack wasn't in New York that entire time," I say, my eyes locking on the dot labeled Pittsburg. "Maybe there are really three other offices those keys open."

Iona drops the keys back in the box and turns away.

"If what you say is true, you can find out the answers by reaching into your pocket."

I look over my shoulder to see her cross the office and sit in Jack's chair. She rests her chin against her knuckles and stares out the window.

What am I doing? I mentally ask myself. *Why am I here? Why do I care?*

This has nothing to do with me.

This isn't my life.

But my hand drifts to my pocket, and I feel the outline of the ring through the thick material.

I've helped grieving widowers. Mourning mothers. Despondent children.

Every one of them was heartbreaking in their grief.

But they were all natural. They lost a loved one. Were

going through the grief process. Were only looking for closure.

But in opening the gate between Jack and Iona, I've found myself tangled in a web of deceit and black veils that now wrap an echo around three hearts.

"I will ask them," I say, sinking onto the couch. "But only if you want me to. Only if you want to find out the truth."

My eyes rise up to Iona, and at first I don't realize what she's doing. She twirls a letter opener between her two hands. Her eyes study it. Never looking away.

A drop of red falls to the wooden floor. Followed by another.

She's pricked every one of her fingertips with the opener. Blood drips from every one of them.

"Iona!" I bark, darting forward to grab it from her hands before she can prick her thumb again. "What...what are you doing?"

I kneel at her side, and looking up into her eyes, I see they're distant. Hazy. Just like when she was up on the rooftop last night.

"Iona?" I say, gripping her arms and giving her a little shake.

She blinks. Once. Twice. And I see her vision come back into focus.

"Your hands," I say, grabbing one of them, holding them up for her to see. Blood drips in tiny trails.

Her face fills with confusion, slight horror.

"Did you even realize you were doing it?" I ask, my voice breathy.

She holds up her other hand, looking at the blood. They begin to tremble.

"Yes," she says. "No. I… I wasn't even thinking. I just… My hands just started doing it and…and I didn't care."

I grip her shoulders, giving her a tiny shake, dragging her eyes to mine. "We have to fix this, Iona. This isn't just obsession, anymore. This isn't just mindless love and a loss of appetite. This is dangerous. This is your life on the line now."

Iona's eyes redden. She gives a tiny, tiny nod.

I nod too, and feel as if every one of my organs has recently been rearranged.

"Why are you here, Sully?" she asks, leaning forward just slightly. Her eyes are locked on mine. "You didn't want me there in Roselock. You weren't kind to me. So, why are you here? And why do you care?"

I lean back fractionally. My eyes shift from one of hers to the other.

I look internally for an answer.

"Because no matter what, I'm going to die in two months and thirty days. I've spoken to the dead my entire life. I know hundreds of souls who reside on the other side of the gate. There is no reason you need to go live there early. And I am the one and only person who can get answers from the dead."

Iona keeps looking at me, giving me a teary nod. And

she leans forward, wrapping her frail arms around my wide shoulders, burying her face in the mane of my hair.

But my mind has moved on from the moment. To the solution.

I can get answers, anytime.

Go straight to the source.

I could open the gate straight to Jack again.

CHAPTER THIRTY-EIGHT

IONA

"Take me home," I tell Sully. I look at my hand, just staring at it. The little drops of blood are already trying to clot.

He immediately stands and waits for me at the door.

I hurt. My joints ache. The amount of energy it takes to get off the chair is astronomical.

But I make it. My knees tremble a little, but I rise to my feet, and I cross the office.

Sully locks the door for me and, side by side, we walk down the sidewalk. And I know I need to move now. Because along every square of this sidewalk, a memory of Jack and I is held.

Where we first ran into each other. Where he first held my hand. He kissed me beside that newspaper stand. When he asked me to go on that camping trip with him.

I have to put some distance between myself and these heavily traveled paths we had together.

"Have you ever loved anyone?" I ask as my eyes travel the rooflines that surround us so I don't see the places we frequented.

I feel his presence beside me, so solid and heavy. His broad shoulders seem to take up all the room on our walk. His long hair blows in the wind. He's a creature of the woods, walking around the city like the world's most obvious imposter.

"Maybe," he says.

"How can you not be sure?"

He doesn't respond immediately. And that's okay. It was a serious question.

"There was a woman, once," he says. "I told you that I left Roselock for a while. I went to South Carolina. Got a degree in music engineering. I had wanted to study in New York, but it was too expensive… So to Charleston, I went. We met the summer after I graduated."

I glance over at him, studying his face.

He looks down at the sidewalk. His green eyes grow distant. His hair hangs into his face, a lock of it tucked behind his ear.

"I always wanted to be with her," he continues. "She could make me smile and laugh without even trying. But…"

He trails off and looks up, his eyes sweeping about, not really looking for anything.

"But, what?" I encourage.

"We had nothing in common," he finishes. "She was light and I was dark. She had a future and I did not. In the end it didn't matter if I loved her or not; Roselock called me home, and I wouldn't have dreamed of asking her to come and live all of that with me."

I tear my eyes away from Sully, looking forward once more. I imagine it. Asking the woman he was with to go home with him, to Roselock. To the church that is falling apart. To the forest of bent trees. To the ground that bleeds.

"You loved her," I say. "You loved her enough to let her be free of that."

Sully takes five more steps before he says, "Maybe."

He makes me eat four bites of a sandwich when we get home, and after that I can't force any more down. He finishes the rest for me, but tells me to expect to eat more in an hour.

Maybe that's how I'll overcome this. Eat a tiny bit at a time, all throughout the day.

Maybe then I won't look like a skeleton.

But eating requires food in the house. So we climb into the ancient car Sully drove here from Roselock and head to the grocery store down the street.

Two thoughts keep rolling through my mind as Sully grabs the cart and starts down the aisles.

One: how out of place he looks here. He looks like he just walked out of the jungle, a wild man meant to live with beasts, not humans. His tall figure, broad shoulders, and wild hair make him intimidating looking.

And two: there are so many people here. I've walked these aisles once a week for years, but somehow, all these people became…invisible to me in the past few months.

And they're familiar faces. People I grew up with. Friends whose houses I once slept over at. People who came over to my childhood home to have dinner with my parents.

No less than three people say hello to me by the time we reach the end of the produce.

"You have deep roots here," Sully says, leaning toward me slightly as Mrs. Catala walks away, my home economics teacher from sophomore year in high school.

I nod, looking back at her, only to find her staring at Sully, a wary expression in her eyes. "That happens when you live your whole life somewhere. It's grown a lot since I was a kid, but I still know all the core people."

"Iona!" a cheery voice greets.

I turn to see Cathy, a woman I once worked with. She's an over-the-top type, with a bubbly personality, and no personal filter.

She rushes over with her cart, a very pregnant belly brushing against the handle.

"It's so good to see you!" she chatters. "I feel like it's been forever. What? Probably two years?"

I nod, trying to smile and be pleasant, but really, it's all very overwhelming. "Something like that."

"I heard you'd gotten engaged," she says, with a coy smile, her eyes sliding over to Sully. "Is this the lucky new husband?"

I look over at Sully, my eyes flooding with panic for a moment.

But Sully extends a hand, arranging a pleasant smile. "Sully. It's nice to meet you."

I'm sure I'm not hiding my surprise very well, but Cathy only looks up at Sully, smiling, admiring the giant beside me. "It's nice to meet the man who snatched up Iona, here. She's an incredible woman."

"She surely is," Sully says, giving me a little smile. "If you'll excuse us, we have some shopping to finish. It was nice to meet you."

And without another word, he pushes the cart forward, and Cathy calls a goodbye.

We turn down another aisle, making sure we're well out of earshot, before I give Sully a side glance.

"What-"

"I didn't think you wanted to tell her the full story," Sully fills in, grabbing a package of pasta. "And I never confirmed that I was your husband, only introduced myself. I thought it was easier."

I look up at Sully and study his face. He searches the shelves for more items to add to our cart, but it feels like he's intentionally not looking at me.

"Thank you," I say, more clearly than I thought I was capable of. "Thank you...for all of this."

He only grunts, and goes to push the cart further down the aisle. My hand darts out, gripping around his wrist, stopping him.

"Really," I say earnestly as he looks back, finally meeting my eye. "You don't have to do this, you fulfilled your end of the bargain. You being here..." I shake my head, my eyes dipping for a moment. "With you here, I don't feel so...dead."

There's something rolling behind those green eyes of his. Serious, and dark, and contemplative. But he nods his head, his lips pressed into a thin line.

We finish our shopping, and go to check out. Eggs, steak, cheese, apples, carrots, all fill the cart. My stomach instinctually tightens at the sight of it. But there's something that sparks in me, anxious to try. To get my life back.

I pay for the food and we walk out to the car. The bags loaded, Sully points us back toward home.

Together, we carry the food up to my apartment. And Sully begins cooking dinner.

"What about inviting your sister over?" Sully asks as he cuts the carrots and puts them in a big pot. "Viola?"

I watch him from the couch, my knees tucked into my chest, my arms looped around them.

I swallow once, the very thought making my heart jump into my throat.

All recent contact with my sisters has resulted in a massive fight. In screaming and yelling and horrible accusations flung.

But I have to *do* something about all of this.

"That's a good idea," I say. But it takes every muscle in my body, giving one hundred percent to climb off the couch and actually go to the phone on the wall. It's far too difficult to press those buttons and spin that rotary.

"Hello?" she answers.

"Viola," I say, trying to sound light and casual. "It's Iona."

"H...hi," she says in surprise.

"Uh," I stutter. I look back at Sully, twisting the cord around my finger. He only gives me an encouraging nod. "I was wondering if you'd like to come over for dinner tonight? With me...and Sully."

She pauses for a long time. For a moment, I'm worried our connection has been lost. But finally, "Yes, that sounds amazing." And her voice is too excited, too happy to quite be casual. "What time?"

"Five-thirty?" I say, looking to Sully for confirmation. He glances at the clock and nods.

"Yes, I'll be there," she says, and I can hear the smile I know is on her face just through her voice.

We say goodbye and I hang the phone back up. I keep looking at it for a moment, and take a big huff, feeling exhausted, suddenly.

"You did good, Iona," Sully says.

I look over at him, and see him giving me a little look, a small smile pulling in the corner of his mouth.

It changes his entire face. Even though it was small, even though it was a little forced, a smile on Sully's face makes him look...different.

CHAPTER THIRTY-NINE

SULLY

I scoop Iona into my arms and cross the small apartment to her bedroom. She hardly even stirs as I lay her down, pulling the covers up and over her. She lets out a little sigh.

My shoulder pressed to the doorjamb, I cross my arms, watching her as she sleeps, just to make sure she keeps breathing.

The dinner with Viola was somewhat forced, but considering everything, it went well. Little, light conversations. Pleasantries. I'd almost forgotten how to converse and talk like a normal human being to other human beings. But I managed. Because I had to for Iona.

At eight o'clock, I walked Viola down to her car.

"Who are you?" she asked me. "And what does my sister mean to you?"

It had taken me half a minute to come up with an answer, as honest of an answer as I could manage. Because this woman cared about Iona, and deserved as much of the truth as I could give her.

"Iona came to me for help, to deal with Jack's death," I said. "I'm trying to help her get the answers she needs for some closure."

Viola's eyes welled with tears. She pressed her lips into a thin line and nodded. "I don't know how you're doing it. No one else has been able to reach her. She just got angry and shut down. She cut everyone out. But you're doing something." She looked to the side as a little strangled sob leaked through her lips. "This tonight, every single minute of it, it's an improvement. She's doing so, so much better."

She closed the distance between us and wrapped her arms around me. "Thank you," she whispered.

I stood there, stiff and awkward, but hesitantly returned her hug. "You're welcome."

By the time I walked back upstairs, Iona was sound asleep on the couch.

I give one last look at Iona sleeping peacefully in her bed and turn to go back into the living room.

I reach into my pocket and pull out the cloth with the ring carefully folded into it. I cross to the counter, placing it on the laminate surface. The fabric falls open, revealing the ring.

I told Iona I would only speak to the three dead women if she wanted me to. If she really wanted answers.

Staring at it now, it's all I can do to not put the cold metal against my skin and rip them from the afterlife into the present.

And I look down the counter, to Iona's purse, where I know Jack's pocket watch still resides.

My hand twitches. Slides a little further down the counter towards it.

I press my lips into a thin line.

I take a step sideways.

A metallic tang sparks in the back of my throat as the dead press closer in on the gate.

My fingers grip the leather of the bag and I pull it toward me.

For five seconds, I wage an internal battle.

I shouldn't do this.

I need answers.

This has to be Iona's choice.

My rage is barely contained.

I yank the bag open, looking down into its contents.

Lip stick. Keys. A tattered book that looks like it's resided inside for months. A package of tissues. Other various things.

And there at the bottom, because it weighs the most, I see the glint of a gold reflection. A chain. And there, tucked in the corner, I see the edge of the pocket watch.

What were you really up to, Jack? I internally ask. *What are you trying to do to Iona?*

I look over my shoulder, back to her bedroom door. It remains slightly cracked open, the apartment utterly silent. In the dark and in the quiet, I hold my breath, fighting the monster of temptation.

My hands grip the bag, and on silent feet, I cross to the door. It squeals only slightly as I pull it open.

A thundering steam machine—that's what my heart is as I storm down the stairs. Out the front doors, and into the blowing snow outside.

I didn't grab a jacket, and the thick snowflakes cling to my exposed forearms. It tangles in my hair, instantly melts onto my neck, running down into my collar. But I don't even feel it as I stalk straight for my ancient vehicle, and yank the half rusted door open.

If anything, it's even more frigid in here. My breath billows out in giant clouds, only slightly illuminated by the streetlight halfway down the block.

For a moment, I just stare at Iona's purse, resting in the passenger seat.

My blood is ice.

My veins are on fire.

The questions burn a wormhole into my chest.

With the force of a man out for murder, I plunge my hand into the bag, and close my hands around the pocket watch.

The cold metal burns my skin. But I grit my teeth hard, yanking it from the bag, casting my eyes around the space.

"Jack," I call, not keeping the distrust and malice from my tone even a fraction. "You better give me some damn answers."

A couple of seconds, that's how long it should have taken Jack Caraway to appear.

But the seconds tick by, and my eyes only search the

small space of the car, the immediate vicinity outside the vehicle.

I cough, hugging tighter around myself as it grows colder. My heart picks up, anticipation eating its way through my blood.

I look around, and still, Jack doesn't appear.

I cough again.

"Jack!" I bellow into the night air. I squeeze the watch tighter and feel the metal begin to bend around my force. "Show your face! I summon you from behind the gate."

I cough again, this one more forceful. My hand raises to my lip, to the spot where I felt the warm wet. It comes away with a splash of blood.

I notice the tightness in my veins. Not just the anger, but a tightness that is physical. As if my entire body is recoiling, trying to force my life essence away from the watch in my hand.

I cough again. More blood fills my mouth.

"Jack," I growl, determined.

I broke my promise to get answers.

I will *get* my damn answers.

My free hand goes to my chest, to my white shirt, clawing at it when it feels too tight. Immediately, it's hard to breathe. Everything in me constricts, revolts against me trying to reach the dead.

It's Roselock, I know it. Telling me that I cannot leave. That I have no right to use its gifts outside of its borders.

I cough again, only there's too much blood and I can't clear it.

I thrash. I throw myself half out of the car door. Spill the blood onto the crisp snow.

Fight.

Live.

I release the watch, letting it clink into the drivers seat.

But the world still goes black, as my brain begs for oxygen.

CHAPTER FORTY

IONA

When I wake, Sully is nowhere to be found.

The dishes from dinner are washed and fully dry by now, lying on a towel. The apartment is relatively clean, part from Sully's cleaning spree I didn't even notice for a day, and partly due to me *waking up* and realizing I was letting my life literally rot away.

I stand in the middle of the apartment, looking around.

I suddenly feel very alone.

Feel a hole in my chest open up.

Where is Sully?

Would he really just leave like that? Without a word? Without any kind of closure? The answers to be found were not for him, but still. He was invested in this now, too.

I don't know what to think.

His jacket rests on the back of the couch. But that's the only trace of him. He very well could have just forgotten it as he left me in the middle of the night. The man is nearly an animal, anyway; I doubt he really feels the cold.

The hurt at his departure cuts deeper than I want it to. I feel his absence in a hollow, cavernous way in my chest.

But I lift my chin. Swallow twice.

I turn, head back into my bedroom. I shower. I dress. Do my hair and makeup. I even force myself to eat a slice of toast before I want to vomit my guts up.

When I go to leave though, my purse is nowhere to be found.

No trace of my car keys. No signs of my wallet.

I stand in the middle of my living room, my eyes wandering. I take a hard swallow.

I don't want to let the words surface.

But they do, anyway.

Would Sully really have taken my purse, with all of my money? Would he have taken my car?

No, *no*, the words echo in my head.

But really, how well do I actually know Sully?

I shake my head, pushing back the sick feeling in my stomach.

No. Something else is going on.

But for now, I have a life to live.

I have to get to work. I'll figure out what's going on later.

My determination to survive, to stare into the void and *survive* this time is short-lived.

I step outside of the building, into the snow-blanketed world.

Across the street, Sully's ancient car still waits, buried in six inches of snow.

The door to the driver's side is open.

I squint through the still dim light, trying to make out the lumpy shape that spills out from the car, onto the road, covered with snow.

I sprint across the street, the snow falling down into my boots. I barely make it across before a plow cuts around the corner, nearly taking me out.

"Sully!" I scream, falling at his side. I sweep the snow off of him, my horror growing threefold when I uncover blood-soaked snow. I dig and dig, shoving aside the snow, uncovering the man who I thought had abandoned me.

"Call an ambulance!" I scream at the first person who walks out into the early morning. The man startles, his eyes growing wide as he sees what I'm doing. "Now!"

He darts into a nearby coffee shop.

"Sully," I whimper as finally, I uncover his face.

His head rests against the concrete, as if he fell out of the car. There's blood spilling from his mouth, frozen against his skin. Snow melted against the warmth of him, and then refroze.

"Wake up," I beg, feeling around his neck, trying desperately to find a pulse.

But his lips are so blue.

He doesn't stir.

"Help!" I scream out into the morning. Frantically, I dig, unearthing him from the snow. He wears only a white t-shirt and his jeans and boots. His lower half is half in the car, half out.

A woman darts over, a gasp and half a scream. She kneels beside me, digging the giant out. "What happened? Was he…was he shot?" she guesses at all the blood.

"I don't think so," I say as the first tears prick my eyes and then immediately fall onto my cheeks. "I…I don't know what he was doing out here."

But as my eyes drift up, I see his right foot balancing on the drivers seat. And half covered in snow, sits Jack's pocket watch.

I know exactly what he was doing out here.

The scream of sirens blares through the morning, and relief and fear saturates my body as I see the flashing lights draw nearer and nearer.

In just a minute, I'm being gently pushed aside as the paramedics hoist Sully up and out of the snow, away from the car. They fire a million questions at me, and I only just have enough time to grab the pocket watch before they're ushering me into the ambulance with Sully.

"Is he alive?" I whisper as I huddle in one corner, staring at him as the two men work on him, checking and pumping and radioing to the hospital.

They don't answer me immediately, and listen to his heart with a stethoscope.

And the tears flood onto my cheeks when he finally gives a slight nod yes.

It only takes three minutes to reach the hospital. I jog

alongside the stretcher as they race into the emergency room, and gasp in pain as they disappear through some doors, telling me I have to wait until the doctor comes to get me.

I'm not sure how long I stand there, just staring at the doors. Probably a few minutes. But eventually a nurse comes to my side and asks me to take a seat. She offers reassuring words, none of which reach me.

I look down at Jack's watch in my hands.

Sully went to get answers. He went outside where I wouldn't hear him speaking to Jack. He looked for privacy and dark.

And along the way, something had gone terribly wrong.

Along the way he had nearly died.

Sully's blue lips flash through my head once again, and my heart fractures.

If he doesn't make it, if he dies, that's on me.

He did this for me.

I ASK THE NURSE FIVE TIMES IF THERE'S ANY UPDATE yet. Each time she tells me no, and to please sit down and wait for the doctor to come out. I pace. Ruin my blouse as I twist and twirl the hem of it with worry.

And finally, three hours later, a man in a doctor's uniform comes back through those doors. There is a smear of blood down his chest.

"Are you the one who found Sully?" he asks, unsure, looking in my direction.

I leap to my feet, nodding.

Heavens, my chest is so tight. I can hardly breathe.

"Are you his wife?" the doctor asks, extending a hand back to the chair I just evacuated, slipping into one himself.

It can't be good if he wants me to have a seat.

I shake my head. "We're…" I hesitate. What do I even define us as? "We're just friends. He doesn't have any family left. He was visiting me when this happened."

The doctor nods, begging me with his eyes to sit down.

I don't want to, with every fiber in me, but I do.

"Sully suffered from hypothermia," he begins to explain. "His internal temperature fell to ninety degrees. That may not sound too serious, but had it fallen any lower, he would have suffered some long lasting, serious physical complications."

"So he's going to be okay?" I ask, and my voice cracks.

The doctor gives a tentative nod. "He's incredibly lucky. We checked the temperatures last night. It got down to twenty-nine degrees, and it sounds as if he was outside all night. He probably shouldn't have survived. I credit it to his size, and well, that mane of hair might have helped save his life."

The doctor chuckles, and I can see why. He himself wears no facial hair, has short, neat hair, and dainty glasses upon his nose. They're certainly polar opposites.

"What about the blood?" I ask. The tension in my chest won't release.

I'm not shocked when a somewhat puzzled expression tugs on the man's face.

"We still aren't sure about that," he answers honestly. "It

came from his lungs, almost as if they were punctured. But there's no signs of physical trauma. Besides the hypothermia, he seems perfectly healthy. The man's as strong as an ox."

Tears once more prick the backs of my eyes. I press my lips together tightly and give a slight nod.

"We'll keep trying to find an answer to why there was so much blood," the doctor says. "But he's going to be fine. We've warmed him back up. I'd like to keep him here in the hospital overnight for observation while we do some more testing. But I expect he will be able to leave tomorrow morning."

I squeeze my eyes closed, forcing a tear out onto my cheek.

"Would you like to see him now?" the doctor asks. "He just woke up."

My eyes fly back open, and my heart breaks out into a sprint. My lips still pressed together, I nod.

Through the sterile smelling halls, I follow the doctor. We pass so many doors that I begin to grow impatient. And then he turns into one of them, pushing it open for me.

Sully lays there, his head turned slightly to the side, but the moment I walk in, his head perks up, looking at me with wide, unsure eyes.

I let the door fall closed behind me.

And I linger by it, just looking at Sully.

I hug my arms tight around me. My chest is still tight. My emotions are a hurricane right now.

Sully just lies there with his insane hair and beard.

Wearing a hospital gown that barely fits him. Looking far too solid and heavy for that poor hospital bed.

He's pale. He looks tired. There are dark circles under his eyes.

Tears prick back into my own.

"Iona," Sully breathes.

I hug myself tighter. I bite my lower lip. I shake my head.

"Iona, I'm so sorry."

My vision swims. Before I give them permission to do so, my feet move me across the room, my arms wrap around him the best they can, and I bury my face in his neck.

I sob.

I sob and sob and sob.

Sully pulls me in tight and I should be worried about hurting him, but he's so solid, such a bear, that all he feels is huge and protective.

"I'm so sorry," he breathes, running his hand down my hair. There's something stiff and awkward about the way he holds me, but he doesn't recoil from my embrace.

I force my breaths to slow. I make the tears stop. I calm the shaking in my chest, in my hands.

Slowly, I sit back up.

And a hot ember of anger lights in my veins as I look into his green eyes.

"You broke your promise," I say flatly.

It's there in his eyes. He knows he broke it. He knows it was deliberate, what he did.

"I know," he says. He brings a giant hand up and wipes away a stream of tears from my cheek. "I was angry. I wanted answers. But it wasn't my place to make that call."

"And somehow it nearly cost you your life."

And I realize *this* is what I'm actually angry about.

Sully nods. He drops his hand, an exhausted move. His head falls back to the pillow, and he turns his head toward the window, gazing outside.

"It was Roselock, punishing me," he says.

"What does that mean?"

He doesn't answer right away. His eyes just keep looking out the window, to the gray skies. The clouds are dark and thick, but for now, the snow is held at bay.

"I've never tried to speak to the dead outside of Roselock," he finally continues. "I told you I left Roselock for six years. I tried to pretend the town and everything associated with it didn't exist. So I never tried to summon the dead while I was away. Last night was an experiment I didn't know I was conducting."

My chest tightens once more. I look away from him, anywhere but at the man who my chest is fracturing over.

"I never," he says, "never would have guessed that would be the reaction to trying to open the gate anywhere but in Roselock. They're running tests, to see what happened. But they won't find any answers."

It makes my hands tremble, thinking of this normal, mundane hospital, and the true answers of Roselock. The trail of pennies through the town. The grave of the lovers. The blood that seeps out from beneath the church.

"We need to get you out of here," I say, and then turn my eyes back to Sully.

"Yes, we do," he says, and he meets mine once more.

"Are you okay to move soon?" I ask. And I don't even think about it when I reach forward and grab his hand in mine. "How are you feeling?"

His eyes drop to our hands. "Tired. Really, really tired. But I'm all right. I can move."

I nod, even though he isn't looking at me. "We'll never get you out of here like this. And your old clothes are covered in blood. I'm going to run to the department store a few blocks away, and then I'll be back."

"Alright," he says. He watches me as I stand and go to the door.

I pause when I pull it open, looking back at him, holding his eyes. I'm not sure what I mean to say. Something angry and vengeful. Something forgiving. All of those words and emotions are caged in my chest without a logical, sensical way to escape.

So I don't voice any of them.

I walk out, closing the door behind me.

CHAPTER FORTY-ONE

SULLY

THAT WAS GENUINE TERROR AND FEAR ON IONA'S FACE.

Those were devastated tears she sobbed all over my hospital gown.

As soon as she leaves, I just keep staring at the door, a hand over my chest. I rub it, as if I can push her tears into my skin, all the way down to my rewarmed, beating heart.

It's been a long, long time since anyone cared if I lived or died. It's been since before my mother passed that anyone cried over me. Iona's reaction was something real and soul bending.

I tell myself that it's a sign of hope, of progress. That even in her grief, her obsession, Iona is still capable of that kind of concern for another.

I have to push that aside.

I remind myself that I'm in the midst of an escape plan.

I ring in the nurse and ask if it's okay if I take a shower. After confirming with the doctor, she helps me into the bathroom and starts the shower. She returns a moment later with seven tiny bottles of shampoo and two towels.

I'm about to shut the door to the bathroom, when I catch her eye, giving me an appreciative look from behind.

I smirk when the door closes, and rid myself of the hospital gown.

The act of cleaning myself is an exhausting one. All my muscles still feel cold and sluggish. The doctor explained to me that they used a machine to draw my blood out of my body, rewarm it, and then put it back inside me.

I feel a little like an alien at the moment, remade. Engineered.

The tiny comb waiting on the bed when I finish showering is just a joke. I get through the bottom inch of my hair before giving up. Shuffling to the window, I look out, and find that the snow has once more broken free from the sky.

I'm worried about Iona driving in these conditions, and I shouldn't be. There should be a line here, between keeping her alive and worrying over her in hour-to-hour moments, but it's beginning to blur.

I huff a sigh of relief when twenty minutes later, the door to my room opens once more, and Iona walks in with two bags in hand.

"I'm not sure if everything will fit," she says, and I notice she doesn't quite meet my eyes. "I had to guess. So…"

She kind of shrugs, setting them down on the bed.

I'm certain now, she's not looking at me deliberately.

"Thank you," I huff, pulling the items out. She dismisses herself outside.

The jeans are a little tight in the thighs, but surprisingly they are long enough. The long-sleeved shirt, however, is perfect. I pull out a thick coat, taking note that she ripped the price tag off of it before giving it to me.

I should repay her. I can't stomach being a financial burden. But I am a man who has had no use for money in years. I've been living off of the small stash in the church for years, on a strict budget, allotted out to last me exactly until May seventh.

I pull my boots back on, the only item of clothing still usable from before last night. I hobble over to the door, pulling it open just slightly, and Iona steps back inside.

She looks me over, taking note of how the clothes fit. But still, she doesn't meet my eye. "Looks like everything will work."

I nod, looking down at myself. "Thank you," I say again.

"Let me help you with your hair," she says, crossing the room, grabbing for the comb. "Other than it, you look ready to walk out of here."

I'm a little startled, taken off my guard. She tells me to sit on the bed, and she kneels behind me, running her fingers through my hair. She gently pulls and tugs through it with her delicate fingers, pulling it back and up. Finally she releases a hair band from her wrist and ties it back.

She climbs off and stands in front of me, assessing her work, but not looking me in the eye.

"You still stand out, but at least you don't look like you just crawled out of a cave."

And her words actually make me smile. And it's the sun dawning in the pit of my heart when she smiles, too.

"Come on," she says, reaching for my hand. "Let's break you out of here."

My hand swallows hers as I take it. She pulls me forward and sticks her head out the door, looking up and down the hall.

She tugs me forward after her, into the hall, and down it we escape.

It's kind of ridiculous, how easy it is to leave. We simply walk down the hall, past the reception desk, and out the doors.

"Your sister, she's a nurse," I say as we begin walking. And I realize Iona's car isn't here because she probably rode in the ambulance with me. "Is this the hospital where she works?"

Iona nods. "She works in labor and delivery, though. She won't see anything."

I just nod in return.

It takes us thirty minutes to walk back to her apartment. In thirty-degree weather, through light snow, it's quite the journey. By the time we make it back to the building, I'm a dead man walking. Iona actually puts a hand under my elbow and helps me up the two flights of stairs.

She unlocks her front door, and steers me straight for her bed.

I only just manage to peel my new coat off before flopping down into the bed, my still-booted feet hanging over the edge of it.

It's not one minute before the heavy blanket of sleep washes over me.

CHAPTER FORTY-TWO

IONA

I watch Sully sleep for a while, just staring at his gigantic form on my bed. He dominates the entire thing. Even if I wanted to, there would be no room for me to crawl into it and curl up against his side.

I swallow hard, pushing that thought away, and turn from the room.

The phone rings, and I already know who it is going to be before I answer it.

It's my boss. I explain that there was an emergency with a dear friend, that's why I wasn't at work today, either. I'm still not feeling well, so I don't think I should come in tomorrow, but I promise him that I will be in to work on Monday.

This is my last chance, the man says with a tone that tells me he doesn't want to fire me, but I've taken too many personal days lately. If I don't show up for work, on time, on Monday, I shouldn't bother coming back in.

I need this job. If I lose it, I might as well pack up and go back to Roselock with Sully.

But the thought sends a shiver down my spine. I recall that yipping laughter in the woods as it grew dark. The many, many graves that rest behind the church. I think about all the bodies Sully told me lie trapped in the mountain.

No, I could never.

I have to keep my job.

Over the next hour, I spend a generous amount of time putting together some oven-baked chicken for dinner.

"That smells amazing," a voice cooed from behind me. A set of arms wrapped around my waist, and a chin rested on my shoulder. "Look at you, my domestic goddess."

I smiled and laughed as I cut the potatoes. "Apparently you've forgotten last week's burnt pork disaster."

"Just added more flavoring," Jack said, kissing his way up my neck, from my collarbone to the hollow behind my ear.

Someone knocked on the door as Jack spun me around, grinding his hips into mine.

"Ignore that," he growled into my neck, a gentle bite into my flesh.

"It's gotta be someone important if they're showing up at my door," I said through a playful smile, attempting to force my eyes open.

They knocked again. "Iona?"

Cressida's voice cut through the door, stabbing me with a jolt of panic.

Jack growled into my skin, brushing his cheek against mine as his lips rose up to take mine, possessive and with force. "She can come back later."

"Jack," I chuckled against his lips.

"Iona, I can hear you two," Cressida demanded impatiently. "Let her answer the door, Jack."

My brows furrowed at that. *Let* me answer the door?

What the hell did she think was going on?

I raised my hands to Jack's hair, running my fingers into it, pulling his face harder against mine. His hands came to my backside, forcefully grinding my hips into his as he pulled my dress up over my thighs.

Forget answering the door. Forget my eldest sister.

A biting chill tugs at the back of my brain.

Cold.

Cold.

So, so cold.

My teeth chatter and my entire body begins to tremble.

Suddenly a gasping breath rips from my chest, and I surge forward into a sitting position. Water sloshes all over the floor, and tiny specks of ice rush away from me.

I'm sitting in the bathtub, stark naked. It's full of frigid water, and I see the last remaining bits of dozens of ice cubes floating around in the water around me.

I hold a hand up. My fingers are well-pruned and utterly purple.

Climbing from the tub, I wrap a towel around my violently shivering body. I look in the mirror, and find my lips nearly completely blue.

The door to the bathroom is wide open, and just outside the door, in the hallway from the living room to the bedroom, lay my clothes.

My brain goes back, trying to recall what happened over the last few...minutes? Hours?

I was making dinner. My thoughts drifted to Jack.

But there's another memory, hiding in the back of my brain, reluctant to show its face.

One of me going to the freezer. Pulling out the four ice cube trays. Dumping them into the tub and filling it with cold water. After refilling the trays and placing them back in the freezer, I stripped my clothes off on the way to the tub, and climbed in.

I breathe hard, my lungs feeling too frozen to work. I look down at my skeletal arms, and somehow, they look even thinner. It hurts to move, and every movement is stiff and jerky.

I don't have enough body fat to insulate me.

I grab my clothes and duck back into the bathroom, cranking up the heat of the baseboard heater. I squat down beside it, but I'm too frozen solid to feel its heat.

That's how I sit, for at least an hour. Huddled by the heater, with the door cracked open, clutching my clothes to my chest. Slowly, slowly thawing.

And I know. I can't deny it anymore.

Something is wrong.

Something snapped in my brain. It's sent me down this path that makes it so I don't even recognize myself, anymore. And if I don't do something about it, I'm afraid I'll soon be dead.

My body still hurts and aches as I pull my clothes back on. I hold my ear to the door and hear the sounds of Sully's deep breathing. I cross to the phone on the wall and call the directory.

"Marvin County Prison, please," I request.

A few minutes later, I'm patched through to the right person. I make my appeal.

"I see here that there was an assault last time you visited Mr. Raymond Douglas," the man with the gruff voice says. "Says here all future visits are revoked."

"Please," I beg. "I need to speak to him. He has some answers I need to get. I promise there won't be another incident."

"I'm sorry, ma'am, there's nothing I can do." He hangs up on me.

I stare at the phone for a long minute, in utter shock.

No. *No.* I need some answers.

But, what else am I supposed to do?

The shuffling of feet behind me draws my attention.

"Are you ready to get the truth?" Sully asks. His expression is open, but empathetic to how difficult every single breath of this is.

I swallow once, and place the phone back on the receiver.

And finally, I nod.

CHAPTER FORTY-THREE

SULLY

AT DAWN, WE MAKE THE DRIVE BACK TO ROSELOCK.

Two hours down the highway. Down the forgotten road that breaks off of it, and then, I feel it.

My heart beats faster. My veins dilate, allowing my blood to flow more easily. The second we drive past the Roselock sign, my chest loosens. I actually lean back in the passenger seat of Iona's car, and sigh.

It's difficult to make it through the town and up to the church. Snow blankets the ground and there haven't been any plows that have cleared these streets in fifteen years, and even then, it was only Mr. Kebler in his truck, with his homemade plow attached to the front.

"Come on," Iona begs her car as we crest the final stretch up to the church. The tires spin and we slide backward a bit. She pumps the gas, and finally the wheels catch and we lurch forward.

She pulls right up to the front doors of the church and

the two of us climb out. She tries to support me as we climb the rotting steps, and I try to hold her upright as well, which leads to an awkward, slipping climb.

The scent of rot and dust is familiar as I pull the doors open. The rows of pews haven't moved at all, there are no new boot prints.

I've been gone for four days, but locking up never once crossed my mind.

Who is around to break in?

I'm still exhausted from my hypothermia. Slowly, I shuffle across the chapel, but only make it to the bench at the organ before I slump down onto it.

Iona sits in the pew closest, looking around. Dread and fear but determination settle into the tiny wrinkles in her forehead and the depths of her eyes. She rubs her hands together, pinning them between her knees.

"I should go start a fire," she says, and steam billows out from between her blue lips.

"No," I grunt. "I'll get it. Just give me a minute."

She nods, and I think she's relieved. She's a city girl. I doubt she knows how to start a fire.

"You said you got a degree in music engineering," Iona says. She looks up at the organ pipes.

I nod. "I wanted to be a producer someday. Work with all kinds of music. Every aspect fascinated me."

"You would have been amazing at it," she says.

My gaze falls to the keys. And like they are magnetic, my hands rise up. My fingers fall to them.

One by one, my fingers depress keys. Bleed out a tune

from the back of my head. They're never ones I've heard before. Just whatever flows into my mind at the moment, demanding that I open the valve and let the notes free-flow out.

My eyes slide closed. My back hunches, my shoulders lean in toward the organ. My song today is a simple one. A hesitant one. One that is scared to learn the truth.

But it's an honest one.

I lay my soul bare, spilling it out of my body.

When the exhaustion takes over and the notes have drained out from my head, I stop. It takes every muscle and ounce of will to move my body and rise from the bench. I grant just a brief glance at Iona as I walk past her. She simply stares blankly at the organ pipes.

A few minutes later, I have a fire started and the flames grow bigger by the moment. I kneel before the fireplace, staring through the glass at the flames. Slowly, so slowly, I feel the heat radiate from it, warming my half-frozen face.

Any normal day, I would be going out to gather roses now, to lay them on the graves of all those individuals I know. Despite the snow, it's something I always do.

Later, I'd gather my family to keep me company, pulling them from the other side to have a grim conversation. Because, in the Whitmore family, every one of them is dark and grim.

But as I rise back to my feet, somehow everything feels different. I don't feel that duty and call.

All that occupies my thoughts is getting Iona's answers.

Iona stands in the doorway to the chapel. Her eyes drift

from place to place on the floor, but she has that far-off look that tells me she isn't really seeing anything. She bites her lower lip and it takes me just a moment to realize why my chest suddenly feels tight.

She's holding her breath. Her chest doesn't rise and fall.

Before I can begin to worry that she's going dark again, she speaks, and releases me.

"This is the hardest thing I've ever had to do, you know," she says. And then, her eyes find mine once more. "To accept…this. Everything that's going on. To realize…"

Her voice trails off and moisture pools in her eyes. "To realize that everyone but me was right. I loved him. Loved Jack with everything in me. So I thought…I thought that seeing him die, losing him was the hardest thing I would ever have to go through. But really, it's this. Doing what we're about to do. It means I'm cutting a piece of me off. A big one. And throwing it on the fire to burn."

Her lower lip trembles slightly. But she raises her chin. She swallows once, twice. And holds herself high.

I cross the room. And tentatively I reach out, and take her hand. She looks up to meet my eyes and nods once, before walking by my side to the Sunday School room.

Dust is thick in the air and the room bites with its bitter cold. A small draft around the window allows the ice cold to blow straight in. Together, Iona and I rearrange the room, just as it was before with two chairs facing one another. We light half a dozen candles, and draw the drapes.

Our eyes lock, each of us mentally preparing for what is about to happen.

Are you really ready? I mentally probe.

I'm scared, but ready, her eyes answer in return.

In unison, we lower into our seats. Iona never once looks away, locked in on my eyes like everything in the world depends on it.

Into my pocket, I reach. I produce the bit of cloth I wrapped around the ring. For a moment, I hold it open-faced. Despite the door being opened to the now roaring fire, the temperature in the room drops.

Iona's hand suddenly darts out, her thin fingers gripping around my wrist.

I look up to find her eyes locked on the ring.

"Their names," she says with a near frantic urgency. "I...I don't want to go into this and not know their names." She looks up at me. "I think it will help make it more real for me."

"Simone," I recall immediately. "She was the last. Joanne and Sharon. Simone is dark skinned with curly, black hair. Joanne has black hair and a sharper looking face. And Sharon is blonde, short. All beautiful."

Iona nods, pale. I wait until she meets my eyes, and then nods, granting me permission to continue, telling me that she is ready.

Holding my own breath for a moment, as if I'm about to slide under ice cold water, I close my fingers around the ring.

"Thank you," one voice immediately cuts through the silence.

"She looks better," another says.

"It's working."

Like a floodgate with a crack in it, the three women come crashing through, drowning me in their surge.

"They're here," I tell Iona.

"All three?" she asks, her voice a quiet squeak.

I nod, looking around the room. Sharon stands in the corner, her arms crossed over her chest, her eyes wide and scared. Joanne paces, a look of anger and possibly disdain on her sharp face. But Simone, she walks to stand at Iona's side, just looking at her.

"Is she really to learn the truth now?" Simone asks. She squats at Iona's side, and watching my eyes, Iona looks in the same general direction.

"She is," I reply. "Please, tell us what is happening."

Simone looks up to Joanne and then to Sharon. The other two take a step or two forward, closing into a circle.

"Jack was the beautiful and charming new psychologist in town," Simone begins. She looks to the others, and both of them nod.

"Where were you all living when you met Jack?" I ask after relaying Simone's words.

"Pittsburg," Simone says.

"Richmond, Virginia," Joanne tells us.

"Long Island," answers Sharon.

"How…" Iona struggles to get her feet under her,

stumbling over her words, but determined looking. "How old was Jack when you met him?"

"Twenty-four," Sharon says. She twists her fingers into her black dress. "I was eighteen when we met. We were together for two years, Jack was twenty-six when he asked me to marry him, and when I died."

"And Jack was working when you first met him?" Iona questions.

Sharon nods, even though Iona cannot see her. "He'd just graduated from NYU and was working with another doctor in town. He was brand new. But everyone really liked him. That's…that's how I met him. He was working with my younger sister and I was usually the one who dropped her off and picked her up."

My fingers tighten around Iona's, an automatic reaction of anger.

She was eighteen. Hardly an adult, and Jack being six years older than her.

I can just picture it, Jack giving a flirtatious smile to the young, naïve sister of one of his clients. Wooing her. The charming, older, professional man and the honey sweet young girl.

"Jack was still twenty-six when I met him," Joanne speaks up next. "We were the same age. He'd been practicing in Richmond for about three months when we met at the movies." She bites her lower lip, her eyes falling to the floor for a moment. I'm sure the recall is playing through her head. "I was there with some girlfriends, and there he was too, all by himself. I wasn't very nice, I guess. I teased him about being on his own. But by the end of the night, he walked me home, and we went out again the very next night."

"And how old was Jack when you…" I trail off, because saying the words feels rude and cruel.

"Jack had just turned twenty-eight when I died," she replies harshly.

"I didn't quite make it to two years like you two," Simone pipes up. All eyes shift to hers, Iona's following mine as I repeat everything that is said. "He was twenty-nine when we met and thirty when I died. I was twenty, and trust me, everything about our relationship was a problem for everyone."

She rises to her feet once more, angling slightly to the side, her eyes fixing on a wall. "We met outside a bakery, where the owner had just thrown me out for having the wrong shade of skin. Jack watched the whole thing and stepped in, putting the owner in a different frame of mind. He bought me a croissant, and insisted on walking me the rest of the way to work."

There are dark scars on this country's history. Certain things may be illegal now, but far too much is still within the law.

"Within six months, that ring you're holding was on my finger," Simone continues. She looks empty and sick at the same time. Hollow disgust haunts her eyes, the slant of her mouth. "But like I said, there were complications at every turn, every direction we faced. Even our upcoming marriage wasn't formally legal. It was going to take time, to figure it all out. So our engagement lasted seven months, and things got more and more dire, before suddenly I decided the bottom of the Ohio River was where I needed to be with pockets full of rocks in the middle of December."

Shivers work their way up my veins, imagining the scene. Iona cringes visibly.

"Jack lied to me." Iona's voice is a croak. Rough words spoken through a dry throat. "He told me he had a fiancée who died. He never said it was suicide. And he also told me she'd died a year and a half ago. But…" She shakes her head, her eyes unfocused. "If Simone died in December… Jack moved to Ander in January. Simone had only been gone for three months when we met."

Her words gain in pitch before trailing off and she shakes her head.

"Thirty?" I say, immediately moving on, because I can feel the tug at the back of my brain saying that our time is limited. "You said Jack was thirty when you met him, Iona?"

There's a distant look in her eyes, and I can see it: she's shutting down. But she nods, her gaze fixed on a blank space of wall.

"So he spent roughly two years with each of you, building a relationship, eventually proposing, but then the end came before he ever married any of you," I fill in, feeling that tug grow stronger, a little more frantic.

Each of the women nod, even Iona.

"And then there was roughly, five to eight months

between each of you, where he moved to another city, established a new practice, and met another woman." Each of them looks around, nodding in unison.

My heart thunders, races, crashes against my ribcage, threatening to stampede as the gate grows heavier and heavier.

"Thank you," I say quietly, my grasp on Iona's hand loosening. "You can rest now. We will see you soon."

And just like that, the three of them are instantly gone.

Iona's hand shakes, but she doesn't leave it in mine for more than a moment once the gate is shut and the room instantly warms before ripping it out of mine and standing.

"I need paper," she says, crossing the room and walking out. "Do you have some paper here, and a pen?"

CHAPTER FORTY-FOUR

IONA

Sᴜʟʟʏ ᴜɴᴇᴀʀᴛʜs ᴀ sᴛᴀᴄᴋ ᴏꜰ ᴘᴀᴘᴇʀs ᴀɴᴅ I ɢʀɪᴘ ᴛʜᴇᴍ with enough force to wrinkle and crease every one of them. He hands over a pen and I drop it in my urgency, half tripping over myself as I walk back out of his room and into the common room, to the couch.

I grab a big, old book from a shelf and lay it on my lap to write against.

SIMONE

JOANNE

SHARON

I write their names in big letters and cross to the old bulletin board that looks half molded, half falling apart and pin them up. Next, I write each of their cities where they met Jack, and how old he was during each relationship.

There. Now I have a timeline.

"You forgot one," Sully says as he watches from one wall, his arms crossed over his broad chest.

I look back at my board with six pieces of paper pinned to it.

Iona.

I forgot myself.

My movements slowing down by the moment as the forced adrenaline I was riding on ebbs away.

IONA.

Ander, West Virginia.

30-31.

When I pin up my own two pages and take a step back, I marvel at the timeframe.

From the ages of twenty-four, to thirty-one.

This has gone on for over seven years.

"How can anyone ever trust their heart?" I say as I look from one name to the next. "He seemed so normal. It was just a love story. You meet all these couples, and they tell you how they met, and it's sweet, but of course never feels as real as your own love story."

I wrap my arms around my waist, hugging myself tight. "I loved Jack. I loved how we met. I loved our story. It was so sweet and…normal. But there were three others. And they loved their stories, too. With the *same* man I loved. And in the end…"

I trail off. My throat feels tight.

"You can't ever really trust anyone but yourself, can you?"

I hear Sully take five steps closer, but something recoils inside of me, and I take two more steps away, toward that back door.

"Iona, you cannot judge the world based on one sick and twisted man. The world is full of good, honest people."

"Then why was I so unlucky to find the worst of the worst?" I ask. I look over my shoulder back at him, daring him to give me a logical answer.

He doesn't have one.

So I push the back door open, and walk outside into the snow.

It was so hot that all the food was drying up.

Mom's potato salad was almost ruined. Cressida's baked beans were looking more like mush. Sweat dropped off of Jack's brow, narrowly missing the grill.

But everyone was in good spirits as we wrapped up the day with dinner, before we would watch the fireworks from the back patio, just like every year.

"How come you aren't spending Independence Day with your family, Jack?" my mother asked as she finished setting out the dishes.

A long table had been set up on the patio, about a dozen different dishes lining the tablecloth. Around was gathered all of my family, my sisters, Cressida's husband Harold, and their three kids. And, of course, Mom.

"My parents passed away when I was at NYU," Jack said as he flipped the burgers. "And being from Canada, they wouldn't have been celebrating today, anyway."

He gave a charming laugh, looking over his shoulder at me and giving me a wink.

But the moment just turned awkward, and no one knew what to say.

"What about siblings?" Mom probed. "Surely they'd like to see you at some point."

"Only child, ma'am," Jack said as he scooped the cooked meat onto a plate. "My parents tried for years to have more children, but I guess it just wasn't in their future."

"Must have been an awfully quiet childhood," Cressida said as she helped Fiona, her oldest, detangle a pinecone from her hair. The second she was done, my beautiful niece took off, chasing after her brother once more.

Jack nodded, removing the last of the patties, and shutting down the grill. "It was. My parents were...involved in their lives. They sometimes kind of forgot that I was there. But they were good people."

It surprised me a little, to hear Jack talking so openly about his childhood with my family. He rarely opened up about it, even with me. I suspected there were some resentful scars there, coming from a family who always seemed dissatisfied that there weren't more children, so their reaction was to pretend there wasn't even the one of them.

None of my family seemed to quite know what to say to that, so instead, Mom just declared that it was time to eat.

I settled down with my plate, cozying up to Jack, who placed his hand on my knee under the table. I leaned in, pressing my lips to his as his dazzling eyes met mine.

Sparks ignited in my chest when he kissed me. Strings of connectivity wound between us with each and every one, drawing me closer to him.

"I love you," I whispered against his lips, smiling.

"I love you, too," he said in a growl that was hungry and possessive.

"I better see you eat every bite on that plate," Cressida's voice cut into the intimate moment. "If you lose one more pound I'm going to start force-feeding Jonah's breast milk down your throat until you put that weight back on."

I forced a little laugh, despite the violence that sparked in my blood. Cressida and her big, bossy mouth, always telling everyone what to do.

I tentatively scooped a bite of the potato salad and put it in my mouth.

It didn't taste like anything, and I wanted to push my plate away, but I looked up at my sister across the table, and smiled.

Jack leaned in, tracing his nose up my cheek, igniting another storm of desire, instantly.

"Don't let her get to you," he whispered. "You're beautiful, any way you are."

So I did as he said. I ignored my sister, and I relished Jack's hand running up and down my thigh underneath the table.

A shiver works its way down my spine as the wind blows through the crooked and bent trees, and I stare down into the open grave. Not a flake of snow makes its way down to the exposed dirt, six feet down.

The two skeletons lie side by side. Clinging together, refusing to be separated, even in death.

I shiver once more, letting out a long, slow breath, clouding the air before me.

CHAPTER FORTY-FIVE

SULLY

I KNEW I SHOULD LEAVE HER BE, LET IONA DEAL WITH her grief and anger in private. Which she obviously wanted, considering she'd walked out the door and away.

But considering all of her recent behavior, considering it was involuntary, I didn't dare let her roam around a town like this on her own.

So I'd waited three minutes before I hauled my aching, sluggish body out the door, following her small footprints through the deep snow and out into the gray day.

Down the road, turning at Penny Ozwaltz's house, and down the lane to the grove of crooked trees.

And then she just settles there, looking down into the grave of the lovers.

And I just watch her, standing there, lost in that head and the past, for two hours.

CHAPTER FORTY-SIX

IONA

"How much time do you think we'll have this go around?" I ask Sully as he greets Simone, Sharon, and Joanne.

"The second time is always longer than the first," he says. "Though, I suppose this is technically the third." He looks around the room, listening for a moment.

"Joanne says she's determined not to be shoved back until we have things figured out," Sully says. "Though I'll remind her that she doesn't really have a choice."

It's so strange, being so outside on all of this. Relying on him to relay every aspect of the conversation. Not being able to see the faces of these other women, when his eyes are tracking all around the room.

But still, he holds my hand tight, my ring in his other hand.

Not my ring. *Our* ring.

It was never just my ring.

If anything, it is Sharon's the most. She probably picked it out.

"We have our timeline established," I say, pushing this along, because as Sully said, we don't really have a choice on how long they can stay. "You each briefly mentioned how you and Jack met. I guess we should just figure out how things went from there."

Sully's eyes slide away from me, going to the same corner he kept looking into this morning. The room is darker than ever, the hour creeping past eleven.

"I fell in love with Jack nearly as soon as I met him," Sully speaks, but the words don't sound like him. They sound young and honey sweet. Sharon, I know from our discussion earlier today. "I talked to him twice while taking my sister to him. And I just…I couldn't get him out of my head. I just wanted to be with him, talk to him."

I nodded. It might not have happened quite so fast for me, but eventually, that's how I was, too.

"Once he asked me out on an official date, it was everything," Sharon's voice says through Sully. "And it seemed like it was for Jack, too. He was always coming by to call on me. We spent every weekend together. It just all…clicked so fast."

Sully's eyes shift, tracing back and forth, as if following someone who is pacing. "I kept thinking to myself that it was weird, how enamored I was with Jack."

It's Joanne.

"We were so opposite. Really, we had nothing in common. But I just wanted to be with him. All the time.

And he was so insistent. So…attentive. It was like he'd put his sights on me and he wasn't going to let anything change either of our minds. And I liked it for some reason. Even though I had never been like that with another man. There was a reason that I was twenty-seven and still single. I didn't buy into the notion of obsessive love and settling down because everyone else did it. But there I was, fully sunk in love with Jack."

"How long?" I ask, my stomach knotting. "Until you knew you loved him?"

Sully's eyes slide over to mine, but I swear it's not him I'm seeing. It's a raven-haired woman with sharp cheekbones and a narrow nose. "Four weeks," she says. "But I'd been fighting it, lying to myself for at least a week. By the time I said the words to him though, it had been four weeks."

Not that quick, but still alarming considering what Joanne knew to be true about herself.

"I told Jack I loved him after just one week." Simone's voice fills the Sunday School room. "After the day we met, we spent every single day together." The longing in her voice, the desire, the love, it opens a familiar ache in my chest, and I have to stop myself from recalling our own first few weeks together when everything was magic and beautiful. "And it was like nothing I'd ever heard of before. Better than books. Better than the movies. He was magic and life and I loved him from that first day."

The crack in Sully's voice is spot on. I look at him, really seeing him instead of the dark, beautiful woman I have pictured in my mind, and I see it. When he opens the gate, Sully is a conduit. He is a puppet and the dead are the masters.

What a gift Sully has. What a curse.

"And that's the part that I hate the most," Simone says. "That I don't know if that first week was him, or me. Because I think that I genuinely fell for Jack. He didn't force me into anything in the beginning. But how can I really know that, considering everything that followed after?"

"So is that the first symptom of what he's done?" I ask, once more propelling this forward, when all I want to do is spend hours mulling this over, absorbing and studying. But time is short. These moments with the dead are limited. "Obsessive love? Because that's exactly how I felt after the first few weeks. He was all I thought about. All I wanted and needed."

Sully looks around, and the three women seemed to concur.

I pull a fresh sheet of paper into my lap and write at the top *obsessive love*.

"Everything seemed perfect from there on out," Joanne's voice comes through again. "Until the very end, I thought everything was perfect, and that everyone else just didn't understand."

A moment of pause, and then Sharon. Sully even nods. "At first everyone was supportive of me and Jack being together. And then they kept saying things weren't healthy."

"And I was just angry at everyone," Sully becomes

Simone. "And I never wanted to spend time with my friends and family. It was all about Jack, Jack, Jack. But that's exactly the way I wanted it."

I look back down at my paper again. I underline the word *obsessive*.

"My family kept telling me that I was getting in too deep with Jack, that it was okay to be in love," I explain. "But that it wasn't okay that I was letting him occupy every day of my life. I thought they were just overreacting and had forgotten what it was like to be in love."

"But looking back, you see that he was there, planting little seeds of isolation in your head." Joanne, once more.

"Did any of you also get really, really thin?" It's Sharon, now.

Sully's eyes shift around and he actually nods. "I couldn't fit into any of my clothes after a few months," Simone comes through. "Everything just fell off. And I couldn't afford to buy new ones, so Jack stepped in, buying me a whole new wardrobe, telling me I was beautiful no matter what."

"I didn't even notice, it felt like." Sharon. "People were telling me that I didn't look healthy, but…I don't feel like I even heard them."

I nod, as something bites at the back of my eyes. I actually feel angry. "I feel sick every time I take a bite. Like…my body has been trained to recoil from all food."

I swear I can feel it when each of them nods, too.

Loss of appetite, I write next on my paper.

Sully's hand suddenly tightens slightly around my left

one. I look up into his face, and I see the message clearly there: the gate is wanting to close again.

"About a month before I died, the dangerous behavior started," Sharon's voice suddenly cuts out of Sully. "Most of the time I didn't even remember doing it. I didn't think about it, I would just do these insane things. And again, my family was concerned, but it was like I didn't even realize, and Jack didn't even seem to notice, either."

"I broke my left leg and got seventeen stitches after I tried to jump from the roof of my house," Joanne affirms. "It just kept escalating for another week and a half. Until finally, I took a gun from a passing police officer and put it to my temple and pulled the trigger."

I flinch, my eyes squeezing closed as the sound of a gunshot gives me an instant headache.

"It was almost like…like a relief, doing all those things," Simone concludes. "It just felt right, is the best way I can describe it. With every dangerous, insane thing I did, I felt like I was doing what I was supposed to. Like…fulfilling my destiny."

It makes me sick, but she's right. With every crazy thing I've done so far, it's felt…good.

Dangerous behavior, I write next.

My hand shakes a little as I move down to the next line, and write

Death.

"Once the dangerous acts start, how long was it until…" Again, Sully can't quite say it.

Until you killed yourselves, is what he wants to ask.

"One month," Sharon restates.

"Two weeks," Joanne condemns.

"Four weeks," Simone says, and every syllable tells me the horror she dealt with in those four weeks.

"Three days," Sully says, looking over at me. "It's been three days since I found you standing on the roof in the wind.

My eyes widen a little.

Sharon was right. I didn't even think about what I was doing. Until this moment, I hadn't thought of that as a dangerous act.

"So, does this mean I have one to three weeks left before I suddenly kill myself?"

And there the words are.

Out.

Finally confessing that this is the end that somehow Jack is leading me to.

CHAPTER FORTY-SEVEN

SULLY

THE CRACKS IN MY CEILING HAVE GROWN TWO inches in the three days that I've been away from Roselock. The cobwebs have grown thicker, more intricate.

I stare up at the ceiling in my bedroom, one arm lying across my forehead, the other hand on my chest.

Three days.

How has it possibly been only three days since I left Roselock for the first time in two years? How has it only been a week and one day since I first met Iona, standing on the front porch of the church?

I close my eyes, hearing the voices of three dead women in the back of my head, and praying that a fourth does not join them soon.

Heat barely makes its way from the fireplace to my room, but the cold is the furthest thing from my concerns at the moment.

The ticking of the clock on the wall sounds every passing second.

For the first time in nearly a week, I am reminded that those ticking seconds are now limited for me.

My death is still coming, one day at a time.

At thirty-three years, three months, and three days.

The faint tug of sleep pulls at the back of my brain when the clock on the wall reads twelve-thirty-one and the sound of footsteps softly pad down the hall toward me.

My door opens with the faintest squeal and I lift my head slightly.

Iona's tiny frame steps halfway in, her big eyes searching through the dark. I can't really see her features, but I feel it when her eyes lock with mine.

She doesn't speak a word. She just stands there for eight breaths.

And then she steps inside, her bare feet not making any noise. She crosses the room. She lifts the blanket and climbs inside.

Not a breath of hesitation, she curls up, tucking herself against my side, her knees pressed into the bare skin of my ribs, her lips and nose pressing against my shoulder.

I adjust the blanket, making sure it's tucked up to her chin, never moving away from the contact of her.

She wraps one hand around the crook of my elbow, pulling my arm a little tighter to her. Without a single word spoken, she closes her eyes.

I lie there in silence, just listening. And not two minutes later, her breathing grows even and calm.

My eyes slide back open, fixing on the ceiling. But every nerve in me is aware of the tiny woman lying beside me, fast asleep.

I wake long before Iona does, but I don't dare move, don't want to wake her. I lie there, utterly frozen. She sleeps with one leg thrown over mine, her arms still curled around mine, clinging tight.

When she stirs as the sun begins to tear through the clouds, I close my eyes and focus on making my breathing even. She slowly detaches from my side, and gently climbs out of the bed, trying not to disturb me.

I keep lying there, feeling the warm spot in the bed beside me until long after I hear her footsteps retreat to the living room.

When I hear her start a bath and the splash when she climbs in, I rise and dress myself.

The pruning sheers on the dresser still hold a little slash of my blood, left there from the day the fawn knocked on the front doors. I retrieve them and walk outside.

The sun breaks out from behind the retreating clouds, promising a warmer and sunny day. Stepping in the snow that is growing glossy as it begins to melt, I make my way to the back corner and begin clipping green stems.

Thorns cut my hands as usual, leading to two small streams of blood dripping down my hand. But twenty minutes later, with an arm full of red roses, I head into the graveyard.

A rose for my neighbor. A rose for my friend, Agatha. A rose for Ben and his wife Karen who used to babysit me. And roses for my grandfathers and their wives. Roses for my father, my mother, and my sister.

I turn at my family's grave and look back at the church. The sun has broken out from the clouds and a waterfall of melt off runs from the roof, drenching the deck and ground around.

Inside is a woman. Here, because of her. Here, because of me.

I never anticipated that happening.

My feet are fully soaked by the time I trudge my way back to the church, in through the back door. The scent of cooking food fills the air.

I take my boots off next to the fireplace, getting a change of socks, before going to find Iona in the kitchen.

She's just finishing making some mush and cutting up an apple from the cellar. She scoops a heaping amount into a cracked bowl and puts some sugar and milk into it. I help her carry everything to the table, and then we sit and I dish it into my mouth, watching her.

The look on her face is slightly nauseated. She just looks at the food for a long minute. But finally, she reaches for the spoon, and puts some in her mouth.

"It's not getting any easier, is it?" I ask as I watch her.

She chews slowly, and it looks like it takes her a great deal of commitment to swallow. "No."

With a huge amount of effort, she takes another bite.

"We'll get this figured out, Iona," I say. I study her, begging her to look up at me, and finally she does.

I want to add, *I promise*. But can I really, truly make that promise?

She just nods, and looks back down to her food, taking another bite.

"We will open the gate one more time," I say, finishing off the last of my breakfast. "We should be able to glean any more information there is left to gather in that time frame. I don't think we can ask any more of them."

"Is there a limit to how many times the dead can handle being pulled back through the gate?" She asks it as she holds a spoonful up, watching as it drips back down into the bowl.

"Everyone is a little different," I explain. "Some can't handle coming back more than a few times. Other's can handle it longer the more they are brought back, like my family. But most wear out, eventually. Generally, three to five times and they're exhausted and in agony."

She meets my eyes again at that, and I know she's looking for the story in my eyes.

The one with a poor grieving mother, unable to let go of her eight-year daughter. She made me open the gate over and over. Eight times.

By the end, it was like the poor girl was dying a death all over again.

The mother blamed me, thought that somehow I was harming the child. She'd tried using violence before she finally just broke down in tears and left Roselock for good.

Besides Iona, that was the worst visitor I've had to endure.

"We'll get what answers are left," I move on. "And then I think we should return to Ander to find answers there."

Iona chews and swallows, forcefully. "I only have two and a half weeks left on Jack's lease. I need to start moving all of his things. It will be a good way to go through everything."

I nod.

This is good. With every day, Iona is coming to accept more and more. She's opening her eyes. She's trying.

I clean up when we're finished eating. Iona follows me as I walk around town, checking on things, making sure nothing is in too bad of disrepair, even though it doesn't matter, anymore.

She and I place buckets around the inside of the church, catching all the leaks.

And at three in the afternoon, we once more go into the dark room and light the candles.

Sitting across from one another, Iona places her hand in mine. I open the ring in my other, and the gate opens.

"Where is Sharon?" I ask when Simone and Joanne appear.

They both look around, as if she's hiding.

"It's getting harder," Joanne says.

Simone nods. "I think this will be the last time we can come."

I nod, relaying the information to Iona.

"Do either of you have any idea as to *why* Jack has done

everything he did?" Iona asks, moving us from point A to B with exactness.

Joanne and Simone look at one another. "It has to be some kind of control thing," Joanne says. "It's some kind of process."

"Practice makes perfect," Simone says. "You were his fourth experiment. But as to the exact reason why… He's sick and twisted, and the world is better off with him six feet under ground."

Even though I feel the venom coming from each of them at her words, I still see the hurt in their eyes. The longing and love there.

"What about how?" I ask. "None of you were Jack's client. Was there ever a time that he was able to…brainwash you?"

All three women shake their heads. "I don't know when. I never felt like he was analyzing me," Simone says.

"No," Joanne says. "It never felt like he was trying to pry into my head."

"There has to be something that he did," Iona speaks up. "He got into our heads. Pretty damn deep. I mean, he's still affecting me now, and he's dead!"

Something sparks at the back of my brain. A possibility.

"Did any of you get matching tattoos?"

Iona's eyes instantly dart up to mine, wide. Her hand rises to the spot on her shoulder and chest.

"No," Simone says. Joanne shakes her head.

"Do you…" Iona begins to ask. "Do you think that has anything to do with it?"

I give a little shake and shrug. "Maybe, maybe not. It's different, at least."

"A tattoo," Simone says. "I don't know what real kind of power it could possibly have. It's only ink on your skin."

Iona massages her tattoo, her eyes glazing over.

"Is there anything else?" I ask, looking back to them. "Anything else at all that might help. Any answers to questions. Any ideas of how to break this?"

The regretful look in each of their eyes is answer before either of them opens their mouths.

"I'm sorry," Simone says. "I wish there was anything... I wish we had answers."

"You can figure this out," Joanne says, a determined look upon her face. "You know now. He's dead. You two can fix this."

The tingle and pull grabs at the back of my throat. It's time.

"Thank you," Iona says. "For everything. I hope you can rest in peace now."

"Stay safe," Simone says quietly. Joanne nods in agreement. Then they're gone.

Iona lets go of my hand and leans back in her chair. She raises her hands up, lacing her fingers into her hair. Her eyes fix on the ceiling.

"Jack did this." Her voice is clear. Sure. But she continues to stare up at the ceiling, and I know these words are not met for me. "Jack did this to me. He tried to isolate me. He somehow made me give up my health. My free will."

She pauses a moment, building her strength again.

"He made three other women kill themselves." Her voice quivers slightly, but she holds on strong. "He would have done that to me, might still do that to me. Jack. Jack Caraway did this."

She sits up straight, dropping her hands, and looks at the ring in my hand.

Jolting to her feet, she grabs it, and walks out the door.

I follow her without a word.

The day is wet and soggy, the sun having melted the snow. Through the cemetery she tromps, past the fence. Out into the woods we wander.

She clutches that ring in her hand, determined.

My heart leaps in my chest for a moment as she seems to veer toward the well, but then she takes a left, and cuts down a deer path.

And then, seemingly randomly, she drops to the ground. With her bare hands, she begins digging in the dirt.

Down. Through rocks, past twigs, she digs.

Six or seven inches deep, and then she sits back on her heels and pulls the ring from her pocket.

"I know a lot of bad things happened here," she says, but I know the words are not for me. They are for Roselock. "And you've punished people for their sins. I don't know if you can punish Jack, anymore. But can you at least make sure all of this ends with me? Don't let anyone ever, ever find this ring again."

She hesitates, just for a few moments, and then drops the white gold with the three diamonds down into the hole.

Over her shoulder, I see it. The ring bounces to rest at the bottom of the hole. And then a moment later, it sinks, slowly, further into the earth. Within a minute, it's completely gone. Iona replaces the dirt she dug, her lips set in a thin line.

It's a promise, between Iona—and Roselock.

Jack's ring will never again be touched by human hands.

"Thank you," she whispers.

Iona kneels there for half a minute more.

And then she climbs to her feet and turns.

"Let's go back to Ander," she says as she walks past me, back toward the church. "I'm ready to rip Jack's life apart to find my answers."

CHAPTER FORTY-EIGHT

IONA

WE WENT BACK TO ANDER. I DROVE SULLY AND I BACK to my home, where we found his car had been towed away. But with no need to worry about that until morning, we went to bed.

I told Sully he was to sleep in my bed tonight, and he didn't question me. That night, I changed into my nightgown and curled up into Sully's side.

Two nights in a row now that I'd slept peacefully. That'd I'd felt safe.

I didn't question if I'd wake in the middle of the night and do something dangerous and hurt myself. I clung to his arm the entire night, felt his enormous hand on my knee there as a protecting presence.

In the morning, we made a plan.

I would go to work. Get my life back on track as much as I could. I would eat breakfast, and lunch when it was time for my break at work. And while I was gone, Sully would rent a truck, and begin moving all of Jack's stuff out. We would go through everything in detail and then take it to the dump.

So that's exactly what we did the next day.

I went to work. I did my job. I smiled at my boss and thanked him for his understanding while I dealt with my latent upsurge of grief and life drama. I talked to my friends in the office, even though everything in me wanted to sit at my desk and pretend that no one else existed.

And during my lunch break, while I forced myself to eat half a sandwich, I wrote a letter to Raymond Douglas.

I poured out my heart in that letter. Telling him that I was sorry for striking him. I told him that he was right to do what he did. I told him about Sully, about what he could do, without disclosing Sully's name or location. I told him how I'd spoken to Simone, his sister, through Sully. The answers she'd given me. About the other women.

I thanked Raymond for saving my life.

Tears stained the pages by the time I folded it up, placed it in an envelope, and put it in my work's outgoing mail. But a heavy stone dropped into my stomach. Because I was giving all the evidence to a man that he was justified in murdering another human, but knew it would never be enough to free him from bars.

So I allowed myself to cry.

And then returned to work.

At five o'clock, I left work, and headed down the road. I walked. Passing all the old familiar places. Down three blocks. I cut behind the building, out the back that butted up to Jack's office.

Sully carries an office chair from the building to the truck, lifting it as if it weighs nothing. He sets it down inside and pushes his hair out of his eyes.

"Anything interesting yet?" I ask, surveying the scene. There are stacks of boxes toward the front of the truck. Random bits of furniture are stacked up. And looking inside, it's a mess.

"Not yet," Sully shakes his head. "I ripped apart the couch that was in his office. Went through every bit of stuffing in it." He indicates the big black garbage bags on one wall of the truck. "Same with his desk. Only a few files for a few clients, nothing interesting in them. Pens, rubber bands, paperclips."

I nod. "Jack was a tidy person. If we're going to find any evidence, it's going to be hidden well."

Late into the night, Sully and I go through his office. Combing through his client files takes the longest. We dig through the secretary's desk. The two of us work until the hour grows dark and late.

Exhausted and feeling slightly disheartened, we close up the truck, lock down the office, and head home.

We repeat the same process the next day.

And I get worried, because we've gone through eighty percent of his office, and at least half of his apartment.

On the third day back in Ander, I feel a sense of dread as I walk from work back to Jack's office. I can't stand the thought that we may go through all this effort, all this pain and confusion, only to find zero answers.

What if he left absolutely no evidence behind?

The thought twists my stomach. I want to throw up the seven bites of food I've consumed today.

"What's wrong?"

Sully freezes in place when I walk inside, holding a box, rooted on the spot, his eyes fixed on mine.

"Nothing," I try to recover, wiping at my eyes, even though I'm not crying. "I just…"

Sully sets the box down and walks over to me. He stops, so close in proximity. "Tell me."

I look up into his face, beneath the long mane. Hidden behind that long beard. To his green eyes.

He stares down at me, every single bit of his attention focused on me.

And now the tears do prick at the backs of my eyes. I bite my lower lip. And I don't even give them permission to do so, but my hands raise up, both of them coming to Sully's cheeks, cupping his face.

I chew my lower lip, ashamed to voice the words inside my head. But he just keeps looking down at me, open, accepting. But there's a spark of flame in those eyes that tells me he's ready to tear through the gate, to destroy souls if only I tell him what direction to aim the fury.

"I just want answers," I speak in a whisper. "And I'm afraid. What if we never find any?"

He hesitates, studying me a moment longer. But then

he wraps those massive arms around me, and pulls me into his chest.

I take a deep breath there, inhaling his pine and moss scent. And instantly, my heartbeat slows.

"I will get you your answers, Iona," he says, the words causing his chest to rumble. "One way or another."

I don't let him go. I just want to freeze the rest of my existence like this, cradled safely in these arms, away from the rest of the world that now feels alien to me.

He lets me. I don't know how long we stand like that. A long while.

But eventually, I know we have to move if I'm going to get any answers.

Through the rest of the drawers in the closet we dig. We fill three boxes with random decorations, all of which we carefully scour for anything hidden inside of them.

I realize, as we go through the things in his apartment, that it should have been more apparent how often Jack moved. He really owned very little. Only a week's worth of clothes. Only four sets of dishes. One small bookshelf of books. And absolutely no clutter.

If we weren't going through all of his things so thoroughly, we could have packed up and moved all of his belongings out in two hours.

I've just finished cleaning out the medicine cabinet, which contained a toothbrush, paste, two bottles of painkillers and an antacid. A brush, and hair gel. And that's all. I throw it all into a smaller box, and reach for the broom and mop in the tall cabinet on the far wall.

But I lift too high to get it around the toilet.

The handles hit the ceiling fan, and I scream and dart out of the way as the cover crashes to the ground.

Sully is inside in two seconds.

"You alri-"

He doesn't finish his sentence.

Because both of our eyes rise to the hole.

Where there should be a box where the fan is installed and operates, there's just a hole into the ceiling.

And poking over the edge, just barely visible, is my own face.

Sully swears. He crosses the bathroom in one long stride. He stands on the toilet seat and reaches up into the ceiling.

My lip immediately begins trembling, but my fingers curl into a fist.

"No," I say. "No. No."

Sully steps down, a handful of papers and pictures. I yank them out of his hands, scattering things all over.

Pictures.

Pictures of me.

Pictures of a blonde.

Pictures of two dark haired women, one light skinned, another dark.

"Funeral programs," Sully says, looking through the stack of pages and pictures. "Simone. Sharon. Joanne. All three of them are here."

Now there really are tears in my eyes. Before I can even

process the images of me, I'm looking at the images of Jack's other fiancés.

His other *victims*.

Joanne, harsh but beautiful looking. Sharon, looking as sweet as I imagined her. And Simone. Absolutely stunning, and I can even pick out a few similar features she has to Raymond.

And there are images of Jack. With these women. They all look so happy. So in love. With all three of them.

With all four of us.

"Simone's, from two years ago," Sully says, handing over the funeral programs. And now I really start to cry. Because Simone was only twenty-two when he made her kill herself. "Joanne, from four years ago." She was twenty-nine. "And Sharon." Who was only twenty.

Every one of them too young.

Every one of them taking their lives against their will.

"When was this picture taken?" Sully asks, holding up a faded looking photograph.

I take it, my hand trembling.

It's an image of my father and I, sitting at Terry's Brew, a pub with fantastic fish and chips. But there's something sinister about what should be a sweet image of me and the father I lost.

It's taken from across the bar, the view slightly obscured.

"About a year ago," I breathe, studying the image. "This would have been about…a month before Dad died. Over a month before I met Jack."

"And this one?" Sully holds up another image.

This one is of me laughing, walking down the street with Viola and her friends, headed to the theater.

Another tear leaks out onto my cheek. My hands tremble as I reach for this one. "Probably, two, maybe three weeks before Dad died."

The first time I met Jack was at my father's funeral. He came to pay his condolences, along with the rest of the town because of the role my father played in protecting the people of Ander.

"He'd been watching you," Sully says. He shuffles through the rest of the pages in his hands. And produces a few pieces of lined papers, all filled with Jack's careful handwriting. "He'd been… Iona, I think he'd been studying you before he introduced himself at your father's funeral."

I cover my mouth with my hand, dropping the box of things from the medicine cabinet. I pull the last picture closer to my eyes, looking close.

And there, in the reflection of the ice cream parlor's windows, I can see Jack. Camera out, pointed in my direction.

"Iona Faye is the middle child of Mason and Willa Faye. She is looked down upon by her older sister, Cressida," Sully reads from the pages. "And seems to help take care of her younger sister. She has all the classic symptoms of a middle child, keeping a level head, but also craving loving attention."

"Please stop," I beg him, letting my eyes slide closed.

My heart is fracturing inside my chest.

Lies.

Lies.

Everything, everything about the past nearly year has been nothing but lies.

Sully folds the pages up and stuffs them into his back pocket. He reaches out for me, to pull me into his arms again, but I step away, wrapping my arms around my waist.

So many lies.

So much darkness.

I sink to the floor, my arms folded over my knees, my forehead resting against them. And I cry.

Jack never really fell in love.

He studied me. Probably studied other women, as well.

He picked me. As his most likely option.

What does that say about me?

That I'm weak?

That I have no backbone?

Do I even have my own personality? Or am I just a moldable doll he knew was weak enough he could get inside of and use like a puppet?

"Iona," Sully says. He takes a step forward.

"Please just leave me alone," I half sob, half bite out.

A moment of deliberation, and hesitantly, he opens the bathroom door again, and steps outside to leave me be.

Jack.

Jack.

Jack, who took me ice-skating and held my hand the entire time.

Jack, who made love to me.

Jack, who would draw little patterns over my back and make me fall asleep.

Jack, who whispered he loved me, every chance he got.

He did this.

All of it.

My chest hurts.

I can't pull in any oxygen.

I can't breathe.

I can't…

CHAPTER FORTY-NINE

SULLY

I DIDN'T MOVE MORE THAN AN INCH FROM THE DOOR. I sat there with my ear pressed against the door.

And I worried when I didn't hear any breathing coming from Iona after she took a slightly deeper breath in than normal.

She was holding it.

But I wasn't sure, until I heard her slump against the side of the tub.

"Iona!" I yell, yanking the door back open.

She lies on the floor, as if she's just sleeping. Once more, she's breathing.

"Iona?" I question softly.

She doesn't stir, but I watch for a moment, and she's breathing evenly. Her chest rises and falls, looking normal.

I bite my knuckle, just watching her.

Did she hold her breath? Forget to breathe, and pass out?

Just when I think things have gotten better, just when I think she's maybe moved past this, she goes and does something insane and dangerous again.

For five minutes I watch her, quietly saying her name every now and then to see if she will rouse. And I debate with myself if I need to take her in to the hospital.

But what would I tell them? That's she's randomly doing dangerous things? That she's on a path to hurt herself, that very likely will lead to her taking her own life soon? They would put her on suicide watch, and then send her home.

I look around the apartment, my eyes sweeping outside the door to the bathroom. And find Iona's purse.

Is Jack's pocket watch still inside?

It's been there, ever present at the back of my mind. I've been the one dealing with most of Jack's belongings, touching them, moving them, destroying them. But this echo's the truth of how often Jack moved, how little he valued in possessions. Nothing I have touched has threatened to bring Jack through the gate.

I'm also sure that he isn't too anxious to come back. Some of the dead race back to see the living, like the three fiancées. Others must be searched after, drug back, like Jack was the first time I opened the gate.

But as I stare at Iona's purse, I begin to realize there is no other option at this point.

I'm going to have to go to the source of all of this if we're going to get any real answers.

I'm going to have to speak to Jack again.

I TAKE IONA BACK HOME. SHE ROUSES JUST BEFORE ten, and she's still out of it and confused, but she wakes enough to somewhat walk back to her apartment. With each step, with the frigid air outside, she wakes, blinking hard and fast.

By the time we get to the front doors of her building, she's coherent enough for me to explain what I think happened.

"I…" she stumbles over her words. "I think you're right. I only remember my thoughts racing, feeling so…betrayed. And then my chest hurt, and my head was spinning."

She shakes her head as she pulls her keys out of the purse I carried for her. Like there was a hot iron inside, I know Jack's pocket watch is within its depths.

She opens the door, and the both of us step inside.

I set to making us some food, even though the hour is late, but neither of us has eaten dinner, and my stomach is ravenous.

"This isn't going away, is it?" Iona says. She sits at the table, watching me as I work on making us sandwiches.

"No," I answer plainly. "I suspect it is only going to get worse."

She rises from her seat and goes to a closet. A moment later she returns with a pad of paper and a pen.

"It sounds like all four of us went through stages," she says. I turn, placing the sandwiches at the table. "We've determined, as best we can, what those stages were."

She writes down the words; *obsessive love, loss of appetite, dangerous behavior*, and then, *death*.

"They didn't all happen at once," she says, looking up, tapping the pen against her chin. "For all of us, it seemed to happen in stages. There…there had to be something that triggered them."

I chew my sandwich, swallowing, and push Iona's closer to her. She doesn't even look down at it. She's in full research mode, so I don't force her to eat for the moment.

"Let's figure out the timeline of when things started," I say. "Maybe that will help you figure out what triggered each of them."

She taps the pen on the first step down into chaos; obsessive love.

"It's hard to know when this really snapped into place," she says. "Like I told you, our first real encounter was a little rocky and I wasn't even sure if I should agree to that date with him. But after the date, things were going well. Every week we spent more and more time with each other."

"When did you first tell him you loved him?" I ask, and it makes my stomach knot. It makes the hand on my knee ball into a fist.

"About a month after we first started dating," she says, and she actually looks over her shoulder, back toward the bedroom. "We…" She hesitates, looking back at me, but not quite meeting my eye. "We'd just made love, for the first time. I'd fallen asleep after, but when I woke up, I told him."

"You said it first?" I ask. This is not a recounting I want to be witness to.

She hesitates, her gaze growing hazy as she tries to recall. "I…I think so. Jack always had sweet things to say, but I do think I was the first to say it."

"So that wasn't it, then," I say, finishing off my meal. "It wasn't triggered by him saying it. So maybe…" I sigh, for a moment, wishing I never got involved in this complicated web. "Maybe it was the sex? You said you'd…done it before you told him. Would you say you were in obsessive love with him before that day?"

She pauses a moment, considering. "I…I'm really not sure. I was certainly falling for him. I wanted to spend my time with him. But…maybe the obsession didn't really kick in until after. I guess I still wanted to see other people, my family I mean, before then. So maybe that is when it kicked in."

She writes that down on the same line as *obsessive love— made love for the first time.*

"What about the loss of appetite?" I question, ready to move on to a different subject.

Iona stands and walks over to the bookshelf. She produces a familiar photo album. The one she brought to Roselock, to show me the images of Jack so I would more easily be able to find him.

She sits back down and opens it up.

Page after page of images of her. She and Jack.

I look to Iona's face as she flips through pages, and am sickened when a faint smile curls on her lips.

Will it ever really go away? That deep down, manipulated, implanted love she has for Jack Caraway?

I look back down, and find she's flipped to the very back, and slowly she flips pages, back in time.

Iona shakes her head, and her expression transforms to disgust. "I hate that I didn't even realize it, how unhealthy I was becoming." And it's there, in her rail thin arms. Her fragile-looking fingers. "I used to have curves. A figure. I…I want those back."

And there, sometime between the spring and summer, is where I begin to see the transformation happen.

"Here," I say, pointing to a picture of Iona at what looks to be a Fourth of July party. "You look thinner here than in this one." I touch an image of her and Jack standing on a beach in bathing suits.

"That was in Florida, that trip we took," Iona says. "That would have been in May, for Jack's birthday. I remember well because everyone was so mad that I missed Mom's birthday."

She looks back and forth between the two images. "I…" she shakes her head. "I don't know what would have triggered this one. Like I said, I didn't even realize it was happening."

Her distress is rising. The confusion. The anger. The burning desire for answers.

I reach out and place a hand on her back, rubbing small circles.

"Write it down at least," I say. "It happened sometime between spring and summer."

She lets out a frustrated sigh, but does it.

"Dangerous behavior," she moves on. She taps the pen to the words just once. "I know exactly when this one happened."

She looks up at me, and I see it there: she may still have moments when the love and desire still rises up for Jack, but she also hates him. With a burning, fiery passion.

"I wasn't acting like this before I came to see you," she says it flatly. "Something got triggered when we spoke to Jack during one of those three times. I didn't realize it at first, but when I left Roselock that first time, I tore out of there like a maniac. I could have killed myself with the way I was driving home. It was during that trip that some kind of switch was flipped."

I sit back, just studying her face. The wheels are turning in my head, a thousand miles per minute.

"Jack is dead, yet he moved you on to the next stage."

Iona purses her lips together, her face pale, and nods.

"This isn't going to end," I say. I curl my hands into fists. "We've seen that. And we have no idea how he's doing this, how it really works. But we know it's just going to continue. I don't know that there is any other choice, Iona. I have to go back to Roselock and talk to Jack again. Alone."

If Iona was pale before, it's nothing to her whiteness now.

CHAPTER FIFTY

IONA

AM I GOING TO KILL MYSELF?

Has it already been triggered? Is it just a matter of time, now? Or did I get lucky, and somehow Jack wasn't able to put that last step into motion?

He's come this far. Done this so many times. I don't know that there's any chance that he gave up and isn't going to finish this final experiment.

These are the thoughts that plague my head all through the next day at work. The thoughts that cause me to mess up not once, twice, but four times at work. What gets me dragged into a meeting with my boss, telling me to pull it together or I can go find work somewhere else.

But I hardly even hear him. This is my life, my death that's on my mind.

The moment the clock hits five, I grab my bag and I'm out the door.

The air is warmer today than it has been in months. The

sidewalks are completely dry, the very last remains of snow from the storm, gone. More people are out and about than there have been since fall.

But I can't even enjoy the sunshine.

Because it's my death that I'm consumed by.

It's my very own mind that I'm scared of. Because it keeps blanking out on me. It keeps telling me to do these insane things.

Sully hauls out the last of Jack's furniture when I get to the office. I look around, the space almost totally empty.

"Anything?" I ask, going for a box on the floor to gather the last few little things.

"No," Sully says.

No.

Nothing.

No answers.

My entire body tightens. Tenses. Wants to fight, to rage. To have something physical to hit.

I turn, finding Jack's diploma on the wall. Gritting my teeth hard, I yank it from the wall, and hurtle it across the room. Glass shatters and wood splinters against the wall and I cringe away, avoiding being cut as debris clatter around the room.

Sully darts inside, his eyes wide and questioning.

"That was me," I promise, holding up my hands. "I swear, I did that on purpose."

He looks at me for a long moment, as if trying to decide if he believes me. And he must, because he turns again, and finishes hauling things out.

Internally cursing myself, I walk over to the broken debris and begin carefully picking up the glass and broken shards of wood.

It seems a shame, to throw out the one piece of solid evidence that Jack spent six years of his life earning this degree, this piece of paper. But it deserves to burn in hell with him.

I grab it to throw it in the box as well, only it slides apart, two individual pieces of paper, one placed behind the other.

The first is his diploma from NYU, his Master's degree in psychology.

And directly behind it, is another certificate. From the New York Hypnosis Training Center.

"Holy shit," I breathe. I hold the piece of paper, my hands trembling. My eyes run over the words, over and over, but only three of them stand out: Jack Caraway, New York, Hypnosis.

"What is it?" Sully asks, crossing the room. He stands over my shoulder, reaching to touch the paper and pull it into his view.

"Hypnosis?" Sully says. I look up into his face to see his brows narrow. "I thought that stuff was all for show. That… that can't really work, can it?"

I step away, leaving Sully with the certificate. I pull my purse from the corner, digging through it, until I yank something cold and hard from its depths.

"Jack always had his pocket watch with him," I say, holding it up by the chain, letting it swing. "*Always.*"

Sully watches Jack's most prized belonging swing back and forth, the item that nearly killed him a week ago.

"That's how he did it," Sully says, not sounding fully convinced of his own words, but starting to fear them. "That's how he got into each of your heads."

"Could he really make us forget the act of doing it?" I ask, studying the watch.

"He made you fall in love with him," Sully says, taking half a step back. "He made you lose your appetite permanently. He made you put yourself in danger. He made those women take their own lives. I'm sure making you forget wasn't too difficult."

I throw the watch. Down. Away from me. Making it crash to the ground with a crushing force.

But it's made of metal. It doesn't bend.

But I do hear something fracture inside.

"I hate him," the words come out over my lips immediately. "I hate Jack. I hate every minute we stayed together. I hate every time I told him I loved him. I hate every time I let him into my body. I hate him."

The words come out as sobs now and I feel my knees weaken. I sink to the ground, resting back on my heels, letting the fury and betrayal wash over me.

Sully walks toward me, but he doesn't reach out to embrace or comfort me. He only places a hand on my shoulder. "At least he's dead now. May he rot in hell."

CHAPTER FIFTY-ONE

SULLY

IONA SITS SILENTLY IN THE PASSENGER SEAT, HOLDING the hypnotism certificate and Jack's diploma in her hands. She stares out the window, not looking at anything.

Through the darkening night, I drive the truck to the dump. With only twenty minutes until it closes, I drive faster than I should. We get there just five minutes before it closes, and three of the employees come over to help me clear it out so they can close up and head home for the day.

I hate it that Iona has to pay for everything. She pulls out her wallet and pays the fee, and my manhood is twisted just a little.

Maybe I'll just get a job.

I internally laugh at myself for the thought. Just imagining it, me working some construction job, before eventually I start vomiting blood. Before I pass out on the scaffolding. Because Roselock will never let me go, especially this close to my death date.

The stretch between the dump and town cuts through fields and farms. Through the dark, Iona quietly directs me back to town where we can return the truck.

Up ahead, I see the bridge we passed over earlier. Only a mile back into the city.

"What sounds good for dinner tonight?" I ask, scratching at my beard. "Tortellini or spaghetti?"

Iona doesn't respond and I glance over at her. She stares out her window, silent and dark.

"Iona?" I probe.

She sets the two pieces of paper on the seat between us.

"Did you hear me?"

I look back forward, making sure I keep the oversized vehicle in my lane as the road narrows to cross the bridge.

The sound of wind rips through the cabin.

Iona flings the door open, and leaps out.

"Iona!" I bellow, slamming on my breaks, causing the back end of the truck to skid, swinging to the left, across both lanes crossing the bridge. Before it has even come to a full stop, I fling my door open and leap out.

My shins bark in pain, but I dash around the front of the truck, smacking a hand down on the hood to catch myself. My feet can't move fast enough, until they see a still figure, wrapped around the first post of the railing of the bridge.

"Iona!" I scream into the night, closing the distance between us. Gravel flies everywhere as I drop to the ground next to her.

Her stomach is pressed up against the concrete post, her legs curled up, her chest against it as well, wrapped around the post. Carefully, I run a hand down the side of her face, only to come away with my palm coated in blood.

"Iona, can you hear me?" My voice quakes.

She lets out a little whimper of pain.

"Iona," I breathe. "Is anything broken? Do I dare move you?"

She lets out another little cry. "Sully?"

"I'm here," I whisper. Carefully, so carefully, I help her roll over.

There's a big gash above her right eye, and the right side of her face looks as if it scraped through the gravel. She winces, holding her right arm, a hiss of pain.

I swear, guilt instantly clawing its way into my stomach. "Your arm? Your collarbone? Do they feel broken?"

She lets out another sob of pain. "I don't know. Everything…" She tries to suck in a breath, but it doesn't want to fully cooperate. "Everything hurts."

"I have to move you, Iona," I say. Panic is eating its way up my spine. Clawing its way through me like a rabid beast. "We have to get you to the emergency room."

As gently as I can, I scoop her up into my arms. She gives a little cry of pain, but not as guttural as I expected. Careful to make my steps as smooth as possible, I half run back to the truck. She bites her bottom lip to hold in a scream as I set her back on the seat, and lock the door before I close it.

I slam on the gas the second I get back inside. And I reach over and take Iona's hand in mine, to give her something to hold on to, and to make sure she doesn't try to jump again.

Five minutes later, I screech into the pull-through in front of the emergency room doors.

It's a flurry of activity as people rush out, as they help Iona onto a stretcher, and all of us race inside.

"She fell asleep on the drive back," I lie on my feet. "She was leaned against the door when it popped open and she fell out."

Lies. Because the truth... Even I don't understand the truth.

We reach the entrance of a room, and I'm told to go back to the waiting room.

I stand outside that room, my hands fisted in my hair. Feeling utterly helpless.

No more.

I can't let this go any further.

Because she easily could have died tonight. She could have smacked her head against that concrete pillar. She could have fallen off the bridge and plunged twenty feet to the river below.

This is getting too out of hand.

"Sir," a nurse says as she walks down the hall. "You need to go back and wait in the waiting room."

I nod, and begin walking back toward it, hoping and praying no one recognizes me from my own stay just last week. But suddenly, an idea dawns on me.

"Excuse me?" I say as she begins walking away. "Is Viola Faye on duty right now? She works in labor and delivery."

"As a matter of fact, she is," the nurse says.

"Can you please help me find her?" I ask in desperation. "Her sister Iona is in that room right there."

CHAPTER FIFTY-TWO

IONA

Such dark weight holds me down. Which is good, because the fog in my brain would probably make me float away.

A sliver of light sears my brain, but instinctually, I flutter my eyes open, blinking five times fast, before I raise my hands up to block out the light. Only something binds my right arm.

And everything hurts.

"Don't move around too much."

A familiar female voice cuts through the cotton in my ears. Gentle hands grab mine, and guide them back down.

"Viola?" I ask groggily as my eyes adjust to the light and blink them open.

"I'm here," she says. And she comes into focus. She sits at the edge of my bed, wearing her work uniform.

I blink, looking around, and remember that I'm in the hospital.

"Where…" I struggle to make my words form. Everything in me is sluggish and tired. "Where is Sully?"

Viola shifts, sliding closer up the bed toward me. "He tracked me down last night and asked me to stay with you. He said he had to go take care of some business and fix all of…this."

And instantly, I'm one hundred percent alert.

Roselock. Jack.

Sully went back to confront Jack.

"What is it?" Viola asks, her own eyes widening. "What's wrong?"

And I realize I've given away too much with my panicked expression. So I force myself to calm down. To lie back in my bed. "Nothing," I lie. "I just wish…wish he didn't have to go."

Viola looks at me intensely. Warily. She's studying me, looking for answers.

"So what's broken?" I ask, turning my attention to my body to put off the hard moments I know are coming shortly.

It works. Viola tears her eyes from mine, looking over my body.

"You've got eight stitches above your eyebrow," Viola says, her eyes rising to look at the spot. "The gravel kind of ate up your face, though it probably should have been much, much worse. You'll have some scarring, but not too bad."

I'm not worried about scarring too much. It's been a

long while since I really cared about my appearance. But I do want to see the damage in a mirror.

"You fractured your right collar bone," my sister continues. "You'll need to keep it in the sling for about two weeks. No big movements or it might actually break."

"Anything else?" I ask, half sarcastically.

Viola's eyes narrow, annoyed. "There should have been a lot else," she says, her tone biting. "What the hell happened, Iona? The doctors all think the door just popped open, but Sully said I need to ask you about the truth."

Internally, I curse.

No. He wouldn't go and do that. Get my sister involved in this craziness.

"He said that I need to ask you about Jack and who he really was."

Ice-cold acid drops in my stomach, burning a hole.

"What did he do to you, Iona?" my sister asks. But her tone eases up. It's pleading, and scared.

I look over at her, not saying a word. Evaluating.

Isolation. That's one of the things Jack made me do.

Isolate myself from everyone I loved, besides him.

I used to be close with my younger sister. We used to be best friends. Were, up until Jack inserted himself into my life.

"You won't believe me," I whisper.

Viola stares intently at me. "Please, tell me," she says as she slides further up, and takes my good hand. "I promise, I will believe you."

There's so much pleading in her eyes. So much sincerity.

"You can't tell Cressida, or Mom," I say. My voice grows quiet. So, so quiet. "They won't understand. They'll think I'm crazy."

Viola hesitates at that. Studies me for a long moment. And I can see her evaluating. Deciding if maybe I am crazy. If I've lost it.

But she nods. "I promise."

I swallow once. My heart rockets into my throat. My entire body breaks out into a sweat.

I'm scared.

So scared to tell anyone the dark secrets of the truth.

But I take a breath, and I tell her everything.

CHAPTER FIFTY-THREE

SULLY

Leaving after dark was a bad, terrible, reckless idea.

But I wasn't going to wait a moment longer.

I took the moving truck, considering I hadn't bothered to find out where my ancient Cadillac had been towed to, it was my only option.

Iona likely wouldn't be driving any time soon, but I couldn't bring myself to take her only mode of transportation.

So, in the moving truck, I took off into the night. I drove the two hours back to Roselock.

At the turnoff from the highway to the town, I stopped. Right in the middle of the road.

With Iona's purse right next to me, sitting on top of Jack's diploma and certificate, proving what he was allowed to practice, I sat in the road, in the dark.

My breath filled the cabin in a cold billow. Crystals of

ice formed in the corners of the windshield. Slowly, slowly, I let off the brake, shifted the truck into gear, and crept forward. The temperature continued to drop with every foot I rolled further into town.

A yipping yelp sounds through the night, the first signs that I have arrived back within the godforsaken borders. It grows louder and louder, more frantic.

My breath pulls in and out of my chest faster.

Don't go out at night.

Don't go out at night.

Something hits the side of the truck, in the back. A small, but fast ping. A moment later, it's accompanied by another.

I push harder on the gas, as more and more arrows strike the side of the truck, coming from every side. There will be no evidence of the insanity of the night come morning, but here in the dark, it's very real.

Gunshots fire through the darkness, hitting the rock beside me, blasting it apart.

Screams echo through the night. Crying grows and grows until it reaches a frantic decibel.

I rip down the crumbling street. Past the homes of my friends and neighbors. Soon, there is the roundabout, and the truck threatens to tip onto two wheels, but moans and settles as I whip around.

Cresting the hill, I feel the drag, as if a dozen hands have grabbed hold of the bumper, and threaten to pull me back.

The tires slip. Spin.

"No!" I bellow, throwing my voice out into the dark. "I must speak to the dead and you will *not* stop me."

A moment of considering hesitation. And then there's a give, and the tires find purchase once more, and I rocket forward.

Cresting the hill, I listen.

The cacophony of the night has quieted marginally. As if they're holding their breath for me. Waiting.

I park in front of the church, and look up at it.

Home.

This wicked, damned place is what I call home.

Ticking, ticking, ticking away the seconds left of my pathetic life.

Taking in a deep breath, gripping the steering wheel like my life depends on it, I steel myself for a moment.

And then I shove the door open and barge out. Immediately, my boots slip in the slick red beneath my feet. The dim moonlight glints on the wet red, but I keep my focus, crossing the half a dozen steps to the entry of the church.

Just as I close my hand around the doorknob, the chaos lets loose once more. I don't look around, don't let the sounds overwhelm me. I yank the door open, step inside, and slam it closed behind me.

Instantly, all sound dies.

This church is my hell and my sanctuary.

Clutching Iona's bag in my hand, I stalk through the chapel. I slide past the organ and through the doors to the private quarters.

It's bone-chilling cold inside, but with the hatred of fury burning in my veins, I don't worry about another dance with hypothermia.

The Sunday School room is the coldest of them all with that draft. Even a little lick of sound drifts out from the cracks around the window, letting in the howling and screaming cries of those long surrendered of this world.

I close the door and set to lighting the candles, barely able to see with the moonlight trickling in through the filthy window.

The pounding in my veins propels me onward. To stand before the seat I put Iona's purse upon. And reach inside.

As if guided, my hand goes straight to the pocket watch and closes around it.

"Where are you, Jack?" I growl into the dim light. Looking around, the world blends with another. One darker, as if looking at everything through a black veil. It's fluid and has motion to it. Ever shifting, ever darker.

"I summon you, Jack Caraway," I say evenly. "I have questions and you *will* answer them."

A shifting movement over my right shoulder draws my eye and I twist, trying to follow it. But it disappears, gone, slithering into another dark corner.

"I won't let you kill another," I say, turning, looking in all the dark recesses of the gate. "You've had your twisted fun. Spare Iona, and move on."

Another movement, and I twist around.

To see Jack Caraway standing in the corner.

"I think you're actually as brave as you look, Sully

Whitmore," he says. He stands with a sly smile pulling on one side of his mouth, his arms crossed over his chest. He leans one shoulder against the wall. "I think after learning a few things about me, most wouldn't be so anxious to speak to me. But here you are."

I stalk forward, my teeth gritted together tightly. I place a hand on the wall behind either side of his head, boxing him in. I bring my face within inches of his.

"How do I reverse what you've done?" I growl.

Jack smiles. Shakes his head. "How do you expect to reverse it, when you don't even really know what it is I've done?"

And suddenly Jack takes a step forward, through me.

It's as if ice-cold acid was dumped over me. So frigid, so arctic. My body immediately shutters for a moment, unable to handle merging with the dead.

But the instant Jack steps through me, I feel human once again.

A growl on my lips, I spin around.

Jack walks casually around the room. Looking down upon the dirt and dust and leaves. He waves a hand casually over the flames of the candle.

"She's got you wrapped around her dainty little fingers, doesn't she?" he asks, finally looking up at me from beneath his lashes. "You keep chasing me down, dragging me back from that horribly lonely place. But this time, she's nowhere to be seen. You're here of your own accord—for Iona."

"Don't even speak her name," I very nearly whisper.

"I will speak her name if I like," he says, that coy smile

beginning to return. "Because, you see, I own Iona Faye. I am Iona Faye."

It's instinct that makes me act. When my fist swings forward, looking for a chiseled jaw to connect with.

But there's only air and ice.

Jack simply laughs and takes three casual steps across the room. "This is entertaining," he says. "Watching you squirm like a dog. Riling you up until you snap your sharp teeth. Only the bite has nowhere to land."

"Better a dog than a poisonous snake," I say, watching as he continues to walk around the room.

"But the snake doesn't have much to worry about, does it?"

That smile of his makes me want to rip his lips from his face, and pluck every one of his teeth from his head, one by one. "Only the shovel coming down on the back of its neck from the grieving brother of the one who was last bitten."

Finally, the smile on his face falters.

"We have about five minutes until the gate to the other side is going to drag you back," I say as I lean back against a wall and watch Jack. "I'm going to get some answers."

"You have no leverage against me," Jack says. And I can see it now, one of the things that must have made him so charming: he has absolute confidence.

"As I understand it, you have no siblings, both of your parents are dead," I say. "You have no friends because you move every two years. So no, I don't have any leverage against you. But know this, that if you had anyone left on earth who mattered to you, I would go after every single one of them. I would do to them whatever it takes, until you talked, until you begged me to have mercy. That is the kind of man that I am, and that is the kind of force I will use to keep Iona from taking things just a little further and ending her life."

His expression is a little more unreadable. Contemplative, angry, considering. He just watches me for at least a minute. There must be some kind of debate going on inside his head, considering how much to tell me.

"So she's close," he says, and a tug of that smile pulls on his mouth once more. "The dangerous actions have started?"

A spark lights in me.

A direction.

A door to some answers.

"She jumped out of a moving truck just four hours ago, barely missing falling off the bridge, just outside of Ander," I explain. "She's in the hospital. It's the most recent of some very terrifying, inexplicable acts."

Jack smiles, something satisfied. "It's impressive, isn't it? That even in death, my little burrow into her mind still holds?"

He turns, looking toward the window.

"Does it have anything to do with the tattoo?" The words leave my mouth before I give a moment to consider them.

Jack looks over his shoulder at me. He bears a complicated expression. Frustration. Determination.

"It was an attempt to further the…bond," Jack says,

looking back to the window. "But it didn't seem to have an effect. All of this is uncharted territory. A task of trial and error."

"So Iona is permanently marked for nothing," I say flatly.

"Not for nothing," Jack says, turning back around. "It's all in the name of science."

"Hypnotism," I say. "That's how you got in their heads."

Jack's eyes slide over to mine. "It was a late night walk with Sharon," he says. He takes a step forward, beginning a slow walk around the room. "She was so tired, but so desperate to spend the evening with me, like a grown woman. She leaned her head on my shoulder and I brought out that watch. It was incredibly easy."

My hands curl into fists. My teeth clench together.

"I caught Joanne just as she was waking up," he says. "There was a group of us on a camping trip. I knew she wasn't going to be easy to…persuade." He smiles. "But I wanted a real challenge."

My hands close around the pocket watch, and I feel the metal give under the pressure of my fingers.

"Simone just thought I was kidding around," he says as he finally stops circling. He leans back against the wall, folding his arms over his chest. "She was laughing, teasing me about being a hack. She thought it was so funny when I swung it in front of her, speaking so calm and even. She walked right into it."

"And Iona?" I ask. I don't really want to know the answer.

Jack's smile confirms that I'm not going to like what I hear.

"We'd just made love," he says, boring into my eyes with a steely gaze. "She'd moaned my name, twice. She smelled like sex, sweaty and utterly satisfied."

My grip on the watch tightens. I hear something snap inside.

Jack's eyes flit down to it, and a snarl crosses his face for a moment.

Good.

"So she was good and tired when I picked up the heirloom you're now crushing with your brutish hands." His gaze burns, embers nearly lighting in his eyes. "It wasn't hard. She fell asleep right after. And when she woke up, everything fell into action."

The first time they made love. That was the day Iona suspected it all started.

Jack just confirmed it.

"I take everything," Jack says. The temperature in the room grows colder. "Bit by bit, I take everything that makes them who they are."

My heart thunders in my chest, rumbling toward a grand finale. The tug of the gate pulls at the back of my brain.

"I call it total occupation," he says at last. "I'm there, in every corner of their mind. I implant the steps. The triggers. And one by one, I set them off. Gliding down the path as I take every one of their elements of humanity."

The breath in my chest stills.

There it is.

He strips them of the basic elements of humanity.

Possessing every one of them.

"And the final, grand finale, that last step where I own every bit of their minds—death. Cementing total occupation."

Jack nearly glows, radiating power and confidence, so assured of himself.

Because he has done this three times before. And very nearly has completed the fourth experiment.

"You said you own Iona," I say quietly. "That you *are* Iona. But really, she is you now."

Jack nods. "If you could look into that brain of hers, it is now more Jack Caraway than Iona Faye."

"How?" I question, stumbling over the words. "How… who taught you to do this? Who would be so reckless?"

"Taught?" Jack barks out, offense in his volume. "You think total occupation can be taught? That someone can learn it out of some kind of textbook? No," he shakes his head, an expression of disgust on his face. "This was my grand opus. My life's work. The greatest experiment ever conducted in psychological history. And I mastered it."

Mad. That's what Jack is.

Brilliant. But insane.

Evil.

"My father was a brilliant psychologist, himself," Jack says, and his eyes become unfocused. "He founded the department at the local university. His name…well, he was rather well known in the field, we'll leave it at that."

Jack wraps his fingers around his opposite wrist, behind his back. "My parents never let me forget, that as a child, I was what you might call…manipulative. With my friends. With my teachers. I knew how to get what I wanted."

A cold smile curls on his lips. "In high school, I began to realize just how moldable people are. I read my father's books, the ones he brought home from the university, and the ones he wrote. If you knew certain things about people, watched them closely enough, you could learn how to work them."

"That's when the idea for total occupation came to you," I clarify.

Jack's eyes slide over to mine. A smile curls on his lips. "Yes." He takes two steps forward, and begins slowly circling the room. "I presented the rough idea to my father. The man was intrigued, perhaps even impressed. But even more so, he was mortified. He told me to forget what I was studying, what I was even trying to practice in some small form. So when he didn't support me, I decided I would study elsewhere."

"You went to New York." Iona has told me the details he didn't lie to her about.

"I studied, for six years. How to speak calmly. How to gain trust. How to wield that pocket watch that had once belonged to my grandfather."

Jack stops, and I feel him studying me.

"There were two women I practiced on during my years at NYU," he continues. "The first didn't stick well. I could never get her to confess her love. And she always regained her appetite after a week or so.

"The second…" Jack smiles. I want to smash it. Crush all of his teeth. Make him bleed. Make it so he can never speak again. "It worked. But not smoothly. She went mad after four weeks. And she took her life just a week after that."

I squeeze the pocket watch, threatening to crush it.

"I thought things were over, that I would never be able to master total occupation," Jack speaks again. "I was overwhelmed, thinking maybe I was just trying something too impossible. But that woman's death, it sparked an idea."

His voice grows quieter, but his eyes widen as he stares at the floor. His shoulders seem to broaden, his balance rising onto his toes just slightly. Excitement builds under his skin, sending him nearly manic.

"She threw my plans askew with her death, but then I realized: that was the finale to my beautiful experiment." Jack's eyes flick to mine. "That would be the final step to total occupation. That I would own them enough to claim *everything*. Even their very lives."

I feel two steps away from snapping. From breaking, with an aftershock powerful enough to drag the entire world to hell with me.

"And I would have perfected it even further," Jack says, taking a step forward. "I would have expanded into other arenas beyond love. I would have created tools to get into any head. Make even the best spy spill their secrets. Get entire colonies to become compliant and accomplish incredible movements and advancements in human society."

Jack stops, just inches from my face. "I could have been a *god*, shaping people as I needed, creating new, better ones."

Over the past few weeks, this has been one of my biggest questions: why?

And here is the answer.

Jack has a god complex.

A controlling appetite like never seen before.

"How did you trigger it all?" I ask. I have to throw water on that bright, hot fire burning inside of Jack.

His face transforms into a smile. "A magician never reveals his secrets, right?"

I stalk forward, only a breath between us. "How do I stop it?"

Eye to eye, Jack and I stare at one another.

"Please," I whisper. "I can't let her die."

Two heartbeats. Three. Ten. Twenty heartbeats.

"You've proven you've mastered this…total occupation," I say. And I'm begging now. Pleading with a dead man. "When the gate closes today, you can go in peace. You'll never see me again. And you'll never see Iona again. So please, tell me how to stop this."

He stares at me a full minute longer. His expression doesn't soften. He just continues to look at me, his brows slightly furrowed. His eyes hard.

"Say the words 'absolution of resurrection' to her."

Jack turns away and walks back across the room. He stands at the window, looking out.

"That's it?" I ask. I take three steps forward. "Say those words, and she's fixed?"

He looks over his shoulder, but not at me. "I've never used the fail safe before. I can't make any guarantees. But everything else has worked so well, I expect positive results."

"Absolution of resurrection," I repeat the words. "Thank-"

But I cut myself off. "No, I won't thank you," I say, turning away. "You're only helping me fix your evil obsession."

"God does terrible things in the name of creation and advancing human society," Jack says. "Am I truly any different? It's four lives in three billion."

A great roar climbs up my chest and I whirl back around. "You are a monster. A soulless, arrogant, viper of a monster. Did you ever, *ever* love any of them?"

Every fiber inside of me hates it when he crooks a little smile.

"I loved them all, Sully Whitmore," he says. "In my own way."

And in the blink of an eye, Jack Caraway disappears once more from the face of the earth.

CHAPTER FIFTY-FOUR

IONA

Everyone is smiling at me.

Smiling at me while I down the slice of carrot cake Mom made for this Sunday dinner.

I laugh, wiping a bit of frosting from the corner of my mouth, looking up to catch their eyes as they smile once more and look away.

Mom—looking genuinely happy to see me for the first time in so, so long.

Cressida, who took one look at me when I showed up for this family gathering, and pulled me into her arms, for the first real hug she'd given me in about a year.

My niece and nephews, they run around without even noticing anything at all has changed.

But even Harold's face brightens at the sight of me.

And Viola. She stays at my side, watching closely. Monitoring me as I use my right hand a little with the aide of the sling.

There's a knowing look in her eye when she glances at me. There's still doubt in it. She doesn't really know whether to believe everything I told her or not. I don't blame her. I probably wouldn't believe all the facts either.

But there she is again. My best friend.

"It's so good to have you here again," Mom says for the fifth time since I walked through the front doors of my childhood home.

I look up at her, and smile. "It's good to be back."

Such a strange thing to say, considering I've hardly left town, other than to go to Roselock. But every one of them catches my meaning. That I haven't really been here in a long, long time.

"Do you want another piece?" Cressida asks, leaning over the cake pan with a knife in hand.

I laugh and shake my head. "I think two was enough. Thank you."

Two pieces of cake. An entire meal of roast, potatoes, carrots, rolls, butter, the Sunday works.

I ate it all. Every single bite on my plate.

I look up at the clock above the kitchen sink and find it reads nine o'clock.

"I better get home," I say. "I can't be late to work tomorrow."

"Are you sure?" Mom asks, and the wrinkles in her forehead deepen just a little. The worry that I'm going to disappear again, and not really return. "It's been such a perfect day."

I smile and step forward to hug her. "It has. Let's do dinner at my place on…Wednesday. Does that work?"

We step back, and the glowing look on Mom's face warms my heart. "That's perfect."

I cross to the bench by the front door and grab my purse. "Do you both want to go to a movie with me on Thursday?"

The flash of doubt on Cressida's face twists my stomach. But there's hope there. A little door opened to me once more. "I'd like that."

Viola bounds across the room, a wide smile as she pulls me into a hug.

She hasn't stopped hugging me since I was in the hospital and opened up to her. "I'll be there."

With smiles, I say goodbye, and walk out into the dark. Fumbling through my bag for my keys, I unlock my car and start the engine.

It's just a short five-minute drive from my parent's home to my apartment. I park and hurry inside, getting out of the cold. Up three flights of stairs, down the hall, to apartment 308.

It's warm and cozy inside when I walk in. Clean floors, a cleared kitchen, and a scented candle burns on the coffee table. I hang my purse on the hook, and breathe a contented sigh.

Sully steps out from my bedroom and leans in the doorframe.

"I'd guess dinner went well?"

I smile, looking at him there. With his wild hair and beard. So solid and so real.

"It was perfect," I say. I lean back against the kitchen counter. "It was just like it used to be. Smiles and jokes and old stories."

Sully smiles. And something cracks in my chest when he does.

I cross the space, and as if sensing what I'm looking for, he steps forward. We meet somewhere in the middle, and I wrap my arms around his middle, his going around my shoulders.

"Thank you," I breathe into his broad chest. "For everything. For hanging in there. For saving me. For knowing how to patch things up with my family."

It was Sully's idea that I needed to go to this family dinner on my own. He'd been around, ever present in the last week and a half. All of my family members met him at the hospital.

But today, Sunday dinner, was about just the Fayes patching things back together.

He'd waited here in my apartment, by himself, until I returned.

"You're welcome," he breathes, pressing his lips to the top of my head.

A week and two days ago, I'd just finished telling Viola about everything that was happening, when Sully burst in through the door.

"Absolution of resurrection," he'd blurted the second his eyes met mine.

It was like a wet, soaked, wool blanket was removed from over my shoulders, my face; a weight lifted.

I…I could breathe.

My chest loosened.

I looked at my sister, and I didn't want to cringe away from her. I wanted…I wanted to hug her, and never let go.

I took one glance at my hospital tray of food and was ravenously hungry.

But the biggest of all: I didn't feel a hollow void in my chest.

Where Jack had once resided, where he had once occupied every corner of my being, even though I tried to ignore him, there was just…me, again.

Thinking on Jack, I felt nothing but hatred and betrayal. No lingering feelings of love. Of obsession.

I didn't love Jack anymore.

And it was all thanks to Sully.

Who had saved me. Literally.

"You should get to bed," Sully says. He releases me.

I look up at him once more. And I just feel happy. Alive. Free.

I turn to get ready for bed, looking over at Sully once more.

Come tomorrow, he will head back to Roselock, because he can't survive being gone for long. And I will go to work.

But when I am done, I will be at the library, researching.

Looking for ways to break his curse. Looking for

anyone who might be able to do something about what is happening in Roselock.

Sully saved my life. I'm determined to save his.

"Goodnight, Iona," he says as he heads toward the couch.

And there is a little empty void when we walk opposite directions.

I miss him there in my bed, a protective presence.

But I've just escaped the clutches of needing a man in a way there was no logical explanation for. I need to make sure I can stand on my own two feet again. That I can do something as simple as sleep, on my own.

"Goodnight, Sully," I call, looking at him one more time, before I close the door behind me.

Every book in the library catalogue referencing curses sits on the table I sit at. There are sixteen of them. Five are fairy tales. Two are old wiccan texts. They're the ones I pour through more carefully, but am the most afraid of. And the rest are textbooks, referencing old witch-hunts and other bloody historical events.

Two days later, I pull up everything I can find on the Native American tribes who used to come through this area of West Virginia.

Sully went home to Roselock Monday morning. I went to work. And then I went to the library.

Every day, from the moment I got off work, until the library closed, I researched.

My head ached.

My eyes burned.

But still, my fingers turned the pages, my eyes continued to scour text after text, hoping and praying for something.

Anything.

And the entire week, I thought of Sully. Alone in that church. Sitting inside it while the town went insane every single night.

My heart breaks for him. Bleeds.

Such a good-hearted man, someone willing to sacrifice so much for another, being utterly alone, waiting for a fate he's resigned that he cannot fight.

CHAPTER FIFTY-FIVE

SULLY

MARCH THIRD HAD ARRIVED.

Throughout the entirety of the day, I had wandered through town, scattering red roses. Thirty-three of them for the souls of the Shawnee tribe who were slaughtered. Four for the settlers who had been killed, as well. Thirty-three for the men and boys trapped in the mountain side.

When I was finished, I returned to my room. I stared at the wall that housed the sorting unit, with those hundreds of little drawers. One by one I brought the dead forth. Paid honor to every one of those who had died before me.

Slowly, the sun slid from one side of the sky to the other. The pace of my heart picked up. Echoes sounded in the back of my head. My heart twisted a little tighter.

March third. On exactly the two hundredth anniversary of the slaughter.

Alone, alone, once more alone, I ate dinner. I washed the dishes. I stoked the fire.

Alone, alone, always alone, I now stand in the chapel, looking out over the town.

The last of the sun's rays slip behind the mountain.

That feral, other-worldly yipping chirps once.

Twice.

Like a breath released from a hundred mouths, all at once, the town moans.

And a scream rips through the night.

I slip my hand into my pocket, and close it around the pendant, the bow, and the hair pin.

"Sully," a soft voice says empathetically. "You should have stayed away on this day. What is the point of staying here, witness to this cursed day if you don't have to?"

My sister stops at my side. Cheyenne's soft face is filled with despair and concern.

"She needs to be her own person," I say, watching as homes are blasted apart. A loud shriek, the sound of a baby crying, cuts through the church. My eyes wince closed. "I have to let her discover who she is once more."

"She cares about you, son," my father says. He walks forward, looking out over the town. He doesn't say anything else, and I wonder if he's thinking about how eight generations of cursed Whitmore men are finally coming to an end, with me.

"Never mind outside sources," my mother says, stepping forward. She reaches for my father's hand, and then my sister's. I cannot touch the dead, but the dead may cling to one another. "Our days together as a family are limited now. Let's not waste a moment of them."

I look to her, disconnected from my family. But not for long. I offer them a sad smile, and go to stand beside them. Watching as the town of Roselock lives out its cursed anniversary.

CHAPTER FIFTY-SIX

IONA

Friday evening, after work, I load up a box of research books into my car, a weekend bag packed full of clothes, and take off in my car.

But little tendrils of doubt begin wrapping around my brain, the further away I get from Ander.

Here I am, again, going out of my normal, in an extreme way, for a man.

About five miles before the turnoff to Roselock, I actually stop in the middle of the highway.

I chew on my bottom lip.

I'd nearly forgotten dinner with my mom on Wednesday. My heart leaped into my throat when I looked at the clock and remembered, and I'd looked like a fumbling idiot when I stumbled through the door five minutes late, clutching the grocery bags.

And then Viola had to call me ten minutes before the movie was to start on Thursday, telling me she and Cressida were already at the theater. I'd been at the library, pouring over my research.

I'd been trying to keep myself from running to Roselock. To keep myself from keeping Sully company as he suffered through the anniversary of the Battle at Roselock.

But he'd asked me to stay away that night.

I'd listened.

Even though it hurt to do so.

I doubt myself now, sitting there in the middle of the road.

I'd nearly forgotten all those things with my family, because I was obsessed with finding a way to save Sully.

I'd been obsessed with a man before.

Cut everything off once before.

This is different, a voice coming from my heart says.

I will never trust my heart again.

But I want to believe it.

Sully is going to die if I don't find a solution. I can't let the man who saved my life die.

I let off the brake, and continue down the highway.

The familiar, terrifying sights of Roselock greet me when I pull off the highway. The rundown buildings. The line of pennies I carefully drive over. And then the sight of the church up ahead.

And I dread the beats that each pound in my chest. Because every one that sounds, is another one counting down to May seventh.

Something tightens in my chest when I step into the

evening light. Brilliant sunshine casts down on the trees that surround me. The sun illuminates the roof of the church. It makes the old stained glass windows glow.

My feet step forward. Propelled faster as my heart screams in my chest.

Truth.

Truth wants to speak to me.

But fear and doubt are ever going to be my constant companions.

The stairs squeal under my gaining weight as I climb them. The porch sags. But I actually smile, recalling the first time I feared I would fall through it.

A lifetime ago.

I knock loudly on the doors.

It's silent for a moment. And my heart sinks, worrying that I'm going to have to go and search for him.

But then, heavy footsteps sound within.

Anticipation burns in my veins.

I shift from one foot to the other.

I bite my lips together to contain the smile.

I hear a hand land on the doorknob. And finally, it swings open.

I actually press a hand to my chest, trying to still my heart. But my smile breaks free of my bite, and spreads on my face.

Sully stands there, so different from the first time I knocked on this door.

First, because his eyes are bright, hopeful. Happy to see me.

And second, because he *looks* entirely different.

He's cut his hair. It's now short, cropped, clean cut. And his beard has been trimmed, now short and groomed, with purpose.

It fractures all those hard walls I was attempting to build when I stopped in the middle of the road.

My body acts of its own accord as I surge forward, wrapping my hands behind his neck, and pull his face to mine.

CHAPTER FIFTY-SEVEN

SULLY

THE FLOODGATES ARE OPENED.

The second I opened the door and saw her standing there, so permanently changed from the scared fawn I found standing there once before, everything came rushing in on me.

I wanted this woman.

I wanted her with me, wherever I was, wanted to be with her, wherever she might go.

I wanted to fight for her, every day, and be there to remind her to fight for herself.

And as she rushes forward and wraps her arms around my neck, I know this is where my heart is going to be for the short remainder of my days.

Our mouths collide without hesitation. Hunger and passion rip through me like a tornado out on the plains. My hands go to Iona's sides, slowly wrapping around her waist as she leans into me.

A hungry sigh escapes her lips and I let her into my mouth, her tongue darting out, tangling with mine. Her lips mold to the shape of mine, promising bittersweet escape from everything in the world.

She leans in harder, and I give two steps back into the church. She follows, her body glued to mine, inch for inch as we move. The door still sits wide open, because who would be around to witness? I slowly work us backward into the church.

Iona's kiss is not gentle. It is not hesitant.

Every one of them claims me. Declares me hers.

A violent and electric storm bites in my veins. Desire and the instinct to claim run savage in my blood as I twist us, backing Iona into the wall as we stumble from the chapel into the common room. Her tiny little body feels so much more feminine even after just two weeks as I grasp her hips and lift, pinning her to the wall.

"Sully," she sighs as she tips her head backward. But I don't slow, can't slow. My mouth moves from hers, over her jawline, down her neck. My hands curl from her hips, under her thighs, holding her up, holding her legs around my waist.

It takes every ounce of control in me not to pound my hips. To not thrust. To not claim this woman as my primal mate.

Mine.

Mine.

Mine.

A medieval voice screams the words through my brain.

But suddenly I jerk back. My eyes go to Iona's.

Because that's what Iona was to Jack.

He owned her. She became him.

And I will never, ever claim possession over her.

"Is this what you want?" I pant, my chest heaving, my body trembling from head to foot. "You've only just found your freedom again, Iona." I struggle to keep my words under control. To breathe evenly. "Is this what you want?"

Those caramel eyes of hers stare back at me, searching, pouring over my soul like a fortuneteller looking through a crystal ball into the depths of my dark and twisted soul. Her breasts heave up and down, her lips already swollen and red.

But there's a stillness that settles over her. Calm. Serene.

She brings her hands to either side of my face, never once looking away from my eyes. Slowly, her hands rise up into my hair, locking in what little is left of it.

"You are a good man, Sully," she says quietly. "I need good in my life again." She pauses, searching me again. "This…this is what I want."

She leans in, slowly, so slowly surely I'll soon be an old man, tortured and waiting for heaven. She presses her lips to mine. She breathes a breath into me.

Every nerve in my body shutters with want. Need.

Steadily, our lips move in sync. Assuredly, our mouths open.

Iona shrugs her coat off.

I kick my boots off as she squeezes her legs tighter around my waist.

She reaches for the hem of her shirt.
And I carry the both of us to the bedroom.

CHAPTER FIFTY-EIGHT

IONA

THE DIM GLOW OF THE SUNRISE TICKLES THE horizon.

I lie on my stomach, looking at the dirty window. It faces north, so my view of the eastern sunrise is blocked, but I can see a trace of light blue dancing behind the tree line.

Sully traces a finger over my bare back. He's quiet, just letting me sort through my thoughts, getting utterly lost in them. But the tip of his finger keeps lazing over my skin, as if drawing a map to some exotic destination where only he and I can exist.

We made love last night. Soul crushing, soul healing love that went on and on through the night. At some point, I finally fell asleep, lying on Sully's chest, skin to skin. When I'd awoken, I rolled over and just looked at his profile in the dim light.

But the moment I turned over, Sully stirred, and then his fingers were there.

My mind is a tangled web of thoughts and questions.

This was different. So under my skin deep, so bend me backward, look at the sky and see to the stars and moon, different.

But…

But there is something broken in my mind now. Something fragile and scared, but willing to fight until my last breath.

But I turn my head, looking back at Sully.

His hair is wild, sticking up in all directions from my fingers endlessly running through it all night, and sleeping finally. But there's peace in his eyes. Light. He leans forward and presses his lips to my shoulder. He takes a deep breath, breathing me in.

I will be frightened. I will fight for myself.

But the truth is there, nesting itself in the center of my chest, so obvious and large that I can't ignore it.

Sully and I. Me and Sully. An ache forms in me when I think of parting from him.

I roll over to my back and look up at him as he hovers, looking down at me. I reach up, placing a hand on his cheek.

"There doesn't need to be words," Sully says. He lies there with his head propped up on one hand, his elbow to the bed. His other he laces with the fingers of my other hand, resting on my chest. "There doesn't need to be any promises. Just, whatever you need, Iona. And I'll do it."

Peace.

Real peace.

And real happiness. That's what I feel.

That's what courses through me as he leans down, gently pressing his lips to mine, bare chest to bare chest.

I'll never trust my heart again. Never, ever say the words again.

But inside, in my heart, I know the truth.

I love this man.

Sully tromps around all that day, going about his duties. He takes care of the town of Roselock. He visits the graves of the dead. He clears debris and speaks to an old friend he summons from an old pair of spectacles.

I watch him. At least once an hour, he finds his way back to me, kissing me deep and long, our hands all over one another. But he goes back out.

I walk around the church, looking all around the base. In the light of day, it looks so normal. Just a crumbling foundation. Just weeds and bushes jutting out here and there.

How…how does it bleed at night?

How do the voices of the dead call out in the dark, for any and all to hear?

How did the town curse Sully?

That night, as we sit together, eating, I ask him, "Is there anything left of the tribe that used Roselock as the burial ground?"

He looks up at me from beneath his dark lashes. "Why?"

I finish chewing my bite. Keep his gaze. "Because there has to be an answer to this. I want to look for clues. Signs. Anything."

He stirs the stew in his bowl without looking at it. "Why?" he asks again quietly.

I'm still as a statue. "Because I can't lose you in two months and four days." My features feel rock solid, unmovable. "I won't lose you."

Sully is true to his word. No promises. No words. Just whatever I need. But I see it there in his eyes. That this means just as much to him as it does to me.

I rise, leaning over the table and let my lips go to his. Letting two lonely souls find companionship.

"Please, there has to be something," I whisper.

I think he suppresses a sigh as he leans back. "Come," he says as he stands. "I'll show you where they were all buried."

CHAPTER FIFTY-NINE

SULLY

ONE PERFECT WEEKEND BECOMES A WEEK OF separation, to be free again, to learn independence once more. And then another weekend brings emotional and physical fulfillment I've never in my life experienced.

And then a trip to Ander for a few days before the call of the dead pulled me back to Roselock.

For a month this was my life. Creating a balance of being with the woman who had come to inhabit my every thought, every direction of hope for me, and letting her find herself again, to reconnect with her friends and family.

And Iona thrived. She laughed with her sisters. She got a promotion at work. She reintegrated into the town she'd lived in her whole life.

But she also desperately searched for a way out of my fate.

Through books. Through phone calls to shaman and priests and professors.

I could only give her a hopeful, false smile, and feel gratitude that someone cared about me enough to go to so much exhaustive trouble.

But I knew the truth. I knew the answer.

There was no answer.

Because the damage had been done, over two hundred years ago. There will never be any forgiveness for the Whitmore family.

I'm a cursed man, forever.

My rose continues to fade from red to white.

But Iona never gave up hope.

And it felt incredible to have someone fight so fiercely for me.

Eight weeks after Iona was released from Jack's black grasp, I drive straight from Roselock to Iona's apartment. Parking across the street, I climb out and cross the street.

The breath of spring whispers across town. Daffodils bud, ready to spring open any day. The trees are just getting their leaves. And the temperatures rise with every passing day.

I walk into the building and up three flights of stairs. Down the hall, and to apartment 308.

Three knocks. I overhear laughter, and it brings a smile to my own lips.

A moment later, the door swings open.

Iona stands there in a red dress. Red lipstick. Her hair done up in an elegant twist.

And she wears a smile that has changed my entire world.

"Hello, handsome," she says with a coy smirk.

I step forward, my hands automatically going to her hips, and am about to press my lips to those tempting red ones, when someone standing from the table draws my eyes.

"Hold it, hold it," Viola says, slinging her purse over her shoulder. "You two can hang on for just a minute until I clear out of here."

Despite her teasing, she crosses the room and wraps her arms around me. "Good to see you," I greet her, wrapping the woman into my arms for a quick hug. "You just get off work?"

"What gave it away?" she once more teases, smirking down at her work uniform. "I'm glad you're back, Sully."

I give her a little half smile.

Viola chuckles and shakes her head. "I have to say, I think I miss the hair and the beard."

I give an exasperated laugh, dropping my hands. "You, too?"

Iona laughs, coming to my side, wrapping her hands around my arm. "I don't know what it is," she says, beaming up at me. "You just looked so dangerous and wild before. It was…sexy. Now you're just…"

"Threatening outback man?" Viola suggests. She pauses in the doorway, looking back over her shoulder at us, giving a wink. "I'll see you two later."

"Bye," Iona calls and I give a little wave.

"You know how long it took me to grow out all that hair you never told me you wanted me to keep?" I say, looking down at Iona as I wrap my hands behind her back.

"Years and years," she answers. There's a playful smile on her lips. But there is also a look of fear that creeps into her eyes.

Because it's there, in the back of our heads. There will be no time to grow it back out. Because I only have three weeks and three days left on this earth.

"You ready?" I ask, moving on, because I won't spoil this night for either of us.

Dodging boxes, Iona goes back for her purse.

Her entire apartment is packed up. She found a new one, across town. Where she will never have to walk the same path she frequented with Jack. In two days' time, I will be moving all of her belongings into a truck, and then into the new building where she will continue to rebuild her life.

But for this day, the night is spent at a fancy restaurant across town. It actually looks out over the river. The evening draws to a close as we clear our plates. When Iona finishes her fish, potatoes, and steamed vegetables, every bite of them, she reaches across the table and takes my hand.

"I have an idea," she says. She keeps looking at my hand. "It's the only thing I can think of. So please listen. *Really* listen."

Maybe my false front of hope hasn't been as solid as I thought it was.

"Of course," I promise her.

She draws two little lines with her finger on my hand,

and I realize it's a cross. "The town was cursed because it was built upon sacred grounds, correct?"

I watch her, moving from the cross, to random swirls and shapes. "It's always been assumed that was the reason. Pain and torture for all the lives lost in that battle. For building upon what we didn't know was there."

Iona nods. In the glowing candlelight of the dinner table, I can't help but think how beautiful she is.

Her cheeks have filled back in, no longer gaunt and starved. Her hips have shape to them. She's still thin, it will take several months more before she's returned to her previous self.

But she's beautiful.

"What if we remove what was wrongfully placed there?" she asks quietly, and her fingers finally still.

Two heartbeats. Three. Four.

"What do you mean?"

She doesn't answer me immediately. She places her hand over mine, holding it lightly. And then, her eyes meet mine.

"What if we burn the town of Roselock to the ground?" she asks. "Level it so it is as if it never existed."

Something pulses in my chest. Throbs. Surges.

"What if we burn all those houses, one by one, until they no longer exist?" she says. "What if we burn the church, as if it had never been built? And then we create some kind of…memorial, for all those lives that were lost?"

There are too many thoughts running through my head to respond. Too many questions. Too many doubts.

"If we fix what was done, we can break the curse, Sully,"

Iona says with hope. "Reverse what was done, as much of it as we can."

Pounding. Racing. My heart doesn't know what to do.

"Sully, we destroy Roselock, every bit of it," she says, the hope and desperation rising in her voice. She leans in closer, her hand tightening around mine. "And we make sure you are nowhere close to it when May seventh arrives. And we save your life, Sully."

Her voice cracks slightly when my name escapes her lips.

I nod. Because that pleading in her eyes fractures every bit of me. "It might…" Even saying the words makes me too scared to hope. "It might work."

She looks at me, not quite daring to believe that I'm opening the door of consideration. But slowly, a smile curls on her lips.

"We can do this, Sully," she says. "I am going to help you. And you are going to live."

I lean in closer, trying so hard to give her what she wants.

The waiter walks up. "Your check, sir," he says. "No rush."

I look up at him, maybe managing a polite thank you. Again, I hate when Iona reaches for it, and then produces the money to pay the bill. Standing, I pull her seat for her, and arm in arm, we walk out the front doors.

With the beauty of the day, we decided to walk. Now that the sun has set, the air is much cooler. I shrug out of my jacket to place it around Iona's shoulders.

She gives a little contented sigh and clings to my arm, resting her head against my shoulder.

"My family likes you, you know," she says as we slowly walk down the sidewalk.

The view is spectacular. The tracks of the train stretch before and behind us, and just beyond that is the grassy bank of the Kanawha River. With the sun set low behind the hills, the sky bleeds gold and red.

"I like them," I say, sliding my hands into my pockets. "Cressida can be a little intense, but I think I'm finally getting used to her."

Iona laughs, shaking her head. "She was certainly born as her own self-assured person. Once you realize you can agree to disagree with her, she's not as scary."

I smile and nod.

Down we walk, along this sidewalk, which will eventually turn, and lead us back into town.

"Do you think it could work, Sully?" she asks. And her steps slow, though she keeps moving. "I've studied and searched. This...this is the only solution I can think of. It has to work, doesn't it?"

"It's a good idea," I say, trying not to sound too doubtful. "Logically, it's the thing that makes the most sense."

She turns her face up toward mine, biting one corner of her lower lip. "It has to work. I don't want to lose you, Sully."

I bend down, lowering my face to hers. And press my lips to her own.

"I won't lie," I confess as I straighten when the blast of the train horn sounds, quickly approaching. "It's hard to imagine. That after two hundred years, all of the insanity of Roselock could come to an end." The sound of the train grows louder and louder, the ground rumbling. "That after my entire life, always knowing exactly when the end would come, to see it all come to some kind of...logical...conclusion."

A stone drops in my stomach.

Because suddenly, Iona's expression slackens.

Something dark sparks in her eyes.

Her grip on my arm loosens.

The tremor of the train's approaching power shakes the ground. The honking of its horn obliterates my ears.

The look in Iona's eyes distances.

"Iona?" I question.

She lets go of my arm.

She turns away, taking a step toward the track.

And just before the train levels with us

Iona jumps.

CHAPTER SIXTY

IONA

It was like a sweet release.

Something snapping.

A cord cut.

I didn't have to hold on to anything. I could just let go. Could just stop trying to keep everything pulled together.

And just give in to the monster.

The monster told me it was time to jump.

So I followed its voice.

I leapt.

And found blissful release from this life.

Now here I stand, watching it all as if in a blurry fast-forward time lapse.

The splatter. The crunch. The spray.

Sully's bone-shattering, earth-moving scream.

The screech of iron on iron as the train skidded to a halt.

The sirens and the screams of ambulances and police cars.

And Sully… Poor, poor Sully.

A blur, that's all I could see. A blur I couldn't touch. Couldn't break through. Couldn't say a word through.

A screaming, crying, mourning family.

A packed funeral.

A grim-faced man who had done so much for me.

And then a cursed town that brought nothing but pain.

CHAPTER SIXTY-ONE

SULLY

A WEEK. AN AGONIZING, PAIN FILLED, CONFUSED, cursed week.

Seven days of repeating the same story over and over. To Iona's family. To the police. To the paramedics. Again, to the police.

What happened?

Why would Iona jump in front of a train?

I endured the screaming accusations of Iona's family.

I bore the questioning stares of half a town at the funeral.

My things and I were tossed out of Iona's apartment the day after.

I only managed to grab two things before they shoved me out.

Her photo album and her purse.

Quickly, I slipped one inside the other, wrapped them

in my jacket, and set them in the passenger seat of my car. I left the town of Ander. For the very last time, ever.

For the last time, ever, I drove down the roads, turning off the highway. Faster and faster, I pressed the gas. Faster to the answers I've now had to wait an entire week for.

The bumpy road of Roselock greets me this fading evening. Over potholes and riveted washouts I work my way through the trees, and then past crumbling homes.

Burn it all down to the ground, she'd said.

I'll do it now, just to spite it all. Just to punish something. Anything.

Something needs to pay for what has been done.

I pull my car into the shed once more, because it will never need to come out again after this day. Carefully, I take the photo album and purse, still wrapped in my jacket, and make my way into the church.

On my way inside, I snap off a single red rose, cutting my hand on the thorns.

The chapel is dusty and dirty as ever as I stalk through it. It is colder inside than it is outside, but I don't bother lighting a fire.

I hook down the hall to the right, and head straight for my bedroom.

There's a shirt of Iona's pushed into the corner.

A spare brush she brought from home rests on the nightstand.

A tube of lipstick sits on my dresser, just under the mirror.

The woman who formed to fit the shape of my heart,

and took up permanent residence there, left traces of herself over every space.

And now she's dead.

My fingers roll into a fist. I throw the photo album to the bed, the rose immediately following it. And I swing.

My fists connect with wood, splintering apart a frame that sat on the dresser. Next, an old lamp shatters. I sweep my hands across the table in the corner, scattering tools and books as a furious cry erupts from my chest.

Everything. After *everything*, she still took her own life.

After everything, even after the fail-safe, Jack still won.

I stand with my hands braced on the top of the dresser, panting. Huffing. My head swims. Into the darkness my mind wants to spiral. To drown. To end the suffering.

But I have to know.

Have to find some kind of answer.

I turn, looking over my shoulder. To the photo album that lies open and facedown on the bed.

Two more calming breaths, I cross the room.

I grab the photo album.

And a rushing warmth filters through my veins.

"Sully."

Her voice cracks, a sob barely contained.

I turn to see Iona standing behind me, by the door.

She looks beautiful. Her skin radiant. Her brown hair braided back. Her cheeks lively and healthy.

But her lower lip trembles. Tears swim in her eyes.

She takes a step forward, her hand gripping the opposite forearm. "Sully, I'm so sorry."

And it fractures me. Splinters apart every ounce of self-control I've executed this week. I take two steps toward her, and fall to my knees, a broken man.

"I'm so sorry, Sully," she whispers in broken words as she stands before me and looks down. "I'm so sorry."

I let my head fall, my emotions breaking. Sobs crash through my chest. The dam is broken, releasing from my eyes.

And I lose myself.

CHAPTER SIXTY-TWO

SULLY

IN THE DARKEST PART OF THE NIGHT, WHEN THE SUN is so far away from me, it's a planet away, when the moon is no more than a tiny sliver of light hidden behind the trees, I take Iona's purse and walk into the Sunday School room.

One candle, that's all I light.

I drop the purse onto the chair, staring death and damnation upon it. My jaw clenched tight, I reach into it. And close my fingers around the cold metal.

The temperature of the room instantly drops. The short, little hairs on the back of my neck stand on end.

"So much for your promises to leave me alone."

Jack appears just to my left. Smug and confident, he stands there, arms crossed over his chest. He smiles.

I just stand there, my gaze fixed on him. My fingers curled around his watch. His tool of destruction.

"It was beautiful, wasn't it?" Jack says. "The moment you see it in their eyes. When mentally they just...cave."

Still no words, I keep staring at the man.

"It's too bad it's just me on this side of the gate," Jack says. He steps forward, beginning a little circle around me. "I would love to speak to her, or any of them, really. To interview them, to really get in their heads, and find what it felt like, when they finally granted me total occupation."

My throat tightens at the same time my other fist does. A spark. A violent streak of lightning flashes through my veins.

But still I don't say anything.

"You're a resolved man, aren't you, Sully Whitmore?" Jack says. He comes to a stop, and he lowers his gaze to meet my eyes. And I see a shift there. To something probing and analyzing. Something that can reach down into a soul's depths and retrieve the contents to look them over. "What is it? Why are you such a...weighed down being?"

I won't answer him. Won't give him anything more than he's already taken.

"You don't have much time left, do you?" Jack concludes. "Somehow...somehow you know the end is coming for you. That's why you aren't more violent. That's why you wear that mask. Because, in the end, you knew your time with Iona was limited, anyway."

Every muscle in my body is tense. Flexed and ready to snap.

But I stand here, frozen.

Jack nods his head, satisfied he's guessed right, which he has. And I loathe that.

"Since you're a man who will soon be taking his secrets

to the grave, I will tell you the truths of total occupation."
Something sparkles in his eyes. Elation. A secret kept and
soon to be shared. An evil plan now come to fruition.
"Open the watch."

I blink once, confused at his simple request.

"Open it," he instructs once more, nodding his head
toward the object in my hand.

I look down at it, and seeing how no more harm could
come, I open it.

The glass inside is cracked, the metal slightly bent from
my multiple times of abuse to it.

"Press your thumb down on the inside face of the lid,"
he continues instructing.

I do, and suddenly, a latch releases, and a thin metal
divider swings open. A folded piece of paper flutters out
and down to the floor. I bend to retrieve it, folding it open.

It's a small piece, only three inches by two inches. Neat,
organized handwriting covers its surface.

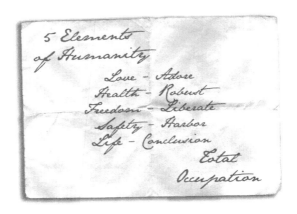

"These are the steps to total occupation, Sully," Jack says, and I can hear the smile in his face. "The five elements of humanity, of freewill and life, and the trigger words to take away every single one of them."

Love—Adore.

"Iona made love to me for the first time four weeks after we met," Jack repeats the story he's already boasted about. "I told you that was when I hypnotized her. It was then that I implanted this entire journey. Every word. The fail-safe. When she awoke, I told her that I adored her, and the *very* next words out of her mouth were that she loved me."

Health—Robust.

"While I could not trigger any physical diseases to compromise her health, I could make her put her own health at risk by taking away a very natural human instinct: the need for nourishment." Jack's wicked smile shifts, displaying his pride. "While in Florida, I told her we could have as robust of a travel life as she would like, and from that moment on, she only ate when others forced her."

Heat builds in my veins. A slow burn, threatening to consume me.

Freedom—Liberate.

"I took away her freedom to do whatever she pleased with whomever she pleased, at a bar when we were out with her sister, Viola." He continues his tale of manipulation. "Every relationship that had been important to her, every spare moment to herself, all turned toward me. Iona never went anywhere, unless it was at my suggestion."

My eyes slide closed, as the heat in me burns so hot, it feels like ice.

"And things would have ended there, with her loving me obsessively, never to have an appetite again, in absolute seclusion, for the rest of her days," Jack says as he takes a step toward me. "Had *you* not come into the picture. Had Iona not sought you out. Had you not opened the gate and let me back into her life."

Safety—Harbor.

"You know that moment I said that word to her," Jack says. "You facilitated that step. And I thank you for allowing me to continue this work."

I snap.

My arm flings out, my fist aiming for his head, only it hits nothing but ice-cold air. So I take a step away, putting some distance between us.

Don't drown, baby, Jack had said to Iona. *I wish I could still be there. Wish I could be your safe harbor. But you have to be strong. Can you do that for me?*

The bastard.

"You gave me the fail-safe," I growl, facing the door to exit the room. "And it worked. It all stopped. She was getting better. She…Iona moved on."

A little chuckle sounds from behind me.

And then a gratified sigh. "The one untested piece to this puzzle," he says. "The fail-safe was installed in case anyone ever began to suspect. In case I ever needed to pause the experiment. It was never a cure. Never a release."

I look over my shoulder at Jack. He looks up at me

from under his eyelashes, the face of absolute evil who does not think any of their actions were wrong.

"Anyone could have triggered any of the stages," Jack says. "It's why I chose such obscure trigger words. Iona was merely on pause. And could have stayed on pause for forever. Until someone said that very last trigger word."

Life—Conclusion.

It's hard to imagine. After two hundred years, that all of the insanity of Roselock could come to an end. That after my entire life, always knowing exactly when the end would come, to see it all come to some kind of...logical...conclusion.

I'd said the word.

I had triggered the final stage.

I'd made Iona take her own life.

"Magnificent, isn't it?" Jack says. My eyes once more meet his. "The power it grants? The master one may become over another? Can you just imagine the possibilities of where I could have taken this, Sully?"

Human nature wants me to argue with him. To tell him how wrong he was. How unnatural and evil it all was.

But looking into those eyes, I find a man who isn't a man. I find a soul that is nothing but black vipers.

Without a word, I fold the piece of paper once more, following its original crease lines. I place it back in its secret compartment, snapping it closed.

Before Jack can say a word, I yank open the door to the Sunday School room and step out.

That little vibration, the disturbance between worlds

sounds as I walk toward the back door. The gate grows too heavy, threatening to close.

But I feel Jack walking beside me, following me.

I pause, for just half a moment at the door, looking through the window out into the dark. The dead of night.

With a strangled breath, I pull it open, and step outside.

Little splatters of blood stain my boots. The sound of muffled moaning floats through the dark.

It's been a month and a half since the anniversary of the Battle at Roselock. The town has begun to quiet at night once more. But it's never a good idea to be outside after dark.

I keep my eyes fixed ahead. I shove through the gate into the graveyard. Past headstones, stepping over my friends.

And then into the woods.

The woods so dark, I can't see more than two feet in front of me.

Tripping. Scraping my skin, drawing blood.

"Is this your epic, grand finale to it all?" Jack taunts. "Your last burial of Jack Caraway?"

I try to ignore his words. To pretend that I cannot hear them.

So I focus on the raging, insane forest around me.

Voices moan out in the dark. A creature not of this world yips, scared, but angry.

Past dark trees, around boulders, through vines and thorns I walk with a dead man.

Until finally, the moonlight hits the tips of two great wings.

I look up into the face of the angel, feeling peace wash over me.

Jack stands beside me, looking up at her as well, finally at a loss for words.

"Never let this kind of evil grace the world again," I ask of her. And then I turn, taking the two steps to the well.

Blood, red and dark fills the well to the brim. I hold the watch out in my fist, hovering over the dark, liquid surface.

"You were wrong," I say as I look back at Jack. "About everything. And I know you don't think that, not for a second. But you're going to burn in hell for what you have done. But the flames will never burn as hot as you deserve."

And Jack's eyes widen for just a moment, before I drop the watch into the well, and Jack Caraway is erased from this world forever.

CHAPTER SIXTY-THREE

SULLY

SHE LIES ON THE BED, LOOKING OVER AT ME THROUGH the dim morning light. On my side, I stare back at her, studying every surface of her perfect skin. That little nose. Her delicate ears. Her soft, pink lips.

I lift a hand, as if to trace it down her shoulder, only she's nothing but ice and air.

"Are you sure about this, Sully?" Iona asks.

She gazes back at me with a mournful expression, sadness running so deep into her eyes.

"It's my time," I say quietly. I rest my hand on the bed, right next to hers, where the back of my knuckles should touch hers, yet I feel only cold. "I don't want to wait around forever. Who knows, maybe the time will finally come, and we can all move on."

She bites her lower lip, and tears swim in her eyes. Because she knows what it means. Once I go, I won't be able to pull her through the gate, anymore. It means we will no longer see one another.

"Please try," she says.

I draw a breath as I roll onto my back. I lay my arm across my forehead, looking up at the ceiling.

Possibility and hope bring pain.

I've endured too much of that in the past three weeks. I can't stand the thought of letting more of it in.

"Come on," Iona says, climbing from the bed and heading toward the doors. "There's only one left."

I watch her for a moment, marveling how she can still sound...hopeful. Happy. Holding on when, for me, there is nothing left to hold on to.

But for her, I climb out of this bed.

I don't even have to put on a jacket, the air already warm outside on this sixth day of May. Out to the back deck. Out to the shed. For the can of kerosene and matches.

Side by side, I walk with the dead woman that I love, down the drive from the church. To the last standing house in Roselock.

Over the past two weeks, Iona has accompanied me as I've burned every house in Roselock down. Turned all of them to ashes and cinders.

Once I've finished dousing the entire inside of the old Rasis home, I light the match from just outside the door, and toss it inside.

It ignites instantly.

"It will work, Sully," Iona says. She stands so close to

me, close enough, the warmth of her body should warm mine. But she's only cold and dead.

I let my eyes slide closed as the blaring of a train and the wet crunch of her body echo through my head.

Jack's smile flashes across my vision.

"What do I have to live for, Iona?" I ask, being overtaken by visions of all the worst times in my life. "There is no one and nothing left for me in this world."

She's quiet for too long. And it makes me open my eyes, and find hers.

"Do you really believe that?" she asks.

I look down at her, wishing I could give her what she wants. I wish I could bring her back. I wish we had had the life together that two normal people would have.

"I'm so tired, Iona," I breathe. She takes a step closer, and we're chest-to-chest, but unable to reach one another. "I'm ready."

Tears swim in her eyes once more, but she doesn't reprimand me. Doesn't get angry.

She just nods that she understands.

I'VE JUST FINISHED CLEARING AWAY THE DISHES OF MY last meal when there's a knock on the door. I freeze with my hand poised over the sink, about to place the plate in the hot water.

The knock echoes through the church once more.

My heart in my throat, I wipe my hands on my pants, and slowly walk toward the door.

A pure white rose resides in my breast pocket.

The air is so calm. As if it's waiting. Holding its breath in anticipation, watching to see what will happen come twilight this seventh day of May.

Through the common room I walk. Through the door to the chapel. Past the kerosene-soaked floorboards of the chapel.

My head throbs. The smell of kerosene is pungent, all too strong now that the entire church has been doused in it.

My hand rests on the doorknob, and finally, I pull it open.

A man with large glasses but a confident expression stands on the sagging porch. Just behind him there are two other men, one holding a microphone, the other a huge, bulky camera.

"Hello," the man before me says with professional charm. He keeps strong control over his face, when it's obvious it wants to contort in displeasure at the smell wafting strongly out to where he stands. "My name is Peter Dit, I'm with Channel Five news. Are you Sully Whitmore?"

Where once upon a time the reporters were only greeted with an angry growl and a door in their face, I'm only cold and calm.

"I am," I answer the man.

Excitement sparks in the reporter's eyes. "I've heard some quite interesting stories about this town. I wondered if you might be willing to talk to me about the fascinating history of Roselock."

My gaze shifts from Peter to the other men behind him. A blinking red light on the front of the camera tells me that the footage is rolling.

"You want the real story?" I ask, looking back at Peter.

I hear something spark from within the church.

"That's what I always search for," the man says, with an ignorant smile.

"Even if it's not what you're hoping for?" I question. A faint smell wafts past me. Smoke. "Even if it makes you squirm? Even if it makes you sick? Even if it makes you run away in fear?"

Finally, Peter's expression falters. His eyes jump over my shoulder, looking into the belly of the church. His mouth slackens a bit, his eyes widen.

"It sounds like a story that would make my career," he responds, his voice quieting.

There's a rushing sound. Like air being sucked.

Peter takes a step back. Down the stairs. The crewmembers behind him scramble back, as well.

They're shouting something. Warnings. Shock. Words come out of their mouths, but I only look down, my hand sliding to my pocket.

"This is the true story of Roselock," I say as my hand touches the paper. "This is the legacy of the name Whitmore."

Eerie calm washes over me.

I planned to burn the church to the ground today. I doused it in kerosene. Come evening, I planned to strike a match, and stand out on the road to watch it burn.

But there was that sparking noise just a moment ago.

And there is heat at my back.

Iona was wrong.

I could never break this curse. Never fight my fate.

I've lived thirty-three years, three months, and three days.

And I'm ready.

"Sully," her voice says as I pull the picture from my pocket. A picture of Iona.

I look to my side to see her standing there. Looking beautiful. Healthy. Peaceful.

"This is the real story," I say to Peter, though I don't look away from Iona. I hear them scramble, shouting, yelling warnings.

The heat of the flames grows closer.

"This is the truth of Roselock." Something pierces the back of my eyes, they sting.

But inside, I just feel peace.

On the seventh day of May, I stand in the home I always resented, staring at the woman I love.

"It's okay, Sully," Iona says. She gives me a little smile. It's sad, regretful. But understanding.

As I hear an explosion, I reach for Iona's hand.

And as I hear glass shatter, and the temperature of the world skyrockets, her fingers lace with mine.

THE END

ABOUT THE AUTHOR

Keary Taylor is the *USA Today* bestselling author of over twenty novels. She grew up along the foothills of the Rocky Mountains where she started creating imaginary worlds and daring characters who always fell in love. She now splits her time between a tiny island in the Pacific Northwest and Utah, with her husband and their two children. She continues to have an overactive imagination that frequently keeps her up at night.

For more information check her out at the following:

www.kearytaylor.com
me@kearytaylor.com

26045932R00223

Printed in Poland
by Amazon Fulfillment
Poland Sp. z o.o., Wrocław